Also by Simon R. Green

The Holy Terrors Mysteries

THE HOLY TERRORS *
STONE CERTAINTY *

The Gideon Sable series

THE BEST THING YOU CAN STEAL *
A MATTER OF DEATH AND LIFE *
WHAT SONG THE SIRENS SANG *
NOT OF THIS WORLD *
WHERE IS ANYBODY? *

The Ishmael Jones Mysteries

THE DARK SIDE OF THE ROAD *
DEAD MAN WALKING
VERY IMPORTANT CORPSES
DEATH SHALL COME
INTO THE THINNEST OF AIR
MURDER IN THE DARK *
TILL SUDDEN DEATH DO US PART *
NIGHT TRAIN TO MURDER *
THE HOUSE ON WIDOWS HILL *
BURIED MEMORIES *
HAUNTED BY THE PAST

And the Deathstalker, Nightside, Secret History, Hawk and Fisher and Forest Kingdom series

* available from Severn House

WHICH WITCH?

Simon R. Green

SEVERN
HOUSE

First world edition published in Great Britain and the USA in 2025
by Severn House, an imprint of Canongate Books Ltd,
14 High Street, Edinburgh EH1 1TE.

severnhouse.com

Copyright © Simon R. Green, 2025

Cover and jacket design by Nick May at bluegecko22.com

All rights reserved including the right of reproduction in whole or in part in any form. The right of Simon R. Green to be identified as the author of this work has been asserted in accordance with the Copyright, Designs & Patents Act 1988.

British Library Cataloguing-in-Publication Data
A CIP catalogue record for this title is available from the British Library.

ISBN-13: 978-1-4483-1353-2 (cased)
ISBN-13: 978-1-4483-1354-9 (e-book)

This is a work of fiction. Names, characters, places and incidents are either the product of the author's imagination or are used fictitiously. Except where actual historical events and characters are being described for the storyline of this novel, all situations in this publication are fictitious and any resemblance to actual persons, living or dead, business establishments, events or locales is purely coincidental.

No part of this book may be used or reproduced in any manner for the purpose of training artificial intelligence technologies or systems. This work is reserved from text and data mining (Article 4(3) Directive (EU) 2019/790).

All Severn House titles are printed on acid-free paper.

Typeset by Palimpsest Book Production Ltd., Falkirk, Stirlingshire, Scotland.
Printed and bound in Great Britain by TJ Books, Padstow, Cornwall.

The manufacturer's authorised representative in the EU for product safety is Authorised Rep Compliance Ltd, 71 Lower Baggot Street, Dublin D02 P593 Ireland (arccompliance.com)

Praise for the Holy Terrors Mysteries

"Charming sleuths and bubbly dialogue add up to an appealing whodunit. A spirited cozy with a supernatural twist"
Kirkus Reviews on *Stone Certainty*

"Fans of Green's Ishmael Jones mysteries will appreciate the supernatural elements"
Library Journal on *Stone Certainty*

"Genuinely frightening. The resolution to the mystery is satisfying, no matter the reader's philosophical bent (skeptics and true believers will be equally happy)"
Booklist on *Stone Certainty*

"Perceptive and witty . . . Great fun"
Booklist on *The Holy Terrors*

"A sleek and appealing . . . homage to vintage whodunits"
Kirkus Reviews on *The Holy Terrors*

About the author

Simon R. Green was born in Bradford-on-Avon, Wiltshire, where he still lives. He is the *New York Times* bestselling author of more than eighty science fiction, fantasy and mystery novels which have sold over four million copies worldwide, including the Nightside, Secret Histories and Ghost Finders series, the Ishmael Jones Mysteries, the Gideon Sable series and the Holy Terrors mystery series.

In the dark heart of an endless night, a full moon blazed like an empty eye, keeping a baleful view on a scene of ancient magic. Miles away from town or city, and centuries away from civilization, on a blasted heath that had long forgotten the great city that once stood in its place, three witches danced around a great brass cauldron. Leaping and howling, wrapped in dark robes like tatters of night, they circled their cauldron like hungry feral creatures. The witches worked their dark arts in the remains of what had once been a noble castle, fallen now to wreckage and ruin, brought down by time and the elements and the arrogance of its builders, who thought the civilization they built would last forever.

The witches hurled themselves around the cauldron, singing songs of horror and hatred, while in the background their followers swayed and stamped through the patterns of a ritual dance older than human memory. A brutal, primitive people, they had fallen far from the days of science and reason, and now wore only scraps of old armour and tanned hide, held together by rusted steel chain. Their snarling faces were blue with woad, their hair fashioned into stiff peaks with caked mud, their eyes bright with the prospect of vengeance on their enemies. In this place of power, a terrible magic was being let loose in the world.

Thunder rolled and lightning flashed, filling the scene with all the unleashed furies of an unnatural world. The witches howled back at the raging elements, and supernatural sounds answered them from the far reaches of the night. More than people had come to this awful place, summoned from distant realms to witness the malevolent magic of three horribly gifted women.

They broke off from their dance to snatch up pieces of old technology from the pile beside the cauldron, laughing at broken circuit boards and parts from smashed machines, before throwing them in. Sacrifices from a lost world: the future that was. The three witches came together before the cauldron and turned to stare out at their audience. The Hecatea, the three ages of woman: Crone, Mother and Maiden.

The Crone raised her voice. 'When shall we three meet again . . .'

But before she could complete the famous line, poisonous fumes boiled up out of the cauldron: a thick choking smoke that sent the three women staggering away, coughing harshly. Other members of the cast ran forward to help them. The supernatural sounds broke off as someone shut down the sound system, and stage lights snapped on as someone ran forward to throw a heavy blanket over the cauldron, smothering the fumes. The blasted heath was revealed to be just a stage, the castle ruins merely a painted backdrop, and all those present nothing more than fretful players, thrust rudely out of their make-believe in the face of a more everyday problem.

The director came storming on to the stage. 'This is the last straw! I refuse to continue with this production until something is done to stop things like this from happening! We can't go on like this!'

People crowded around the director, doing their best to soothe and calm him down, without any notable success. At the far side of the stage, Macbeth and Lady Macbeth stood together, observing the situation. Macbeth shrugged heavily.

'The man's not wrong. You expect a certain amount of disruption with a play as famously unlucky as *Macbeth*, but this many accidents and interruptions makes me wonder whether someone is trying to sabotage the show. We can't go on like this, but what else can we do?'

Lady Macbeth smiled briefly. 'I may have an idea.'

She moved off to one side, reached inside her long gown and brought out a mobile phone. She selected a number, waited a moment, and then her face lit up as she heard a familiar voice.

'Bish! It's Diana. We're needed.'

ONE
And All the Stage a World

Late on a cold grey afternoon, Bishop Alistair Kincaid strode purposefully down London's Berwick Street. He was still unclear as to why Diana needed his help. It had to be some kind of mystery, because that was their calling, and she had mentioned that something like witchcraft might be targeting the people she was working with. Alistair smiled slightly despite himself. Just another day's work for the Actress and the Bishop.

People nodded and smiled as they recognized him from all the early-morning television shows he'd appeared on, as the acceptable face of modern Christianity. Alistair smiled and nodded back but was careful not to slow down. Ever since he and Diana Hunt had acquired a reputation for solving mysteries, it seemed the public just couldn't get enough of them.

Alistair paused before a gentleman's outfitters to admire the elegant three-piece suits on display. Works of art cut from the very best cloth, modelled by smiling mannequins too perfect to be real. Alistair had always found them just a bit creepy. He took a step back to better observe his reflection. Tall and sturdy, in his late twenties, Alistair wore his traditional dark suit and dog collar as a kind of armour to keep an intrusive world at arm's length. Rimless glasses helped take the edge off what the tabloids liked to call his classically handsome features. Alistair had always thought of himself as just another face in the crowd; throw a stick and you'd hit a dozen just like him.

He set off again, past rows of canvas-covered stalls offering everything from ethnic foods to fashionable items that might or might not be all they claimed. And then the whole character of the area suddenly changed as the street came to an abrupt end. Alistair frowned at the decrepit buildings before him, brought low by time and long neglect. Grim grey frontages of worn-down stone and distressed brickwork, like scars on a beaten face. Paint peeled from doors that rarely got a chance to open, and windows stared emptily like so many blind eyes. A forgotten street in a neglected neighbourhood that might once have served a purpose but now only took up space as it hung around hoping to catch a developer's eye.

Alistair made his way slowly down the deserted avenue, until he reached a particularly gothic frontage boasting scowling gargoyle faces and jutting stone promontories. The whole effect suggested a building putting on a good front, like any working girl past her best, while wondering if it was still worth the effort. A faded sign proclaimed *The Theatre of Dreams*, though the exterior suggested that whatever dreams still haunted the place were of a more troubled kind these days.

A massive front door with frosted glass panels and gilded decorations looked as if it might still offer access to the occasional wonder, but its shabby state suggested whatever remained was almost certainly draped in cobwebs. Alistair considered the door thoughtfully, like a knight in armour standing before a cave and wondering if the dragon within really needed slaying.

Since he was there to visit a member of the cast, tradition demanded he go round the side and use the stage entrance. But since he was a bishop, Alistair always made a point of using the front door as a matter of principle. That way, everyone knew where they stood. There was no bell or knocker, so Alistair tried the handle and raised an eyebrow when he found it wasn't locked. He pushed the door open and stepped into an echoing open space half hidden by deep, dark shadows. He called out his name, but answer came there none – just a faint susurrus of echoes, like a crowd of extras murmuring in the background.

Alistair let the door swing shut and looked about him, allowing his eyes time to adjust to the gloom. A little light spilled in through the door's glass panels from outside, the narrow beams picking out dust particles hanging like specks of frozen time in the cloudy spotlights. What had once been a stately and even elegant lobby gradually emerged from the shadows, revealing bare floorboards that hadn't been waxed or polished in ages and cracked plaster walls without even a single poster to boast of past glories or announce the Theatre of Dreams' new lease on life.

Alistair found a light switch by the door, and dusty bulbs in old-fashioned chandeliers flickered reluctantly to life. He wondered whether he should call out again. He'd told Diana when to expect him. He moved slowly forward, his footsteps sounding out loud and distinct in the suffocating quiet, like the tick and tock of some great clock. And then Alistair frowned as he realized he could hear another set of footsteps. He stopped and looked quickly around him. There was no one else in the lobby. He glanced behind him, but the door was still solidly shut. No one could have entered the lobby without him knowing.

Alistair started forward again, and the other footsteps moved along with him, each separate sound clear and deliberate, as though whoever was responsible wanted to be sure Alistair could hear them. He half wondered whether it might be some kind of delayed echo, but when he concentrated on the sounds, he realized they were coming from above him. As though someone was walking on the ceiling. He stopped and looked up, but the bare ceiling stared blankly back. The other footsteps had stopped as well, as if taunting him. Alistair could feel the hackles rising on the back of his neck. He was completely alone in the lobby. He could see that. He just wasn't sure he believed it.

He looked carefully around him, checking every detail and searching every shadow. He still couldn't see anyone, or even sense the pressure of unseen watching eyes. All he could be sure of was that he wasn't as alone as he should be. He scowled up at the ceiling again and examined the chandeliers for any sign something might be hiding in their recesses, but everything was still and quiet. Apart from whatever had emerged from the theatre's past to haunt the present and make it clear he wasn't at all welcome.

Witchcraft, Diana had said. *Maybe black magic too. I need you, Bish.*

Alistair took a deep breath and set off again, only to stop almost immediately when he realized the other footsteps were no longer accompanying him. Which ruled out any possibility of an echo. And then Alistair's head snapped round as he heard new footsteps approaching from inside the theatre. He turned to face the door at the far end of the lobby, his hands clenched into fists. It slammed open and Diana burst into the lobby. She let out a whoop of joy the moment she saw Alistair, hurried forward with outstretched arms and swept Alistair into a hug so fierce it all but crushed the breath out of him. He lifted Diana off her feet and swung her around, and she threw back her head and laughed out loud. After a while, Alistair set her down again, and they stepped back and smiled happily at each other.

Diana Hunt was a tall, striking woman in her early thirties, well built and proud of it, as magnificent as ever in a baroque evening gown of deepest burgundy adorned with a great many ruffles and flourishes. Her long dark hair had been artfully piled up on top of her head, so there would be nothing to distract from her famous features, dominated as always by her bright eyes and wicked smile. Though her makeup was still so extreme it practically had a personality of its own.

'It's good to see you again,' said Alistair. 'This must be some mystery you've invited me in to solve – I've only been here a few moments and already I've heard someone walking around on the ceiling. Is that the kind of thing you wanted to talk about?'

Diana frowned. 'Not really, no. Strolling on the ceiling is something new. But it is typical of the kind of things that have been driving all of us out of our minds. You would not believe the weird stuff that's been going on in this theatre.'

'Is anyone in danger?' said Alistair.

'I think we could be heading in that direction,' Diana said carefully. 'Someone really doesn't believe that the show must go on.'

'Then it's a good thing I'm here.' Alistair smiled at her. 'We've been apart too long, Diana. Caught up in our own careers.'

'You're the one who insists on keeping me at arm's length,' said Diana.

'I have responsibilities to my Church,' said Alistair.

'I have responsibilities to my reputation,' said Diana.

They laughed softly together. Alistair had no doubt they would arrive at a solution to their problem eventually. He was looking forward to it.

'The tabloids are fascinated enough by us as it is,' he said.

'You were the one who dubbed us the Holy Terrors,' Diana said cheerfully.

Alistair winced, just a little. 'I could have lived without that catching on.'

'No such thing as too much publicity,' said Diana. 'Particularly when I'm stuck in a dog's breakfast of a show like this.'

Alistair felt justified in raising an eyebrow. 'You told me this was a big prestigious production.'

'Well, it was, darling,' said Diana. 'Right up until the spooky stuff started happening. We could use your calm and analytical mind, Bish.'

'I'll do everything I can to help,' said Alistair.

'Of course you will,' said Diana. 'That's what you do.'

Alistair considered her thoughtfully. 'Your summons was rather cryptic. What exactly have I been called in to investigate?'

Instead of answering him, Diana frowned at the ceiling as though she could compel it to give up its secrets.

'Did you really hear someone walking about up there?'

'I heard footsteps,' Alistair said carefully. 'I didn't actually see anyone. Have people here been seeing, or hearing, similar things?'

Diana slipped her arm through his and pressed it firmly against her side. 'It's complicated, darling. Come along with me, and I'll introduce you to everyone.'

'Will things become clearer then?'

Diana smiled brightly. 'I doubt it.'

Alistair had thought the lobby was grim, but it was nothing compared to the dimly lit corridor on the other side of the far door. Bare walls and an uncomfortably low ceiling conspired to produce a purely functional passageway, designed to channel people from one place to another without any threat of distraction or enjoyment. Diana couldn't hold back a smile as she took in the expression on Alistair's face.

'The magic of the theatre always disappears the moment you go backstage. It's like visiting the kitchen at your favourite restaurant and seeing what they put in the stew.'

'Tell me about the play you're doing,' said Alistair.

'It's a new interpretation of Shakespeare's *Macbeth*,' Diana said briskly. 'The background has been changed from the past to the future, after the collapse of civilization. To take the story out of history and into legend. There are other changes too, most of them guaranteed to leave the purists spitting feathers. Which might explain some of the unfortunate events that have been plaguing us.'

'Choosing a theatre this old couldn't have helped,' said Alistair. 'It's probably only stubbornness and inertia that's keeping this ancient relic from collapsing around you.'

'Oh, please!' said Diana. 'This is just rehearsal space. A major West End theatre is just waiting to welcome us with open arms, the moment its current production breathes its last so we can boot it out the door.'

'The business of theatre, red in tooth and claw,' Alistair said solemnly.

'It's a jungle out there,' said Diana.

'Tell me what's been happening,' said Alistair.

Diana nodded slowly. 'Right from the beginning, things started going wrong. Scripts disappeared when no one was looking, and props and costumes went astray, only to turn up again once it was too late. At first, we thought we had a practical joker in our midst . . . But then people started hearing footsteps, and movements, and voices, when there couldn't have been anyone else around. Dim figures have been glimpsed, staring silently from the shadows, but there was never anyone there when the braver souls went to challenge them. Sometimes a member of the cast would hear a knocking on their dressing-room door, but when they called out for whoever it was to come in, there was no response. And when they opened the door, the corridor was always empty.'

'Actors can be very superstitious,' Alistair said carefully. 'How much of this could be down to their imaginations?'

'Trust me,' said Diana. 'No one here is that imaginative. The show's producers hired special security people to keep an eye on things, but they ended up more spooked than the cast and walked out, rather than work here. The producers keep promising us replacements, but no one wants to know. It seems word has got around that the Theatre of Dreams is an unquiet place.'

'How will the play's director feel about my being called in?' said Alistair.

'Richard will be very grateful,' Diana said firmly. 'If he knows what's good for him. He needs all the help he can get.'

'So far, it all sounds very . . . circumstantial,' said Alistair. 'Is there anything specific you can point a finger at?'

'Scenery has collapsed when no one was anywhere near it,' Diana said flatly. 'A stage light fell from the gantry and almost hit Macbeth. I finally called you after poisonous fumes suddenly started boiling out of the witches' cauldron.'

'Was anyone hurt?' said Alistair.

'No, just some runny eyes and a lot of coughing.' Diana met his gaze steadily. 'Someone has got it in for us, Bish.'

'You should have contacted me before things got so out of control,' said Alistair.

'It took me till now to realize they had! Actors are used to bad luck when it comes to putting on the Caledonian Tragedy.'

'Really?' said Alistair. 'That's an actual thing?'

'Hard to say, darling,' said Diana. 'Give a play a bad name for long enough and it becomes a self-fulfilling prophecy. What worries me is that some of the problems we're facing do seem to have a supernatural aspect.'

She shot Alistair a challenging look, but he just nodded.

'You mentioned witchcraft . . .'

Diana shrugged quickly. 'Something sinister is going on.'

'Including black magic?' said Alistair.

'Could be,' said Diana.

Alistair frowned. 'Those are two very different things, though neither of them should ever be treated lightly. What sort of occurrences are we talking about?'

Diana was careful to keep her voice calm and factual. 'You can't keep a plant alive anywhere in this building. They just die. It's always darker than it should be – what light there is seems spoiled, like it's gone off. Strange mystical symbols have been found, carved into the woodwork. Everyone's luck has turned bad. Some people have started talking about being stalked by a presence that can only be glimpsed out of the corner of the eye. And sometimes . . . it feels like there are more actors on stage than the scene calls for.'

Alistair kept his face carefully non-judgemental. He didn't want Diana to think he wasn't taking her seriously. He could hear the strain in her voice. She sighed suddenly and leaned against him.

'Someone painted an inverted cross on Macbeth's dressing-room door. In blood. And just recently . . . I found a doll in my dressing room, dressed in my main costume. Someone had driven a silver pin through its heart.'

'Did you feel any pain?' Alistair said interestedly.

'Of course not!' said Diana. 'But if I did believe in things like that, I think I'd be getting seriously worried!'

'Remember our last case, in the stone circle?' Alistair said gently. 'The dead body that had been pinned to the ground with a pitchfork to suggest witchcraft? But that turned out to be just a distraction to keep us from seeing what was really going on. This could be the same kind of thing.'

'I wish I could believe that,' said Diana. 'Things have been getting seriously scary, Bish. No one feels safe.'

'The whole point of a sustained attack is to wear people down,' said Alistair. 'Has anyone walked out?'

'Not yet,' said Diana. 'But people are talking about it . . .'

'What's stopping them?'

Diana's chin came up, and Alistair smiled as a familiar stubbornness appeared in her eyes.

'This play is a major opportunity for all of us,' she said firmly. 'A chance to be part of a substantial success. And that happens a lot less in the theatre than you might think. Actors will put up with a lot to grab the golden ring just once in their careers. But if this insanity continues, someone is bound to crack, and that could be the start of a general exodus.'

'Most of the things you've been describing could turn out to have perfectly rational explanations,' said Alistair.

'Stick around,' said Diana, 'and I guarantee you'll see something to put a chill in your bones.'

'I did study witchcraft and black magic, back when I was at the seminary,' said Alistair.

'Of course you did,' said Diana.

'Most persecution of witches was really nothing more than disguised attacks on women,' said Alistair. 'For political or religious reasons, or to grab land that had been left to them. But there are written accounts of some who sought out the dark arts – and embraced them. Witchcraft promised power and a chance to punish one's enemies. But it was mostly about messing with other people's minds, to make them believe what the witches wanted them to. The power of suggestion can be very strong. Something like that could be happening here.'

'Someone is trying to break us!' said Diana. 'But no one can figure out who, or why.'

'Once we've worked out the why, that should give us the who,' said Alistair.

Diana smiled brightly. 'I knew I'd called the right person.'

'All right, I've put this off as long as I can,' Alistair said resignedly. 'Tell me about the ghost. Because every old theatre has one.'

'I'm not sure if it means anything,' said Diana. 'But there is an old story . . . about an actor who suddenly left the stage in the middle of a scene, for no apparent reason, and was never seen again. No one knows what happened to him. Legend has it that his ghost can still be felt in the wings, waiting to go back on and finish what he started. And quite a few of us have sensed something, when we've been standing there alone.'

'What would you do if you actually saw the ghost?' said Alistair. He was genuinely interested in what she would say.

'Ask him what he needs to move on,' Diana said immediately. 'Poor old thing, still waiting to take his final bow. To be fair, I don't know anyone who's actually seen him, but then we've all been a bit busy seeing other things.'

'You called, and I'm here,' said Alistair. 'What do you need me to do?'

'Help me work out what's really going on,' said Diana. 'So we can put everyone's minds at rest. And we have to do it fast! This is my big chance to play Lady Macbeth in a major West End run, and I'm not having anything getting in the way!'

Alistair nodded. 'Perfectly good reasons. I'll get straight on it.'

'Damn right you will,' said Diana. 'You didn't think I called you here just for your company, did you?'

'Perish the thought,' said Alistair.

Diana smiled and leaned her head on his shoulder.

'It is good to see you again, Bish.'

'I know,' Alistair said solemnly.

* * *

Diana pushed open a heavy door, and the two of them were suddenly standing at the back of a brightly lit auditorium packed with rows of empty seats, a raised stage at the far end. Alistair was immediately struck by the huge painted backdrop depicting a ruined castle. It looked so real he felt as though he could walk right into it. But apart from a small crowd of actors standing around looking sullen and rebellious and not in any way acting, the stage was empty of furniture or props. Alistair turned to Diana.

'Is this supposed to be the blasted heath?' he said politely.

'We're currently in between sets,' said Diana. 'Our beloved director took one look at the proposed designs and said none of them were up to his high standards. So the set designers were sent weeping and gnashing their teeth back to their drawing boards, with instructions to do better or be replaced.'

'Bit of a perfectionist, your director?' said Alistair.

'Like you wouldn't believe,' said Diana.

The actors were wearing everything from rags and tatters interspersed with bits of armour to exaggerated military uniforms and gorgeous evening gowns, in a collection of styles from periods that didn't so much clash as openly threaten each other.

'An interesting look,' Alistair said finally. 'Reminds me of the *Mad Max* movies.'

'I'm pretty sure that's what the director is going for,' said Diana.

'And he chose that look because . . .?'

'Because he can! The theatre is all about making an impact and getting yourself noticed. Now, you see the joyless individual holding everyone's attention, whether they like it or not? That is our revered director, Richard Sutton. A superbly talented, profits-generating, general pain in the arse.'

Alistair nodded at a woman hovering uncertainly beside the director. 'And who is that unhappy-looking person?'

'Josie Turner,' said Diana. 'Costumes mistress, for her sins. Richard has been putting her through hell, because he will keep changing his mind every ten minutes. The only reason she hasn't had a complete nervous breakdown and buried her pinking shears between Richard's shoulder blades is because she can't find the time.'

Josie was half hidden inside an oversized black leather jacket and trousers, topped off with a peaked cap pulled down hard over a mass of dark curly hair. Her sharp features were mostly hidden behind a pair of enormous sunglasses. She looked to be in her late thirties, but fighting it hard. Her whole body radiated tension as she scurried after the director, anxiously waiting for his approval of her latest costumes.

Richard was medium height, lean and lanky, in a sweater-and-jeans combination so determinedly sloppy it had to be a statement. Barely into his late twenties, he had dark floppy hair that gave every appearance of never meeting a comb it liked, and a face dominated by a scowl so deep it had to be a default expression. He stalked back and forth, almost crackling with nervous energy as he snapped out one instruction after another: to change this, rearrange that and bury something else so deep it would never be found.

The costumes mistress did her best to keep up with him, jotting down frantic notes and nodding quickly at each new decree. Some of the cast shot her quiet looks of betrayal, but she avoided their gaze. The director finally gave Josie his grudging approval, subject to all the latest changes being carried out, and she sprinted offstage before he could come up with something else to make her life more difficult.

The director turned back to his actors and lowered his head like a bull getting ready to charge. The cast visibly braced themselves. But before Richard could get a word out, Diana's voice cracked across the auditorium like a velvet whip.

'Richard, darling, there's someone here you really need to meet!'

The director spun round to hit Diana with the full force of his glare, ready to let loose with something loud and cutting, and then saw who she was with and thought better of it. He hurried down from the stage and strode over to join them. Alistair's first impression was that the director seemed more mad at the world in general than anyone in particular. The kind of anger that had to be constantly stoked and maintained, because it had a lot of ground to cover. Richard slammed to a halt in front of Alistair and looked him over as though searching for some defect he could use as ammunition.

'Play nicely, Richard,' Diana said quickly. 'The Bish is here to bail us out.'

'God knows somebody needs to,' said Richard. 'I've never known a production as cursed as this.' He sniffed loudly and straightened his back to give him more height, so he could look down his nose at Alistair. 'You took your time getting here, Bishop. Make yourself useful; we need a high-energy, pedal-to-the-metal, bell-book-and-candle blessing on this production, to cancel out all the negative energy that's interfering with my work.'

'That isn't really what I do,' said Alistair.

'You can manage a few words,' Diana said encouragingly. 'Put on a bit of a show, calm everyone down. You know . . . the usual.'

'Put some backbone into them!' said Richard. 'God knows they could use it.'

He turned on his heel and strode back to the stage. Alistair and Diana exchanged a glance and strolled unhurriedly after him. Just to make it clear they weren't going to be ordered about. Richard stomped up on to the stage and glowered impartially at his cast.

'Pay attention!' he said loudly. 'This is the bishop from the Holy Terrors, come here specially to save your arses. So listen to what the man has to say! Because otherwise you haven't got a prayer.'

The cast looked on Alistair like drowning men who'd just been offered a glass of water. He smiled easily about him.

'Always remember that even the longest run of bad luck will end eventually. And that not everything that might seem weird and uncanny is necessarily anything of the kind. Try not to worry so much; there are no rods so harsh as the ones we make for our own backs with our darkest imaginings. But just in case, I will pronounce a blessing on this show and everyone in it. If you'll all please bow your heads . . .'

He waited for everyone to adopt a suitably respectful pose, or fake it as best they could, and then just started talking and prayed the right words would come.

'May the good Lord bless this production and this cast. Let everyone in this theatre be safe from whatever walks in the darkness or plots in the shadows, and from all bad influences. I invoke Heaven's protection against every unfriendly force and malign intent. Let there be peace and harmony, and may the only voices raised in anger be those on stage.'

There was a brief murmur of laughter and a general nodding of heads.

'Nice one, Bish,' Diana said quietly.

The director looked at Alistair in an *Is that it?* sort of way. Alistair stared right back at him, and the director turned abruptly and bustled off into the wings, as though he'd just remembered somewhere he needed to be. One of the actors stepped forward.

'Todd Nelson,' Diana murmured to Alistair. 'Playing Macbeth.'

'Good to meet you,' said Alistair, but Todd didn't even look at him. He was too busy scowling at Diana.

Well into his late twenties, tall and imposing, Todd was wearing a stark but stylish military outfit. Dark-haired and dark-eyed, he was so generically handsome that his face was almost completely lacking in character, but his gaze was fierce and challenging as he loomed over Diana.

'I told you not to call this man. We don't need his kind of help.'

'First,' Diana said sweetly, 'you're not the boss of me. And second, he's exactly what we do need.'

'It's all just people's nerves!'

Diana smiled. 'Well, they're not looking so nervous now.'

'And how long do you think that will last?' said Todd.

'Long enough for the Bish and me to figure out what's really going on,' said Diana.

Todd finally deigned to scowl at Alistair, in a way that said *I'm important and you're not.*

'I've read about the Holy Terrors,' he said. 'Whenever you turn up, it means people are going to die.'

'I'll do my best to prevent that from happening,' said Alistair.

'And if you can't?'

'Then I will make sure the guilty parties face justice.'

Todd didn't quite sneer. 'No one was ever arrested on your previous cases. The bad guys just died.'

'I can't take any responsibility for that,' said Alistair.

'Are you saying it was God's justice?' said Todd.

Alistair could tell he'd been pulled into an argument he was never going to win, so he just smiled calmly at the actor.

'The Lord does have a fondness for mysterious ways . . .'

Todd scowled at Diana. 'Keep your pet on a leash. Or I'll muzzle him.'

He showed them both his back and strode off. Diana glanced apologetically at Alistair.

'Sorry about that. You're not seeing Todd at his best. He's carrying all the weight of playing the lead, as well as struggling to cope with all the bad things that have been happening. Don't take anything he says too personally. It's just the strain getting to him.'

'The way it's affecting the director?' said Alistair.

Diana smiled briefly. 'Not really. You can sometimes reason with Richard.'

Another actor emerged from the crowd to join them, wearing a similar military outfit to Todd's, though perhaps a shade less impressive, to make it clear he wasn't the lead. Average height, late twenties and strikingly handsome, with light blonde hair and a neat goatee beard. He wore his uniform as though born to it.

'Paul Gerhard, our Banquo,' said Diana.

Paul nodded affably to Alistair. 'Don't mind Todd; he spends most of his time convinced the entire world is out to get him, so he has to get his retaliation in first. He'll ease up when he sees you really are here to help.'

'Have you known him long?' said Alistair.

'Oh, Todd and I go way back,' said Paul. 'Worked together on all kinds of things. But this is our first big Shakespeare, and that's enough pressure on its own without all the nonsense we've been having to put up with.'

'Do you believe anything out of the ordinary is going on?' said Alistair.

Paul was shaking his head before Alistair had even finished speaking.

'I haven't seen a single thing that I'd put down to other-worldly forces. No, this is sabotage. Has to be. Some rival company has got it in for the producers. Unless it's a personal vendetta against someone in the cast.'

'It wouldn't be that difficult to get into this theatre without being noticed,' said Alistair. 'When I arrived, the front door wasn't even locked.'

'Oh, not again,' said Paul. 'We have got to get some new security people! But I'll tell you this much, Bishop: a witch in a pointed hat could go flying over the stage on her broomstick, throwing exploding black cats in all directions, and Todd and I would still rise above it. We've spent our entire careers waiting for a break like this, and no one is going to rob us of our big chance.'

'Some of what I've been hearing does sound like intimidation,' said Alistair. 'But has there been any real threat aimed at an individual?'

Paul thought about it. 'It feels more like the bad stuff is aimed at the production in general. Since Todd is the lead, he's had to put up with more problems than anyone else, but apart from a falling stage light, which didn't even come close to hitting him, despite all the noise he made, I don't believe he's ever been in any real danger. Same with me, and Diana. And we would have talked about it; the three of us have become pretty close during rehearsals.'

'Macbeth and Banquo are being played as a bromance,' said Diana. 'With Lady Macbeth as the third point in the love triangle.'

Alistair limited himself to a raised eyebrow, but Diana wasn't going to let him off the hook that easily.

'Feeling a little bit shocked, Bish?'

'Does the text support this new interpretation?' said Alistair.

'It doesn't *not* support it,' said Diana. 'It's all in the way you say the lines.'

'And the way we look at each other,' said Paul.

'Body language can add a hell of a lot,' said Diana.

'Especially with a body like yours,' said Paul.

They grinned at each other.

'And all of this was the director's idea?' said Alistair.

'Oh, Richard is brimming over with ideas,' said Paul. 'Some better than others. At least this one gives us some interesting subtext to play with.'

'Are there any love scenes?' Alistair said calmly. 'A little provocative nudity, perhaps? I understand that's very fashionable in modern Shakespeare productions.'

'Unfortunately, no,' said Diana. 'I keep telling Richard, if he'd only let us off the leash now and again, we could really heat up the stage, but he just keeps saying that would be distracting. Of course it would! That's how you can tell I'm doing my job!'

'You'll have to excuse me,' Paul said suddenly. 'But I can see Todd getting himself into yet more trouble. I swear, protecting that man from himself is a full-time job. Some days I'm amazed he's survived this long without an armed bodyguard.'

He hurried over to where Todd was exchanging angry words with a handful of actors in colourful military outfits. Alistair looked to Diana.

'Thanes,' she said shortly. 'The aristocracy always get the best costumes.'

Alistair watched interestedly as Paul walked right into the argument and simply raised his voice until it drowned out Todd's. He then carried on talking unruffled good sense until Todd just gave up and turned away. Soon enough the Thanes were laughing along with Paul, knowing he was laying on the charm but ready to let things slide. It was clear they had a lot more respect for their Banquo than they did for their Macbeth. Paul finally left the Thanes chuckling over some particularly scurrilous piece of gossip and moved away to drop a companionable arm across Todd's shoulders. He led him away, talking quietly and persuasively. Alistair shook his head.

'Todd would appear to be his own worst enemy.'

'I don't know,' said Diana. 'There's quite a queue . . .'

'Tell me about your director,' said Alistair. 'What did Richard do before this?'

Diana looked at him. 'Oh, come on, darling, even you must have heard of his hit musical, based on *The Swiss Family Robinson*. An entirely unexpected success that's turned into a phenomenon. It's made so much profit even show business accountants couldn't hide it. People in a position to know are saying it's going to be even bigger than *The Lion King*, and that's made so much money you can see it from space.'

'I had heard about the musical,' said Alistair. 'I just didn't recognize the director's name.'

'Not many do, outside the profession,' said Diana. 'It's not like the movies, where the director's name comes before anyone else. In the theatre, the public only ever cares about the stars. But inside the business, Richard is seen as a proven money-maker, which means he can do no wrong. Everyone wanted him for their next big project, and the producers of this show couldn't believe their luck when he agreed to do it.'

Alistair frowned. 'If Richard is so well off, why does he feel the need to be working again so soon?'

'To prove his first success wasn't a fluke,' said Diana. 'Right now, everyone wants to get into bed with Richard so he can make them rich too. But those of us who've had the dubious pleasure of working with the man aren't as convinced. His idea of dealing with any problem is just to throw the producers' money at it until it goes away. Sooner or later, they're going to have to tell him no, and that's when the shit will hit the fan so hard it will gum up the works. But the producers know that if they fire Richard, or let him walk, they'll lose their chance at a guaranteed hit. Except that there's no such thing in this business.'

'So we're talking about a man who makes enemies easily,' said Alistair. 'Could he have behaved just as badly during the *Swiss Family Robinson* musical? So much so that someone in that cast is still nursing a grudge?'

Diana shook her head slowly. 'I haven't heard of any feelings hurt that badly. Richard must have enemies, just because of the way he is, but I honestly couldn't suggest any names. Actors will put up with a lot when a director is as talented and successful as Richard, in the hope some of it will rub off on them. Besides, it's obvious when he starts shouting at people that he isn't mad at them personally, just at the problem they represent. It's all to do with the difference between the performance in his head and the one in front of him. The raised voice and flailing arms are always all about the play. Actors get that.'

'What about the producers?' said Alistair. 'If Richard has been throwing their money around like there's no tomorrow . . .'

'So far, they've been careful to keep their opinions to themselves,' said Diana. 'Rather than risk upsetting the goose who might still lay sizeable golden eggs.'

'The love of profits is the root of all evil,' Alistair said solemnly.

Diana took Alistair firmly by the arm. 'You need to talk to our witches.'

She hauled him over to three women standing to one side, dressed in flowing black robes and chatting cheerfully together.

They broke off as Alistair and Diana approached, and Diana hugged his arm against her side to make it clear he was her property.

'This is the Bish. My partner in crimes.'

The witches studied Alistair with open interest. He smiled politely back at them.

'I know. You thought I'd be taller.'

'I was looking for the halo,' said the older of the three witches.

'That was Roger Moore,' said Alistair.

'These are our Hecatea,' Diana said grandly. 'Between them they represent the three archetypes of woman: the Maiden, the Mother and the Crone.'

Alistair looked at her. 'The concept seems to have broken down mid-alliteration.'

Diana smiled brightly back at him. 'No one likes a smart arse, Bish.' She nodded at the youngest of the three women. 'This is Jenny Sweet, playing the Maiden. Made her name in a *Downton Abbey*-style sitcom – *Where's My Monocle?* – playing the downstairs maid who turns out to be smarter than all the aristocracy put together.'

Jenny smiled politely at Alistair. Tall, blonde and willowy, barely into her twenties, she was pretty enough in a generic kind of way. Alistair couldn't help thinking that while that might be good enough for television, she might have trouble standing out on a stage. Though she did wear her dark robes with a certain style.

'This is my first Shakespeare,' she said in a light breathy voice. 'And my first big stage production. I'm learning so much from everyone! But I never went to university, so every time people start talking about exploring the subtleties implicit in the text, I can't help feeling just a bit out of my depth . . .'

'You're doing fine, dear,' said the middle-aged woman next to her. 'Just act like you understand what you're saying, and the audience will go along.'

'Angela Harrison, playing the Mother,' said Diana. 'Come to us after a long run as the family matriarch in that ever-popular soap, *Cockney Sparrows*.'

Angela's sweeping robes couldn't disguise a more-than-ample frame, but she had a pleasant enough face and a knowing smile.

Alistair thought she had the look of a woman who'd seen it all before and was determined not to let it happen again. She nodded easily to him.

'I know what you're thinking. Did she jump from the soap or was she pushed? To tell the truth, it was a bit of both. I'd been playing the part so long I could have done it in my sleep, and sometimes it felt like I had. The writers saved all their best material for the young leads.' She shrugged. 'So I resigned before they could fire me. That always plays better in the media. I thought I'd done really well to land this role until I discovered the whole production was cursed. Things around here couldn't feel more supernatural if we had vampires hanging from the lighting rig and werewolves taking a dump in the wings. I keep expecting to look in my dressing-room mirror and find I've developed real warts instead of these fake ones makeup insist on plastering all over our faces. I swear, one good sneeze and they'd fly across the stage like shrapnel.'

'I don't believe in curses,' said the third and final witch. 'We make our own luck.'

'Sarah Warner,' said Diana. 'The Crone.'

Sarah nodded shortly to Alistair, just to make it clear how unimpressed she was by him or his title. Alistair was impressed she could squeeze so much meaning into one small gesture. Medium height and just a bit stooped, Sarah was late middle-aged but made up to look older, and wore her robes as though someone had deliberately forced them on her to undermine her performance. She fixed Alistair with a flinty stare, her mouth compressed into a thin line.

'It's going to take a lot more than a prayer packed full of platitudes to stop whoever's behind this.'

Alistair just smiled politely. 'So what do you think is going on?'

Sarah snorted loudly. 'It's all just practical jokes and nasty tricks, designed to undermine our confidence and sink this production. Someone has it in for us, though don't ask me why.'

Alistair nodded. 'Does anyone in the cast have an enemy that you know of?'

Sarah didn't snort again, but she looked as if she wanted to. 'No one gets far in this business without stamping on a few toes.

People who believe they should have been given our parts, or are convinced they could have done it better if only they'd had the chance. But we've all talked about this, and no one can put a name to anyone who's been hurt badly enough to justify this much malice.'

'What did you do before you came here?' said Alistair.

For the first time, Sarah's gaze faltered just a little. 'You're probably too young to remember, but I used to be a scream queen back in the eighties.'

'Of course I remember,' said Alistair. '*Hellblazer Apocalypse. Nightmares in a Damaged Soul. Tales of Ghostly Horror.* I watched every single one of them on late-night television. Of course, these days I have them all on Blu-ray, so I can immerse myself in the behind-the-scenes extras. I love a good *Making of.*'

Sarah clapped both hands to her cheeks in mock horror. 'Oh, dear Lord – a fan! I never did understand what people like you saw in my movies. Isn't the world bad enough as it is, without making up more things to depress us?'

'Coping with a false fear can help you cope better with a real one,' said Alistair.

Sarah did manage another snort for that. 'For me, it was always just another job. I screamed on cue, took the money and ran. But, inevitably, there came a time when the directors stopped casting me in favour of some younger bit of stuff. I ended up touring the memorabilia shows, signing old photos and telling the same half-dozen anecdotes over and over again. Didn't take me long to get seriously tired of that . . . So when Richard said he wanted me as one of his witches, I jumped at the chance. Turns out he's another one who's seen every one of my films. Who knew I had so many followers?'

'So that's us,' Angela said comfortably. 'The three ages of woman. Magic and mayhem a speciality. But honestly, Bishop, there's no real witchery going on here. It's just someone messing with people's heads, for reasons of their own. So . . . what are you going to do to sort all of this out?'

The three witches stared unwaveringly at Alistair. He took his time, to show he wasn't going to be hurried or pressured.

'Can any of you name someone who's seemed in actual danger?' he said finally.

Jenny shook her head quickly. 'If things had got that bad, I wouldn't still be here.'

'There's never been any real threat, as such,' said Angela. 'It's all things you can't quite put your finger on, or get your head around. That's what makes it so unnerving.'

'Whoever it is,' Sarah said heavily, 'they don't know a damned thing about real witchcraft. I've spent years studying Wicca and the pagan way. I know all kinds of special-effects tricks that would make people sit up and take notice, but can I get our genius director to pay any attention?'

'He never listens to any of us,' said Jenny. 'He just wants the Maiden, the Mother and the Crone. It's so limiting! So I am playing my witch like Sabrina, in the TV show.'

'While I have decided my character sold her soul to the devil for power to fight the patriarchy,' said Angela. 'I am a supernatural freedom fighter.'

'I'm playing my witch as a faded femme fatale,' said Sarah. 'Because that's what I'm good at. I've been pushing the body language so hard it's practically grabbing people by the lapels and shouting in their faces. You should have seen me vamp Macbeth during the prophecy scene; he didn't know where to look.'

'He wasn't alone in that,' said Angela.

Jenny nodded solemnly. Sarah glared at both of them.

Alistair cut in quickly. 'Wasn't there a character called Hecate, who was head of the witches?'

'Richard thought she got in the way of the three archetypes, so he cut the role and shared her lines out among us,' said Angela.

Sarah sniffed. 'It's always dangerous when a director starts rewriting Shakespeare. Gives them ideas above their station.'

'Richard must know what he's doing,' said Jenny. 'I mean, look at how much money his last production made . . .'

Sarah shook her head firmly. 'Just because he can turn out a hit musical, it doesn't mean he's got what it takes to direct Shakespeare.'

'How has Richard been treating you?' said Alistair.

The three actresses glanced quickly at each other, as though sensing a trap. They each considered their answer carefully, as though not wanting to say anything that might incriminate them.

'He doesn't bother us much,' said Angela.

'He always has lots of good ideas,' said Jenny.

'He's a pain in the arse to work with,' said Sarah. 'But there's no denying the boy has talent.'

Alistair just nodded and changed the subject. 'How do all of you think the play is going?'

The witches relaxed a little now they were back on safe ground.

'I'm just doing my best not to be overwhelmed,' said Jenny.

'You're doing fine, dear,' said Sarah, patting Jenny's arm comfortingly.

Angela shrugged. 'Mostly, it's just business as usual. Turn up on time, say the furniture and don't bump into the lines.'

'Is this your first Shakespeare?' said Alistair.

Angela hit him with a hard look. 'I started out with the Royal Shakespeare Company at Stratford, playing all the usual serving wenches, maids and walk-ons. Until I realized they were never going to give me anything better. So I told them they could take their pecking order and shove it, and I left, for better parts and better money in films and television. But I still had a yen to play in a great Shakespearean production, so when Richard offered me this role, I grabbed it with both hands. I don't care what kind of nonsense is going on; they couldn't get me out of here with a crowbar.'

'Same here,' said Sarah. 'I decided a long time ago that I was going to die with my makeup on, because I don't have anything else. There was only ever room in my life for me and my career. I am in this for the duration, no matter how many dirty tricks someone throws in my direction.'

'Aren't you even a little bit excited at the prospect of appearing in a West End run?' said Jenny.

Sarah shrugged. 'Too little, too late.'

The director raised his voice from the other side of the stage.

'Would the three witches care to join the rest of us in working for a living, if they can find the time?'

'Oh God,' said Angela. 'Little Miss Hissy Fit is out of her pram again.'

'That man seriously needs his ashes hauled,' said Sarah.

'There are limits to how far I am prepared to go, for the good of the show,' Jenny said coldly.

The actresses closed ranks, like soldiers preparing themselves for the fray, and went to join the rest of the cast. Seeing that Alistair and Diana were now free, one of the few actors not required for the scene took the opportunity to approach them.

'This is our King Duncan,' Diana murmured to Alistair. 'Mark DeWald. A big name in his day, for those who can remember that far back.'

Mark advanced on them with a slow and ponderous gait. An extremely large and powerful figure, he wore an exquisitely tailored suit of armour that had to struggle to contain his oversized frame. Mark's once-handsome face showed the ravages of a long life enjoyed to the full, with all the broken blood vessels you'd expect from the truly determined drinker, and eyes like piss-holes in the snow. It was like looking at the ruins of what had once been a noble edifice. Not without its charms, but with evident cracks in the façade. Mark swayed to a halt before Alistair and Diana, and addressed them in a hearty booming voice.

'Delighted to make the acquaintance of the celebrated Holy Terrors! Mark DeWald, at your service. Once a big name, now just a big man! It's been a while since I was in a production destined for greatness, but by damn, it's good to be back. I feel like some old soldier sniffing blood and grapeshot on the air.' He leaned forward and lowered his voice a little. 'These days I mostly run a pub and restaurant down in Cornwall, but I'm always happy to emerge from semi-retirement for the right role. And it did help that the money was good, for a change. The restaurant business isn't what it used to be.'

'So this is your comeback?' said Alistair.

'Could be, could be,' said Mark. 'If all goes well, which, as you must know, it really isn't just at the moment. Hopefully, you are here to do something about that.'

'I'll do my best,' said Alistair. 'Apart from the weird stuff, how are you enjoying the production?'

Mark spared a brief glance for the director. 'I don't know if *enjoying* is quite the word I'd choose. It's hard to give of your best with so little encouragement. If dear Richard didn't have a bad word to say, I doubt he'd talk to me at all.' He sighed heavily, his great chest rising and falling. 'Once upon a time, I was a noted face on the London scene. The most promising talent of my generation, or so the critics said. But instead of concentrating on refining my craft, I gave myself over to good booze and bad company. Happy times and excellent memories, but when I think of who and what I might have been . . .'

A sudden melancholy overtook him, like a shadow falling across his face. He turned with a certain slow majesty and moved off like a galleon under full sail. A much younger actor immediately hurried forward to take his place. Tall and lean, with just a hint of gangling, he had the kind of face that needed more life experience to bring it into sharp focus. His dull grey uniform marked him as a servant, rather than a lord. He insisted on shaking Alistair's hand enthusiastically, while Diana stayed carefully out of range.

'Chris Grant, playing Seyton!' the young man said loudly. 'That's Macbeth's sidekick. On stage a lot, but not too many lines. I'm so glad you're here, Bishop! We're all spending so much time looking over our shoulder that we can't concentrate on what we're supposed to be doing.'

'Are you saying there's a chance the show might not go on?' said Alistair.

'Oh, Richard will keep everything on track,' Chris said immediately. 'Nothing ever throws Richard.' And then he broke off as all the conviction ran out of him, and he stared pleadingly at Alistair. 'You will sort this mess out, won't you?'

'I'm sure the two of us can manage something,' said Diana, just a bit pointedly.

Chris actually blushed. 'Of course! I meant both of you! I'm a huge fan of the Holy Terrors. I've read everything I could find about your previous cases.'

'There were only two,' said Alistair.

'But they were both absolutely fascinating!' said Chris. 'I don't know how you kept your wits about you, with so many supernatural phenomena going on.' He tried for a smile but couldn't quite bring it off. 'Trust me; you're going to feel right at home here . . .'

'How do you feel about the play?' said Alistair.

Chris brightened immediately. 'Oh, I'm having a great time! It's an amazing reinterpretation, and I can't believe how lucky I was to get cast.' His smile flickered on and off. 'I keep expecting someone to turn up and say they cast the wrong Chris Grant, and I'll have to give up the role . . . So I keep coming up with new ideas and bits of business, to prove I deserve to be here.'

He started to tell Alistair all about them, but Diana quickly interrupted.

'Chris, dear, I think Richard is looking for you . . .'

'Oh! Right! Must dash!'

And just like that, he was sprinting across the stage to see what he could do for his director. Alistair looked at Diana.

'Keen, isn't he?'

'Like you wouldn't believe.'

'Is there anyone important left, that I haven't met?'

'Just the two angels backing this show.' Diana paused to pull a face. 'Our revered producers: David Jordan and Micah Friedman. They're not even a little bit theatre people; they work in loans and lettings and acquired the Theatre of Dreams when they bought the Paradise Hotel next door. Apparently, they'd always had ambitions to be part of the glamorous world of showbiz, and moved heaven and earth to put together the finances that made this production happen.'

'How much money are we talking?' said Alistair. 'Millions?'

'Lots of millions,' said Diana. 'Putting on a show in the West End eats up money faster than a shark in a feeding frenzy. We're all just hoping David and Micah weren't dumb enough to invest any of their own money.'

'Will I get to meet these backers at some point?' said Alistair.

'Unfortunately, almost certainly,' said Diana. 'They will insist on just dropping by, to see how things are progressing. Really, all they want is an excuse to hang out with the cast, rub shoulders with the glamour and pretend they're part of the show. We're always very polite, of course, but they're not part of the company. Money and talent should never mix.'

Alistair had to smile. 'You are such a snob.'

Diana shrugged. 'Showbiz has always been terribly feudal, darling. But the producers have proved useful on occasion; they've arranged rooms for the entire cast and crew in the hotel next door. It's not what you'd call comfortable, or even welcoming, but it's close at hand and it's free.'

Alistair looked at her steadily. 'What exactly are you expecting me to do here, Diana? This could turn out to be nothing but a run of extremely bad luck, possibly exacerbated by some practical joker stepping up to take advantage.'

'The atmosphere is bad, and getting worse,' said Diana. She suddenly sounded very tired. 'Even if this is just some form of sabotage, I get the feeling it could turn dangerous if that's what it takes to shut down the production. We have to figure out what's really going on and put a stop to it – before someone gets hurt!'

'Sounds like a plan to me,' said Alistair. 'But then, being a friend in need has always been part of my job description.'

TWO
The Play's the Thing

Richard planted his fists on his hips and looked around the stage with the light of battle in his eyes.
'We are going with King Duncan's big arrival!' he said loudly. 'First positions, everyone! Warriors, try to remember you are supposed to be extremely dangerous people and not just a bunch of models on a catwalk! Thanes, remember you are aristocrats, which means you are warriors with an extra layer of subtlety that makes you even more dangerous! Everyone else . . . just concentrate on the character types we've already established. If you can remember that far back. Anyone not needed for this scene, get the hell off my stage. Now, where the sweet suffering hell is my throne?'

A young dark-skinned woman in a classic Spice Girls T-shirt and grubby jeans strode on to the stage, scowling fiercely at everyone and everything, followed by half a dozen backstage people in brown coats bearing a large and seriously impressive throne on their shoulders. The armrests ended in polished human skulls, and the intricately carved seat back was topped with crossed battle-axes, their gleaming steel heads caked in dried blood. It was the kind of throne from which executions were ordered and wars declared. Alistair turned to Diana, and she smiled approvingly at the new arrival.

'Our props mistress, Caitlin Hart. One of the few people who'll actually stand up to Richard and shout back at him.'

'I hope he values that,' said Alistair.

'Does he hell,' said Diana. 'But he's lucky to have her, and they both know it, so he's careful to never let their arguments get too far out of control.'

The backstage people deposited the throne on the stage with a resounding thud and then moved away to mutter under their breath and massage aching backs. Caitlin ignored them all as she fussed around the throne like a mother ensuring her child was properly turned out for their first big appearance. Richard called out to her, in what wasn't quite a heckle.

'Is the paint dry this time?'

Caitlin didn't even look up. 'If you actually gave me the advance time you promised, there wouldn't be any problems.'

Richard sniffed loudly. 'Genius has its own timetable.'

'Let me know when you bump into one,' said Caitlin.

She gestured sharply to where Mark was standing at the wings. He strode forward, and the moment he set foot on stage, he was every inch a king. His great bulk became impressive, even intimidating, and he exuded strength and authority. The rest of the cast watched, fascinated, as Mark flexed acting muscles from a time before they were born.

Caitlin stepped back from the throne, and Mark lowered himself carefully into position. He took his time settling his weight, and parts of the throne made seriously unhappy creaking sounds. Mark looked around him, smiling.

'Was that me or the wood?'

Laughter broke out among the cast, helping to ease the mood a little. Richard gestured sharply to the waiting Thanes. Three of them moved in on each side of the throne, took a firm grip and heaved it up off the stage and on to their shoulders. They couldn't hide the sheer effort involved, and some couldn't suppress quiet groans. Mark gripped the armrests tightly and stared straight ahead, his gaze fierce and determined, as befitted a warrior king. The Thanes glanced at each other to make sure they were in the right positions to handle the weight, and then looked to Richard. He nodded quickly, and they started forward.

Alistair's imagination kicked in, showing him a warrior king of old, soaked in the blood and horror of successful ambition. Who had seized his crown by slaughtering everyone who stood in his way, till his battle-axe dripped with brains and gore. Torches flared and braziers smoked, while horses stamped and neighed, and soldiers duelled each other in preparation for the battle ahead. A fierce barbaric scene, from a history yet to come. King Duncan looked down on it all from his high station, an accomplished fighter brought low by age, but still a very real danger to anyone who threatened him or his land.

The Thanes carried the throne steadily onward, showing honour to their king, while doing their best to keep the increasing stress out of their faces.

'Get a move on!' yelled Richard. 'This is supposed to be a victory parade, not a saunter through the park!'

The Thanes gritted their teeth and did their best to step up the pace. Alistair could see rebellion growing in their straining faces. Couldn't the director see how difficult this was, and how hard they were working? Alistair couldn't hear what they were muttering to each other at such a distance, but he could guess.

He's put on weight.
He was hardly going to lose it, was he?
Whose stupid idea was this?
Whose do you think?

Elevated on his throne, King Duncan rose above it all while waving regally to the crowd, who applauded loudly with every appearance of good cheer and approval. Todd and Paul, as Macbeth and Banquo, stepped briskly forward, looking every inch the professional soldier in their smart uniforms. They crashed to a halt before the throne and saluted their king. Duncan acknowledged them graciously. He started to speak, and then one whole armrest broke away and fell to the floor. Without its support, the king lurched to one side. Thrown off balance by the suddenly shifting weight, the Thanes staggered back and forth and then scattered with panicked cries as the throne tore itself out of their grasp and crashed to the stage. Duncan just had time to let out a bellow of shock and outrage before he slammed into the hard wooden boards with enough impact to shake the whole stage. He groaned once and then lay still amidst the wreckage of his throne.

For a moment, everyone stood where they were, staring at the ruins of the scene. Todd and Paul were the first to race forward and pull the broken pieces of what had been a throne away from the fallen king.

'Are you all right, Mark?' said Todd.

'Are you injured?' said Paul.

Mark sat up slowly, scattering bits and pieces of his throne with great sweeps of his arms.

'I've had better days . . .'

The volume in his voice reassured everyone. Mark felt himself all over, as though checking everything was still properly attached, and then glared around him.

'I'm fine. Don't fuss! It doesn't feel like anything's damaged, apart from a seriously bruised ego. If anyone happened to see where my dignity ended up, I'd be obliged if they would return it to me . . .'

Todd and Paul tried to help Mark to his feet, but the sheer inertia of his weight defeated them. They had to wait until he could gather enough strength to force himself up on to his feet, swaying like some ancient colossus rising from its tomb. Richard watched it all, saying nothing. Diana slapped Alistair on the arm.

'This is what I've been talking about! What were the odds of something like that happening?'

'Perhaps a little higher than usual, now I'm here to see it,' he said quietly.

Diana looked at him sharply. 'You think someone deliberately arranged that? As a warning to the rest of the cast that even the Holy Terrors won't be enough to save them?'

Alistair nodded judiciously. 'All the saboteur had to do was saw through the right supports, all of them hidden from casual view, of course, so everything would seem fine until Mark was in place.'

'But to sabotage the throne that thoroughly, they would have to know all the ins and outs of its construction,' said Diana. 'You saw Caitlin check the throne over, before she let Mark anywhere near it.'

'Unless she was just making sure everything would go as planned,' said Alistair.

Diana smiled at him admiringly. 'Once you start working a case, you really don't trust anyone, do you?'

'Let's just say no one is above suspicion,' said Alistair. 'It's always a good idea to look for someone on the inside, when things start to go wrong.'

'But why would Caitlin sabotage her own work?' said Diana.

'Good question,' said Alistair. 'Maybe we should ask her.'

'You go right ahead and do that,' said Diana. 'I'll go find something to hide behind.'

The cast muttered uneasily among themselves, spooked by

such a serious accident so soon after the bishop's blessing. Richard glared into the wings.

'Caitlin! Get your useless arse out here, right now!'

The props mistress stormed on to the stage and glared right back at him.

'You ever talk to me like that again, and I will build a coffin specially so I can nail you inside and bury it!'

'What just happened with your throne?' said Richard.

'It was fine when it left my workshop!' said Caitlin. 'Someone must have got to it when I wasn't around. I told you, Richard: I will walk away from this show if you can't protect my work from outside interference!'

'Who else had access to your workshop?' said Richard.

'Are you kidding me? Everyone in this place and their evil twin!' Caitlin shook her head disgustedly. 'Until we get some proper security people, there's nothing to stop anyone from going anywhere they want backstage!'

'It's your responsibility to protect your department,' said Richard.

'In this madhouse?' said Caitlin. 'Where no one trusts anyone?'

Richard shook his head hard. 'I've told you before: I don't want to hear talk like that.'

'Ignoring a problem won't make it go away!' said Caitlin. 'We are under attack!'

'I'm still in one piece, if anybody cares,' said Mark, deliberately raising his voice to drown out both of them.

He advanced steadily on Richard, with Todd and Paul moving anxiously on either side, ready to offer support if necessary. Mark nodded brusquely to them, but was careful to keep his arms to himself so everyone could see he was walking unaided. He needed them to see it would take more than one bad landing to stop an old trooper like him. His efforts won him a good-natured round of applause. Mark made a point of pausing to smile at Caitlin.

'I felt very kingly on your throne. If you can put the pieces back together, I would be happy to sit in it again.'

Caitlin shot him a grateful smile. 'Good to know there's one real professional in this show.'

Mark finally swayed to a halt before Richard, took a moment

to get his breath back and then hit the director with his coldest stare.

'Perhaps we could do without the whole raised-shoulder-high bit in the future. I don't walk away from falls as easily as I used to.'

Richard just nodded shortly, not actually committing himself to anything.

'You look all right,' he said ungraciously.

Mark sniffed. 'I've endured worse disasters on stage. You should have seen my Lear.'

Alistair was pretty sure Mark had been more seriously affected by his fall than he was admitting, but was going out of his way not to show it. He watched carefully as Mark took a deep breath and showed Richard something very like a polite smile.

'Richard, dear boy . . . would it be all right if I popped back to my dressing room and put my feet up, just until you need me again?'

'I can't continue with the scene anyway, until Caitlin has superglued your throne back together,' Richard growled. 'All right, take a break. But no little pick-me-ups while you're waiting.'

Mark met his gaze steadily. 'I promised you I wouldn't drink during this production, and my word is good.'

Richard looked as though he wanted to say something but had the good sense not to.

Mark turned slowly, aimed himself at the wings and left the stage with slow and studied dignity. He couldn't quite disguise the occasional wince as one pain after another hit home. Alistair spoke quietly to Diana.

'He really should go to A and E in a taxi, so they check him out for internal injuries. Maybe even a concussion.'

'He wouldn't go,' said Diana. 'He's too afraid that if he's seen as weak or incapable, he'll be replaced.'

'Would Richard actually do that?' said Alistair. 'Mark's name must bring a lot to this production.'

'Legends of the theatre are ten a penny these days,' said Diana. 'You can't move in the BBC car park for dames and national treasures.'

They watched the backstage people gather up what was left of the throne and carry it off in armfuls.

'I hadn't realized it took so many people to make a play happen,' said Alistair.

'It takes a village to put on a show,' said Diana.

'Don't leave any mess on my stage,' Richard said loudly to Caitlin. 'And I want a detailed report by the end of the day, explaining what just happened.'

'Hell, I can tell you that right now,' said Caitlin. 'Someone is messing with us.'

She turned her back on the director before he could say anything, and followed her people off stage. The actors murmured uneasily together, until Richard scowled them into silence.

'I want everyone ready for the next scene: Banquo's assassination. If you're not a part of that, make room for those who are! But don't go too far, because God help you if you're not around when I need you!'

Most of the cast filed off the stage. Some looked relieved to be going, as though they didn't feel safe there. Todd and Paul took up a position next to the wings, while Richard talked to three young actors in heavy black cloaks and hoods. Alistair suddenly noticed that Mark had stopped in the wings, to look back at the director. He seemed suddenly older, tired as well as hurt. Perhaps because everyone had already forgotten about him, and the rehearsal had moved on like the remorseless juggernaut it was. He allowed himself a small sigh and then disappeared into the enveloping curtains. Alistair turned to Diana.

'Was what just happened typical of what's been going on?'

'Pretty much,' she said. 'We're all jittery as hell because none of us can depend on anything.'

Alistair looked at her sharply. 'Is that why there's no furniture or props on stage? Because no one can trust them?'

'Wouldn't surprise me a bit,' said Diana. 'I know Caitlin had to do a lot of fast talking just to persuade Richard to use the throne. It'll probably disappear from the scene now.'

'Because Mark wouldn't get back in it?' said Alistair.

'Of course he would,' said Diana. 'You heard the man. He's still game, like the old trooper he is. But the Thanes would refuse to carry him, in case they couldn't get out of the way fast enough next time.'

'I think we need to have a quiet word with Richard,' said Alistair.

'I think we need to pin him to the wall and shout into his face,' said Diana.

'Let's try polite first,' said Alistair.

'And if that doesn't work?'

'Then we pin him to the wall and shout into his face.'

They moved over to join the director as he studied a heavily annotated script. He addressed them both without looking up.

'Not now. I'm working!'

'You're always working,' Diana said ruthlessly. 'This is important.'

Richard slammed his script shut and glared at them. 'What do you want?'

'That business with the throne had to be sabotage,' said Alistair. 'You and your production are under attack by some outside agent.'

Richard's shoulders slumped, and he nodded reluctantly.

'I know. Mark could have been killed. And no show is worth an actor's death.'

'Caitlin wasn't wrong when she said security backstage is a joke,' said Diana. 'Haven't you heard anything from the producers about replacements?'

'They keep saying they're working on it,' said Richard. He looked around to make sure no one was close enough to listen in. 'But I'm not sure how much I trust them. They're not listening to me any more. I'm not sure anybody is.'

'Of course they are, darling,' said Diana. 'You're the one person here who's proven he knows what he's doing.'

Richard was already shaking his head. *The Swiss Family Robinson* was just a fluke. No one expected that stupid musical to be such a hit – least of all me. I did my best with the material, I always do . . . But it wasn't that good.'

'The public can't get enough of it,' said Alistair.

'What do they know?' said Richard. 'I've done much better work in my time, where not only did the public not turn up but they phoned everyone they knew and told them not to come either. I came back to the theatre to prove to everyone that I know what I'm doing . . . But now all I do is constantly second-guess myself, because I've lost faith in my own judgement. And now you're telling me someone is determined to drag this production down and put my people in danger? Maybe I should just pull the plug and walk away.'

'You concentrate on the play,' said Alistair. 'Diana and I will sort out what's going on.'

Richard shook his head slowly. 'I should never have agreed to do a play as famously unlucky as *Macbeth*.'

'I don't believe in curses,' said Alistair very firmly.

'I didn't use to,' said Richard. 'But there's more to this than just someone messing around in the shadows. You must have picked up on the atmosphere in this building . . . It feels like we're all whistling in a graveyard every time we turn up for work.'

'I don't believe in witches, either,' said Alistair. 'Diana and I will find whoever's responsible and drag them out into the light.'

'And then stamp on them hard,' said Diana.

'Well, yes,' said Alistair. 'That goes without saying.'

Richard glanced at the cast on stage, and at those watching from the auditorium, and then walked away to put the patiently waiting assassins through their paces. His voice was suddenly loud and carrying, and accompanied by any number of extreme gestures.

'He's putting on a good performance,' said Alistair.

'He's playing to the audience,' said Diana. 'Hoping that if he can convince them, he can convince himself.'

Alistair nodded slowly. 'Do you think he'll hold together long enough for us to get to the bottom of this?'

'Hard to tell. There's more riding on Richard than anyone else,' said Diana. 'If this show does collapse, the critics will eat him alive. The only thing they enjoy more than building someone up is tearing them down. Wait a minute, hold everything . . . Mark said he was going straight back to his dressing room, but he's still hovering in the wings. And look who's with him.'

Alistair followed her gaze to where Mark and Sarah were arguing fiercely and paying no attention at all to what was happening on stage. Mark seemed to have forgotten all about his aches and pains, while Sarah looked ready to stab him in the chest with a furious finger at any moment.

Alistair and Diana exchanged a look.

'Feeling curious?' said Alistair.

'Always,' said Diana.

They drifted over to the wings, as though they just happened to be heading in that direction, and eased to a halt just far enough away that it wouldn't seem as if they were eavesdropping. Sarah seemed a lot smaller with Mark's enormous bulk looming over her, but she was still holding her own.

'What the hell are you still doing here, Mark? You're in no fit state to be working.'

'I am shaken but not stirred,' Mark said heavily. 'My second wind should kick in any time now, as soon as I've had a chance to knock back an entire box of paracetamols and wash them down with a pint of adrenalin.' He shook his great head. 'I have to do this, Sarah. I can't give Richard any excuse to replace me.'

Sarah sniffed. 'And I thought I was the paranoid one.'

'You are,' Mark said crushingly. 'I've worked with you before, and like the elephant, I never forget.' He sighed heavily. 'I thought my career on the stage was over. Duncan is my last chance to shine. I won't let a few bruises take that away from me.'

'No part is worth putting your life at risk,' said Sarah.

'What life?' said Mark. 'I tried playing mine host at my very own watering hole, but it didn't take me long to realize I was horribly miscast. I was meant to be an actor, Sarah. When everyone applauded me just now, it felt like waking up from a long nightmare.'

'They were celebrating your being alive, not your talent!'

'I can build on that,' said Mark. 'This is where I need to be, Sarah. You of all people should understand that.'

'Of course I do,' said Sarah. 'I just . . . worry about you.'

Mark smiled. 'I am in this till I drop.'

'Just like me,' said Sarah. She smiled suddenly. 'You're looking surprisingly good, old bear, despite all those years hiding inside a bottle.'

'We're survivors,' said Mark. 'Still here despite everything the world can throw at us. When I think of some of the projects we got talked into . . . Remember that terrible low-budget horror movie, *Ghouls Just Want To Have Fun?*'

Sarah winced and shook her head. 'I'm amazed you even

remember that, given how drunk you were all through filming. It couldn't have been more of a dog if they'd replaced all the dialogue with barking.'

Mark smiled at her fondly. 'You were still glamorous. While I was no longer the slim and handsome figure of my gilded youth.'

'You still had presence,' said Sarah. 'There was a real power in your performance.'

'And not just in front of the camera,' said Mark. He waggled his bushy eyebrows suggestively.

Sarah laughed and patted him on the chest. 'Down, old bear. Those days are behind us.'

'But what about the nights, hmm?' said Mark.

They both looked around sharply, as the young witch Jenny came tripping cheerfully over to join them.

'Sorry to interrupt,' she said, entirely oblivious to the conversation she was interrupting because she always was, 'but you did promise me you'd help run my lines, Sarah.'

Sarah sighed and nodded to Mark. 'You'll have to excuse me, dear. Leaving the child to her own devices would be like throwing a puppy to the piranhas.'

Jenny pouted. 'You know I don't get Shakespeare. It's like someone shouting at me in a language I don't understand.'

'You mustn't be so insecure, dear!' Sarah said sternly. 'Just say the lines and let them do all the hard work. And don't allow Richard to intimidate you; underneath all that storm and fury, he's more nervous than you are.'

Jenny stared at her, wide-eyed. 'But he's so big and successful!'

'He's just a director,' said Sarah. 'We're the ones who work for a living.'

'Never let them see they've got you worried, Jenny,' Mark said firmly. 'They'll only take advantage. If Sarah's too busy to work with you, drop by my dressing room any time, and I'll help you with your part. And maybe you can help me with mine.'

He waggled his bushy eyebrows again, and Jenny giggled. Sarah glared at her.

'Try to hold something back for close friends, dear.'

'But I have so many friends,' Jenny said innocently.

'You're not fooling anyone.' Sarah turned back to Mark. 'Even you must have noticed that things have changed, and you can't get away with chatting up actresses a quarter of your age?'

'Hell,' said Mark. 'She's a quarter of my weight!' He shrugged heavily. 'Old habits die hard, even when I know nothing's going to happen.'

Jenny put back her shoulders, to better show off her bosom, and hit Mark with her best sultry smile.

'Never say never, you big old king, you.'

Mark grinned.

'Leave the girl alone,' Sarah said severely. 'Jenny has real potential, and a role that could be the making of her. I don't want her distracted.'

'Can't I want her to succeed as well?' said Mark.

He walked away without waiting for an answer. Sarah looked accusingly at Jenny.

'Don't tease Mark. He's an old friend, and I don't want him hurt.'

Jenny shrugged indifferently, completely uninterested in Mark now he was gone.

'A girl uses what she has, to get on. I would sleep with the Devil himself for a chance at fame and fortune.'

'Lots of actresses feel that way,' said Sarah. 'But some reputations are easier to earn than leave behind.'

'You should know,' said Jenny. She took in the expression on Sarah's face and understood she'd gone too far. She took a deliberate step closer and smiled warmly at Sarah. 'You know you'll always be special to me.'

She put her arms around the older woman and kissed her on the lips. After a while, they walked away together.

'A very revealing conversation, I thought,' said Diana.

Alistair nodded. 'It must be hard to get old in an industry that places so much importance on youth and good looks.'

Diana raised an eyebrow. 'Are you trying to tell me something?'

'Heaven forfend,' said Alistair.

'I am a thing of beauty and a joy forever!' said Diana. 'Even if I end up having so much work done my ears meet at the back, and I have to cross my legs to get enough slack to try for a facial expression. You wait till your classically handsome features start

Which Witch? 41

to slip, and see how fast those morning television shows decide to book someone younger.'

'That would actually be a relief,' said Alistair. 'I've sat on enough sofas for one lifetime.'

Diana started to say something, saw that Alistair was entirely serious, then started again.

'Would it matter to you if I wasn't quite as beautiful as I am now?'

'You'll always be beautiful to me,' said Alistair.

Their eyes met steadily, and Diana put a gentle hand on his arm.

'Forever, Bish.'

'Forever and a day,' said Alistair.

Diana turned away to look out across the stage.

'Of course, the moment you start to lose your looks, I will kick you to the gutter and replace you with a more recent model. My fans would expect it of me.'

'Of course,' said Alistair. 'While I will do the decent thing and join the French Foreign Legion to forget.'

'Forget what?'

'Give me a moment; it'll come to me.'

They laughed softly and then fixed their attention on what was happening on stage.

Chris had cornered Richard and was talking earnestly at him. Richard looked very much as though he wanted to run away, and might have done if there hadn't been so many witnesses. The three assassins had resigned themselves to working on their own, and moved through a series of violent actions as complicated as any dance routine. Todd and Paul were chatting easily, comfortable enough in their lines that they saw no need to rehearse them. Alistair and Diana drifted casually over to see what Chris was being so intense about.

'Just shadow Macbeth,' Richard said heavily. 'I want you right there with him, whatever he's saying or doing.'

'I'm doing my best!' said Chris. 'But Todd keeps telling me not to get between him and his audience.'

'I'll talk to him,' said Richard. 'Make him see that if you're doing your job right, it'll only add to his performance.'

'Can I suggest a new bit of business?' said Chris.

Richard didn't actually flinch, but he looked as though he wanted to. Chris chose not to see that and plunged on, keen to impress.

'You know I have the famous line, *The queen, my lord, is dead*? Well, I've been thinking about how I can put that across in some way that hasn't been tried before. And I think I've got it! I could come on carrying the queen's body in my arms, present her to Macbeth and then say, *The queen, my lord . . . is dead!*'

'No,' said Richard, very firmly.

'Why not?' said Chris.

'Because the scene isn't about you!' said Richard.

Chris pouted and stared at his feet. 'I'll bet Queenie would be up for it.'

'Diana would embrace anything that allowed her even a few extra seconds on stage,' said Richard.

'I have lots of other ideas . . .' said Chris.

'I don't doubt it for a moment,' said Richard. 'Dear Lord, spare me from actors with ideas.'

'I thought I could dress up as one of the three witches . . .'

Richard walked away while Chris was still talking, and all the warmth and eagerness dropped out of the young actor's face. He looked suddenly cold and calculating as he considered his next best line of attack. Diana and Alistair exchanged a glance and swept down on him.

'Chris, darling!' said Diana.

'Could we have a quick word?' said Alistair.

Chris quickly put his game face back on and looked so completely cheerful and enthusiastic that Alistair actually wondered for a moment whether he might have misinterpreted the actor's earlier expression. It would seem Chris was a much better actor than most people realized. The young man started to say something, but Diana raised a hand.

'First rule of the theatre, darling: not everything that seems like a good idea *is* a good idea. And I wouldn't let you carry me anyway. You'd probably drop me.'

Chris looked at her reproachfully. 'You might have given me the benefit of the doubt.'

'She'd probably bounce,' Alistair said cheerfully.

Diana glared at him.

'I just need to feel like I'm contributing something,' said Chris. 'And I have so many ideas!'

'When in doubt, refer to rule one,' said Diana.

Chris stopped smiling and looked at them both steadily, allowing them to see a little of the hard centre within.

'I will do absolutely anything to get on in this business.'

Diana showed him her own hard smile. 'You're not the first to come up with that one, darling. But there are no short cuts. The theatre, despite all appearances, is a cooperative venture. We all strive together to produce a whole greater than the sum of its parts.'

Chris did his best to look as though he believed her, realized it wasn't working and changed the subject.

'Have either of you seen Jenny?'

'I believe she's rehearsing her lines with Sarah,' said Alistair.

Chris looked as if he'd chewed on something sour. 'She said she wanted to rehearse them with me!'

'I wouldn't worry about it,' said Diana. 'If Jenny is at all interested in you, she'll find some way to let you know.'

Chris smiled, just a bit sadly. 'I suppose stranger things have happened.'

Alistair coughed politely and gestured at the director. 'I think Richard wants to discuss something with you.'

'Of course he does!' said Chris, and he rushed off to confront the unsuspecting director.

'Why, Bish,' said Diana, 'I didn't know you had it in you to be so cruel.'

'They deserve each other,' said Alistair. He looked thoughtfully at Diana. 'Is there something going on between Chris and Jenny? I'm always the last to notice these things.'

Diana sniffed. 'She'd eat him alive. But backstage romances are often a good thing. They take people's minds off the pressures of putting on a play.'

'From what I've read, in the kind of magazines I never used to look at before I met you,' said Alistair, 'you have a famously romantic nature.'

'Oh, I do, darling,' said Diana. 'I have a large and generous heart. But what you and I have is different, Bish.'

'I trust that's a good thing,' said Alistair.

Diana hit him with a smile packed full of promise. 'You have no idea . . .'

'If I could have everyone's attention!' Richard said loudly.

He took up a position in the centre of the stage like a general marshalling his troops and glared around him impatiently. The actors stopped what they were doing and did their best to appear interested, while Richard looked back at them in a way that made it clear he wasn't even a little bit fooled.

'For now, we're going to concentrate on Banquo's assassination, so all I need is him and the three hired killers. Everyone else, take a break. Learn your lines, work on your characters and, above all, rehearse your entrances! You've all been coming on a beat or two late. And people . . . try not to have anything too unpleasant happen to you in the next few minutes, so we can get some work done.'

Most of the remaining cast filed quickly off stage before Richard could change his mind, and headed for the stalls, to sit down and take the weight off. Todd clapped Paul on the shoulder to wish him good luck and joined the exodus, taking his time to show he wasn't being intimidated. Richard gestured for the three assassins to come forward and looked them over critically.

'Will you please try to look more like thugs for hire! You are paid killers, ruthless men, prepared to do anything for money.'

'Shouldn't be too difficult,' said one of the killers.

'We are actors, after all,' said another.

The third assassin just nodded solemnly.

Richard glared off into the wings. 'Props! Where are you?'

Caitlin burst out of the curtains as though she'd only been waiting to be summoned, and presented the director with three ornate knives. Richard looked them over critically.

'These are my daggers? I've got more lethal-looking knives than these in my kitchen drawer.'

'I think that says more about you than it does about the knives,' said Caitlin. 'What you've got there are completely historically accurate. And strictly speaking, they're dirks, not daggers.'

'Three guesses as to whether I care,' said Richard. 'And the first two don't count.'

He handed out the blades to the three assassins, who immediately started cutting and thrusting in a self-conscious sort of way.

'There's no need to hold back!' said Caitlin. 'My dirks have no points and no edges, and the blades retract into the hilts on impact. You couldn't hurt anyone with those if you tried. So stab away – and put some effort into it! Don't make me look bad.'

Richard raised his voice. 'I'll do the directing, thank you.'

'Let me know when,' said Caitlin.

Richard ostentatiously turned away and ignored her loud sniff as she stalked back into the wings. Richard ran the three assassins through their upcoming attack, while Paul walked unhurriedly across the stage, doing his best to look as though he was just out for a stroll. Alistair murmured to Diana.

'Shouldn't Banquo be accompanied by his son?'

'Another alteration,' said Diana.

'Why?'

'Honestly, darling, I've given up asking,' said Diana. 'But in this case, it wouldn't surprise me if it turned out to have something to do with Richard's not wanting to work with children.'

'There were children in the *Swiss Family Robinson* musical,' said Alistair.

'And I'm sure there's a connection between those two facts,' said Diana.

Paul got to where he was supposed to be, realized Richard was still fine-tuning the assassins' attack, and went back to the wings so he could walk through it again. The second time he reached the right spot, Richard had withdrawn, and the three assassins were lying in wait. Paul made a point of not noticing them, right up to the point where all three of them jumped him with flailing daggers.

Once again, Alistair's imagination showed him the scene as it should be. A bleak and desolate moor, far from anywhere civilized. Banquo, off on his own for a little privacy, understanding too late that he'd gone too far to be able to call for help. His hand dropped to the sword at his side, but the assassins swarmed all over him like attack dogs, snarling viciously as their daggers rose and fell.

Banquo crashed to the ground, crying out piteously, only to break off suddenly and swear loudly. He shoved the three assassins away from him, and they were so startled they let him do it. Paul lurched back on to his feet, clutching at his right arm, and Alistair was startled to see real blood soaking Banquo's sleeve. Suddenly, the illusion was gone, and it was merely four actors on a stage.

The assassins backed quickly away. One of them saw blood on his dagger and threw it away in revulsion. He stared accusingly at Caitlin as she emerged from the wings.

'You swore they were safe!'

Richard came hurrying forward. 'What's happened now?'

Paul pulled up his sleeve to reveal a thick trickle of blood coursing down his arm.

'I've been cut!'

Caitlin snatched up the discarded dagger and examined it carefully. 'This dirk's been sabotaged! The blade's been jammed, so it can't retract into the hilt!'

Richard took a close look at Paul's wound and frowned. 'Do you need to go to hospital?'

Paul started to say something emphatic and then stopped himself.

'No, I don't think so. It's not that bad.'

Todd hurried up on to the stage to support Paul, who nodded gratefully.

'I'm fine. Honestly.'

'It's barely a scratch,' Richard said quickly. 'No need for health and safety to get involved. It was just an accident.'

'You honestly believe that?' said Todd.

'It could have been a lot worse,' said Paul.

'I made those knives safe myself!' said Caitlin, almost defiantly.

'You should have tried harder,' said Paul. 'If you don't believe me, try it on your own arm!'

'Don't you dare, Caitlin,' Richard said quickly.

'None of this is my fault,' said Caitlin. But she sounded as if she was trying to convince herself of that.

Todd moved in beside Paul. 'Come with me. I know where there's a first-aid kit backstage.'

Paul winced. 'No antiseptic. Stings . . .'

They moved toward the wings. Two of the assassins did their best to comfort the one who'd wielded the unfortunate knife. He was on the edge of tears.

Which Witch? 47

'I could have really hurt him!' he said plaintively.

'Yes, you could,' said Caitlin, careful to maintain a respectful distance. 'Someone went to a lot of trouble to put an edge on this particular blade, as well as wedge the hilt shut. Good thing you didn't try for Banquo's throat.'

All the colour dropped out of the assassin's face. The other two had to help him off stage, muttering about medicinal brandy. Caitlin started to go after them, only to stop abruptly as the third assassin glared back at her.

'You had a responsibility to make sure those knives were safe before you put them in our hands!'

Caitlin looked hurt and turned to Richard for support, but he was staring at his script, lost in thought. Caitlin glared at him for leaving her to cope on her own and stalked off stage. Once Richard was sure there was no one left to put on a brave face for, his shoulders slumped. He had the look of a child who kept being hit and didn't know why. He trudged off into the opposite wings, with the air of someone in desperate need of answers he knew he wasn't going to get.

'A director doesn't just have to worry about the performances of everyone on stage, but he's responsible for all the backstage problems as well,' said Diana. 'Directing is hard, brutal work, and you couldn't pay me enough money to do it. Don't you ever tell Richard I said that.'

'Will he be all right?' said Alistair.

'Him?' said Diana. 'Hard as stone, that one. He'll bounce back. But now you know what we've been facing, Bish. You can't trust anything.'

'It's definitely not a run of bad luck,' Alistair said carefully. 'This is all part of a carefully planned and orchestrated attack.'

'But who's behind it all?' said Diana.

'I'm still working on that,' said Alistair.

He nodded for Diana to take a look at Todd and Paul, who'd come to a halt just short of the wings. They seemed to have forgotten all about finding a first-aid kit in favour of discussing something, quietly but forcefully. Alistair and Diana moved quickly over to listen in.

'I have had enough!' said Paul.

'Oh, come on,' said Todd. 'It's just a graze.'

'Someone is going to end up seriously injured, maybe even killed,' said Paul. 'And it's not going to be me!'

'Get a hold of yourself,' Todd said sharply. 'All we have to do is see this through and we'll never have to worry about money again. We'll be able to pick and choose whatever roles we want.'

'If we live that long,' said Paul.

He suddenly noticed Alistair and Diana, and tapped Todd on the arm. They turned quickly and stood together, closing ranks against the outsiders.

'Diana said we could depend on you, Bishop,' Paul said loudly. 'But Mark's been hurt in a fall, and I could have been killed. So much for your stupid blessing.'

'I was brought in to discover who is threatening your production,' Alistair said calmly, 'not to hold your hand. That's more Diana's department.'

Paul blinked a few times, taken aback by the blunt reply. 'So we can't expect any protection from you?'

'I'll help where I can,' said Alistair. 'That's part of my job description. But the best way to help all of you is to identify the problem.'

'He's very good at that,' said Diana.

'With your help,' said Alistair.

Diana smiled at him dazzlingly. 'Well, that goes without saying, darling.'

Paul turned his frown on Todd. 'You honestly believe we're better off staying in this bear pit?'

'Don't lose your nerve,' Todd said steadily. 'Not when we're so close to having it all.'

Paul sighed heavily. 'I can't go, if you won't. So it seems I'm stuck here. You know, my arm really is starting to hurt.'

'Let's go find the first-aid kit,' Todd said kindly.

Paul walked quickly off stage, his body language all but shouting that he wanted to be on his own. Todd shook his head and looked steadily at Diana.

'Could we have a word in private?'

Diana looked to Alistair, who nodded easily.

'Don't let me stop you.'

'As if you could,' said Diana, with just the slightest toss of her head.

Todd led Diana off to one side. Alistair looked ostentatiously in another direction, while still listening hard. Todd lowered his voice.

'What do you see in that man, Diana? I mean, bishops are famously not noted for their forgiveness when it comes to sins of the flesh. Given some of the people you've knocked around with, I'm surprised he can stand to be in the same room as you without first hosing you down from head to foot with holy water.'

'My previous romantic adventures are none of your business,' said Diana. 'Any girl knows that if you want to find a prince, you have to kiss a whole bunch of frogs first.'

'But the bishop . . .'

'Is his own man,' Diana said firmly. 'And if you can't see what makes him so special, I can't explain it to you.'

Todd scowled and looked at Alistair, almost in spite of himself. 'You really think he can help us?'

'Have faith in him,' said Diana. 'I do.'

And that was when the three witches burst out of the wings, grinning all over their faces.

'Don't mind us!' Angela said cheerfully. 'We've just been listening in! And for the record, the bishop is hot!'

Jenny gave Alistair her best sultry look. 'Seriously yummy.'

'I could eat him alive,' said Sarah.

'Back off, witches,' said Diana, just a bit dangerously. 'The man is spoken for.'

Alistair smiled calmly at the three witches to show he was taking it all in his stride, and nodded easily to Diana.

'You should see some of the online comments I get after each new appearance on morning television. I had to go online to look up some of the things they were suggesting, and I have to say, I was shocked.'

'You must tell me all about that later,' said Diana. 'You never know – might give me some new ideas.'

'Like you've ever been short of those,' said Alistair.

'Hush, Bish,' said Diana. 'Not in front of the thespians.'

'I need to see how Paul's doing,' said Todd.

He hurried off into the wings. Alistair couldn't help noticing that none of the others seemed that upset to see him go.

'Isn't Todd hot?' he said mildly.

'He might be,' said Jenny, 'if he wasn't so cold.'

Angela cleared her throat. 'I think we could all use a nice cup of tea. I've got some brewing in the kitchen, if anyone would care to join me?'

'Tea is always a good idea,' said Diana.

Angela led the way backstage to a door that didn't want to open until she hit it with her shoulder, and then it fell reluctantly back to reveal a very basic kitchen that Alistair immediately decided was in desperate need of a good clean. Preferably with a flamethrower. The wall tiles might have started out as white, but now looked like milk that had not so much soured as decayed. A long, jagged crack meandered across the ceiling, with such open menace that no one wanted to stand beneath it. The floor looked grubby and felt sticky, and Alistair winced with every sound the soles of his shoes made.

'Typhoid Mary would refuse to work in conditions like these,' he said flatly. 'I can feel plague seeping out of the walls, getting ready to mug us when we're not looking.'

'It's not that bad,' said Angela.

'I've seen worse,' said Sarah.

'Then I'm amazed you're still here,' said Jenny. 'Though I guess at your age you've built up an immunity to most things.'

'You do like to live dangerously, don't you?' said Sarah.

Jenny grinned. 'You love it.'

'All the appliances in this room are so out of date they could have been designed by Isambard Kingdom Brunel,' said Diana. 'On a day when he was indulging a really big grudge against humanity. Do we have to stoke them with coal to get them working?'

'I've already tried them all, and, so far, nothing's gone up in flames,' Angela said briskly. 'Just don't look inside the oven. I swear something's evolving in there.'

A modern electric kettle had already been plugged into a grimy wall socket and was steaming merrily away. Alistair took in an assortment of various ill-matched mugs set out on the countertop, and raised an eyebrow. Diana smiled at him.

'We all travel with our own mugs, because they're part of an actor's luck. But we hand them over when we arrive, just for moments like this. Private gatherings in kitchens, where people can moan and complain and gossip about everyone else, are a necessary part of keeping a cast sane.'

'If I'd known,' said Alistair, 'I would have brought my special *The Power of Christ Compels You* mug. For when I make tea with holy water.' He looked around. 'That was a joke . . .'

'Very nearly, dear,' Diana said kindly.

Angela opened a number of small paper parcels, which appeared to be full of dust.

'Powders and potions, oh my,' Jenny said lightly. 'Have you been studying up on witchcraft as well, Angela?'

'Act your age, dear,' said Angela. 'They're herbal teas. Very good for the digestion, the liver, the kidneys . . . They can even help balance your chakras.'

'And greatly increase the number of times you need to visit the toilet,' said Diana.

Angela sniffed and produced a carton of generic T-bags. 'I did bring these, for the unadventurous . . .'

She tried not to look too upset as everyone went for the cheap and standard, leaving only her to mix a delicate blend of herbal infusions. Her mug bore the silhouette of a traditional witch on a broomstick, accompanied by the motto *Magic is in the Air*. Angela gave her tea a good stir, sipped the result and nodded approvingly.

'Don't know what you're missing . . .'

'And perfectly happy to leave it that way,' said Diana. She passed her mug to Alistair. 'Here, darling, you can share mine.'

Alistair accepted the mug and considered its motto: *The Actress Is Always Right*.

Sarah produced a paper package of her own and tilted the contents into her mug while murmuring something under her breath. She looked up to find everyone else staring at her.

'Just a little something,' she said defensively. 'To help get me through the day.'

'Not surprising at your age,' Jenny said sweetly.

Alistair quickly cleared his throat to draw Sarah's attention. 'Was that a charm you were muttering over your tea?'

'Just some old-time Wiccan, for good luck,' said Sarah. 'The best thing about the whole blessed bit is that it seems to work whether you believe in it or not.'

Alistair nodded. 'I feel much the same way about acupuncture. I refuse to accept it works for the reasons people say it does, but it did a lot of good for my frozen shoulder.'

Angela opened the dented fridge in the corner and produced a carton of long-life milk. Everyone took a little with their tea.

'No sugar, I'm afraid,' said Angela. 'I don't use it myself, so I always forget to bring any.'

'Proper tea breaks should be written into our contracts,' Diana said firmly. 'They're an essential part of refuelling actors. We should organize a roster.'

Sarah sniffed loudly. 'I did not spend all these years making a name for myself, to end up making the tea.'

'Get Chris to do it,' Jenny said sweetly. 'You know he loves being useful.'

Diana looked meaningfully at the three witches. 'I think we've all been polite long enough. What do you think is going on?'

The three women looked at each other, waiting for someone else to go first.

'It's hard to know what to believe,' Angela said finally. 'So much bad luck, for so long, flies in the face of statistics. Even when you're putting on *Macbeth*.'

'You all seem surprisingly casual about using the name,' said Alistair. 'Don't theatre people think that's unlucky?'

'We've moved beyond that,' said Diana. 'We tried not saying the name, we tried referring to the play as MacB and the Caledonian Tragedy, we even tried calling Todd Gladys just on general principles, but none of it made a blind bit of difference. The bad stuff just kept on happening.'

'So now we use the name openly, as an act of defiance,' said Jenny.

'Because we need to feel we're doing something to fight back,' said Angela.

'I can't help wondering if someone is trying to send us a message,' Sarah said slowly. 'That this place is dangerous, and we should all get the hell out before it's too late.'

Jenny shook her head firmly. 'I am not being cheated out of my big break.'

Angela nodded approvingly. 'Quite right, dear.'

combination of charm, determination and viciously sharp elbows, followed closely by the three witches. They all had the same fixed smile on their faces as they descended on the producers like cheerful but determined vultures. Alistair drifted along in their wake, keeping everyone else at bay with a thoughtful look.

Diana got to the producers first and kissed each of them on the cheek in a way that left them in no doubt that they'd been kissed by a star. The witches exchanged a glance, acknowledged that they'd been out-glamoured and settled for warm handshakes and bright smiles.

David Jordan was a large, hulking figure, though, unlike Mark DeWald, there was some substance to his bulk. He wore a smart three-piece suit that seemed out of place on a man like him. He looked more as if he should have been standing on a building site somewhere, overseeing construction. A great lumbering bear, with a mane of grey hair and a jutting grey beard, he was doing his best to appear a man of some standing. But Alistair hadn't missed how David had blushed like the fan he was when Diana kissed him.

Micah Friedman was smaller, slighter and more intense. His suit had been tailored to within an inch of its life to give him an air of authority, but he didn't need the help. Micah's gaze was fierce and piercing: the look of a man perfectly prepared to walk right over anyone who got in his way. He took Diana's kiss in his stride.

The actress called the bishop forward and introduced him, and, just like that, the two producers forgot all about the cast. David grabbed Alistair's hand and shook it firmly.

'Micah and I have read so much about you, Bishop,' he said happily. 'I feel so much better for knowing you're here. Maybe you can dispense some much-needed reassurance and common sense and give the boot to all these silly rumours.'

'I'll do my best,' said Alistair.

Micah shook Alistair's hand very briefly, as though seeking to get the whole business over with as quickly as possible.

'We should have known that where Diana was, you wouldn't be far behind,' he said coolly. 'I suppose you're here to fight fire with fire, and superstition with superstition.'

'I'm just here to help,' said Alistair.

And then they all looked round sharply as the sound of loud and hearty voices was raised in the auditorium.

'It's them!' said Jenny, clapping her hands together delightedly. 'They're back!'

'The angels!' said Angela.

'Money on legs,' said Sarah.

The three actresses slammed down their mugs and raced out of the kitchen, followed at a more discreet pace by Diana and Alistair.

All of the cast, and a lot of the backstage crew, had already assembled on stage to surround and greet two middle-aged gentlemen in business suits. The new arrivals seemed very happy to be there, which was more than Alistair could say about Richard, who was clearly struggling to be polite. The three witches bobbed unhappily at the back of the crowd, unable to force their way through. Alistair hung back a little and looked to Diana for enlightenment.

'Angels?'

'Our beloved producers,' said Diana. 'The money behind the art. I told you about them earlier; David Jordan and Micah Friedman.'

'Of course,' said Alistair. 'The theatrical wannabes.'

'Indulging themselves with another visit,' said Diana. 'Always unannounced, because if Richard knew when they were on their way, he'd find some excuse to put them off.'

'It's not that they're unpleasant,' Angela said quickly.

'They're perfectly sweet,' Jenny said firmly.

'Only because you see both of them as potential sugar daddies,' said Sarah. 'You think you can squeeze money out of them with your thighs.'

'A girl has to think about her future,' said Jenny, devouring both producers with hungry eyes.

'They're really just fans,' said Angela. 'At least they don' want autographs or selfies.'

'I'd give them something to remember,' said Jenny.

'Put on your game faces, girls,' said Diana. 'It's time to g make nice with the money.'

She powered her way through the crowd with a winnir

'That's what they all say,' said Micah.

'Play nicely, Mike,' David said quietly. 'You're not in the board room now.'

A brief silent communication moved between the two producers: two men of long acquaintance who knew each other so well they didn't need to put some things into words. They nodded quickly in unison before turning to face the waiting cast.

'You'll have to excuse us,' David said to everyone, in a way that made it clear he wasn't asking.

'We need a quiet word with our good friend the bishop,' said Micah.

They each took Alistair by an arm and hustled him off to one side. He didn't try to break free; he was interested to discover what they would say in private that they couldn't in public. Diana tried to go after them, but Micah stopped her with a look. Diana smiled graciously and stayed where she was. And perhaps only Alistair saw the anger behind the professional smile. Diana hated to be left out of things.

The producers didn't stop until they'd reached the far wings, well out of earshot of the very intrigued crowd. Alistair pulled his arms free, just easily enough to make it clear he could have done it at any time, and that there was a limit to what he was prepared to put up with. Both David and Micah seemed to take heart from such a show of strength, and actually relaxed a little. Micah nodded to David, and the big man took the lead.

'Mike and I have been in business together for most of our lives. We started out as teenagers, following our guts and our instincts, found we had a gift for making money and never looked back.'

'In case something might be gaining on us,' said Micah.

'Our success is the result of hard work and a constant eye to the main chance,' David insisted. 'We know what we're doing.'

'We get things done,' said Micah.

'But we've always been great fans of the theatre,' said David. 'And we always hoped that someday we'd find a way to get involved. We never thought we'd be part of a production as prestigious as this.'

'But now it's all going wrong,' said Micah. 'And we're damned if we can figure out why.'

'If it was a part of our business, we'd see in a moment what the problem was and do something about it,' said David. 'But show business is still new territory to us.'

'We need someone who can navigate its hidden ways,' said Micah. 'And get to the heart of the matter.'

'We're hoping that will be you,' said David.

'You do have an excellent reputation when it comes to solving mysteries,' said Micah.

Alistair just nodded. 'How did the two of you become so fond of the theatre?'

'My parents took me to see musicals as soon as I was old enough to sit still,' said David. 'And I loved it! The music, the glamour, the beautiful people . . . How could you not fall in love with every bit of it?'

'For me, it was always all about the stories,' said Micah. 'In a musical, all your dreams come true, right in front of your eyes.'

David nodded. 'The stage is one of the few places in this world where magic is real. And where illusions can be realer than real.'

Micah looked challengingly at Alistair. 'I believe in the theatre. But I don't know what to make of any of this witchcraft nonsense.'

David fixed Alistair with a stern gaze. 'Would you be prepared to perform an exorcism?'

'That is not something that should ever be attempted lightly,' Alistair said steadily. 'And I would need a lot of convincing before I was ready to accept things had got that bad. I haven't met anyone here I would say had been touched by Hell.'

'It's not the people who need exorcising,' said Micah. 'It's the building.'

'There are such things as bad places,' said David. 'Mike and I deal in property; sometimes you only have to walk into a house to feel an atmosphere poisoned by its past.'

Micah nodded. 'Genius loci – the spirit of the place.'

'In my experience,' said Alistair, 'bad people make bad places.'

David and Micah exchanged a glance and nodded quickly.

'That is what we would prefer to believe,' said Micah.

'Exactly,' said David. 'We would much rather put our faith in the logical thinking that allowed you to solve your last two cases. We want you to find evidence that we're being targeted by some

Which Witch? 57

kind of professional saboteur hired to bring down the show, and only using the appearance of the supernatural to hide their true purpose.'

'You'd know all about that,' said Micah. 'Right, Bishop?'

'I have some experience in that area,' said Alistair.

David laughed and clapped him hard on the back. The sheer weight of the blow would have sent most people staggering, but Alistair saw it coming and braced himself, and hardly swayed on his feet. David nodded approvingly.

'You have our full support. Do whatever it takes, but please . . . find out what's really going on here.'

'And put a stop to it before we lose our shirts,' said Micah. 'Our pockets are not bottomless.'

Alistair raised an eyebrow. 'You've invested your own money in the production? I was given to understand that was a bad idea . . .'

'Our money, our show,' said David. 'We didn't see why we should share our dream with anyone else. Or the profits.'

'Richard made a great many people's dreams come true with his last success,' said Micah.

'So you understand why we're taking these attacks so personally,' said David.

'And why we keep turning up – to keep an eye on things,' said Micah.

'I'll do everything I can for you,' said Alistair.

The producers went back to enjoy some quality time with the cast. Alistair stayed where he was, concentrating on his own thoughts. Diana hurried over to join him, bringing with her the costumes and props mistresses, Josie Turner and Caitlin Hart. Caitlin sneered down her nose at Alistair, entirely unimpressed. Josie lowered her sunglasses and peered tentatively out from under her peaked cap. Alistair made a point of greeting both of them by name.

'Well remembered, Bish,' Diana said briskly. She nodded to the two women. 'Tell him what you just told me.'

Josie had to swallow hard before she could speak. 'None of what's been going on is anything to do with us . . .'

'Right,' said Caitlin. She stood stiffly upright, her arms folded tightly across her chest. 'There was nothing wrong with that throne when it left my workshop. I brought Mark in specially, just so he could sit on it and test its strength. It made a few worried noises, but all within acceptable tolerances. He should have been able to jump up and down on that throne without breaking it.'

'Have you had a chance to examine the damage?' said Alistair.

Caitlin scowled. 'As best I could. Mark smashed most of the throne to firewood when he landed on it. But I did find a few pieces that might have been sawn through. It wouldn't have taken that many to destabilize the throne.'

'Do you have enough evidence to show the police?' said Alistair.

Caitlin shook her head reluctantly.

'Who else had access to your workroom?' said Diana.

'Pretty much everyone,' said Caitlin. 'We discovered when we moved in here that a lot of the theatre's keys had gone missing, and with no security, anyone can go anywhere.'

'Which is perfectly normal behaviour on every other show I've worked on,' said Josie. 'Because most of the time it doesn't matter . . .'

'And besides, I'm not convinced most of the people in this cast would know one end of a saw from the other,' said Caitlin. 'Given everything that's been happening, our saboteur has to be a pro. And almost certainly masquerading as one of us.'

'Don't,' Josie said miserably, thrusting her hands deep into the pockets of her oversized leather jacket. 'I don't want to believe that I can't trust anyone.'

'I can see how that would be a problem,' said Caitlin, 'given how many of the cast you've slept with.'

'I like to take an interest in people,' said Josie. 'Which is more than you do.'

Caitlin smiled at Alistair and Diana. 'It's always the quiet ones . . .'

'Is there anyone you feel like pointing a finger at?' Alistair said patiently.

Caitlin scowled, but shook her head.

'It has to be sabotage,' said Josie. She made a determined effort to pull herself together. 'My costumes only go missing when I'm called away to listen to Richard's latest changes or make running repairs.'

'Can't your assistants keep a watch over them?' said Alistair.

Josie looked as if she wanted to stamp her foot. 'There aren't any, even though I was promised a full support staff before I signed on. Now I'm told they won't show up until we make our move to the West End theatre. I'm having to do everything myself, and still end up getting shouted at by everyone!'

She looked as though she might make a break for it at any moment, and Alistair quickly gave her his most reassuring smile.

'I'm not shouting, just trying to understand.'

'I make sure all my costumes are right where the actors need them to be,' Josie said stubbornly. 'But they keep disappearing! Someone is playing games with us . . . At least we haven't had any wardrobe malfunctions.'

'I have volunteered to provide some,' said Diana.

'Imagine my surprise,' said Alistair.

'Some outsider is trying to destroy our professional reputations!' said Caitlin. 'You've got to do something about it!'

'That is the plan,' said Alistair.

Caitlin growled something under her breath, turned abruptly and strode away. Josie shrugged apologetically and hurried after her friend. Alistair looked to Diana.

'So,' he said, 'are we going with sabotage?'

'Seems likely,' said Diana.

'The theatre is your world,' said Alistair. 'What do you think we should do next?'

Diana frowned. 'We need to figure out who stands to profit most from Macbeth's failure. I'll ask around to see which other shows wanted our West End theatre, before we took it away from them. I'll also check what shows currently running might see Richard's new success as a threat to their continued good box office.'

'You're going to be very busy,' said Alistair.

'Thank God for the mobile phone,' said Diana.

She looked back at the crowd, who were still being studiedly nice to the two producers. Some were showing signs of becoming genuinely friendly. Diana scowled.

'Never encourage a stray dog, or you'll never be free of them.'

David and Micah chatted happily with the cast and showed no sign of going anywhere. Jenny was hanging on to David's arm and doing her best to look as though she belonged there.

'Follow the money . . .' Alistair said slowly.

Diana frowned. 'But David and Micah only stand to make money if the show becomes a success. Why would they want to prevent that?'

'They could see continued funding as throwing good money after bad,' said Alistair. 'Especially if Richard has been wildly overspending.'

Diana shook her head firmly. 'I've seen their type before, drunk on the glamour of being part of show business. They'll keep the money coming, just so they can carry on chumming around with the actors. Desperate to touch the magic, in the hope they can steal some of it for themselves.'

'We have to keep on asking questions,' said Alistair. 'Until someone tells us something they didn't mean to.'

'I was hoping for more of a plan than that,' said Diana.

'If we make ourselves enough of a nuisance, the saboteur is bound to come after us,' said Alistair.

Diana stared at him. 'You really think setting ourselves up as bait is the best way to go?'

'They'd have to come out into the open to stop us,' Alistair said patiently. 'And then we'll have them.'

'Assuming there is no real witchcraft involved,' said Diana.

'I think that's a safe assumption,' said Alistair.

Diana looked around her. 'I'm not so sure. Some of the things I've seen and felt in this theatre defy explanation . . . You said yourself you heard someone walking around on the lobby ceiling when you arrived.'

'A performance almost certainly arranged just for me,' said Alistair. 'You should know by now that in cases like this you can't trust anything to be what it seems.'

Diana grabbed his arm. 'Come into the wings. There's something I want to show you.'

'That sounds promising,' said Alistair.

Diana grinned. 'Down, Bish. Working.'

She led him into the hanging curtains at the side of the stage. The shadows felt pleasantly cool after the brightly lit stage.

'This is where the theatre ghost is supposed to manifest,' Diana said quietly. 'I'm not the only one to have felt a chill, standing here waiting to go on.'

Alistair took a good look around him. 'Can't say I'm feeling anything . . . Not even a cold draught.'

Diana's head snapped round. Alistair turned quickly to follow her gaze, but he couldn't see anything. The open space beyond the wings was draped in shadows dark enough to conceal any number of things. Diana moved cautiously into the backstage area, straining her eyes against the gloom. Alistair stuck close beside her.

'What are we looking for?' he said quietly.

'I'm sure I heard someone moving around back here,' said Diana, just as quietly. 'And anyone who has any business being backstage is currently out there, fawning over the producers.'

A floorboard creaked under Diana's foot, and a sudden circle of flames burst up to surround her. She cried out and flinched from the searing heat, but no matter which way she turned, she was trapped inside a ring of blazing fire. Alistair looked frantically around for an extinguisher, but there wasn't one. Diana's clothes began to scorch and smoulder, and she had to cover her face with her hands to protect it. Alistair tried to reach through the flames to grab Diana and haul her out, but his instincts wouldn't let him. So he lowered his head, squeezed his eyes shut and ran straight at the fire. He plunged through the flames without flinching, slammed into Diana and snatched her up, and carried her out the far side of the fire. They both fell to the stage, holding desperately on to each other.

Leaping flames filled the whole backstage area with a fierce light. Alistair wrapped his body around Diana's to protect her from the heat. And then the flames just disappeared, all the glare and heat gone in a moment. Alistair sat up slowly, his face and hands smarting just from their brief exposure to the flames. Diana pulled herself up and leaned against him, and he put a comforting arm around her shoulders. They were both breathing hard, and so close they could feel each other's heartbeat. Alistair finally eased Diana away from him so he could look her over carefully. Her face was reddened but unburnt, though some of her clothes were singed. His quickness of thought, and action, had prevented anything worse.

'Those flames would have killed me,' said Diana. 'You saved my life . . .'

'I'll always be here for you,' said Alistair.

Diana grabbed his face with both hands and kissed him fiercely. 'My hero,' she said finally. 'How am I ever going to reward you?'

'Later,' said Alistair. 'We're working.'

He got to his feet and helped Diana up on to hers. They both brushed themselves down and then took a good look at where the ring of fire had been.

'I'm not seeing anything there,' said Diana. 'How is that even possible?'

'Good question,' said Alistair.

He pushed her gently away from him and knelt down to run his fingertips across the floorboards.

'There's no sign of charring on the floorboards,' he said slowly. 'No damage at all . . .'

'Witchcraft,' said Diana.

'Not necessarily,' said Alistair

'What else could it have been?'

Alistair rubbed his fingertips together. 'I can feel something . . . greasy. I think someone laid down a circle of accelerant, just enough to support the flames until it was all burned up.'

'How could the accelerant have caught alight, without someone right there on the spot to supply the spark?' said Diana.

'Professionals have their own trade secrets,' said Alistair. 'But I did hear a floorboard creak under your weight, just before the flames appeared.'

'Stop being so stubborn!' said Diana. 'We've been through some weird stuff before, but this is the first time someone has tried to kill me with black magic!'

Alistair took his time rising to his feet. 'Look on the bright side. We must be getting close to the truth if our saboteur is prepared to attack us this openly.'

'But we don't know anything!'

'Apparently, they don't know that.'

Diana hugged herself, as though to make sure all her important parts were still where they should be, and then held her hands out before her.

'I look like I've overdone it at the tanning salon,' she growled.

'On you, it looks good,' said Alistair.

And then he charged right past Diana as he caught a glimpse of a dark shape watching from the shadows. The figure turned and bolted. Alistair plunged on, vaulting discarded props and piles of coiled-up rope. He could hear Diana following behind him, struggling to keep up but determined not to be left out of anything.

'Stop!' Alistair yelled to the figure ahead of him. 'You can't get away!'

'Yeah, right,' said Diana. 'Because that always works . . .'

A door slammed shut ahead of Alistair. He hit it at a dead run, burst it open and found himself in a maze of empty corridors and passageways. There was no sign of the running figure anywhere, and he couldn't hear any footsteps. He pressed on anyway, trying to look in every direction at once, until he was finally forced to stop when the corridor ahead branched abruptly in several directions. Alistair leaned against the nearest wall and fought to get his breathing under control. After a while, Diana caught up and leaned on the wall beside him.

'I am not built for sprinting,' she said sternly.

'There's no point in going on blindly,' said Alistair, forcing himself upright. 'Our runner could have gone to ground anywhere.'

'Did you see who it was?' said Diana.

'Just a dark shape,' said Alistair.

'I told you someone had been watching us from the shadows!'

'So you did.'

They looked up and down the deserted corridor. All the doors were closed, and everything was eerily still and quiet.

'At least now we can cross witches off our list,' said Alistair. 'That was a very real and very fast-on-their-toes person.'

'Witches are still people,' said Diana.

'But far more likely to throw a spell than turn and run,' said Alistair. 'Unfortunately, we're still no nearer working out who we're dealing with.'

'When we do finally track them down, I will punch their head through a wall,' Diana said grimly. 'Look at the state of my clothes! I'm covered in soot!'

'Suits you,' said Alistair.

Diana slapped his shoulder.

* * *

They made their way back through the corridors to the stage and stepped out of the wings to find everyone staring at them.

'Where the hell have you been?' said Richard. 'And what happened to your clothes? You look like you've been standing too close to a barbecue.'

'We have come face to face with the forces of Hell!' Diana said grandly. 'And made them run like a baby!'

Alistair kept his voice carefully calm and collected as he explained what had just happened, and everyone made appropriate sounds of awe and wonder. When Alistair was done, a chatter of raised voices took over. Lots of people claimed to have seen a dark figure in the wings or somewhere backstage, but when pressed for details, they fell silent.

'Far more likely you were all just jumping at shadows, or your own imagination,' Richard said cuttingly.

'What we just chased was no shadow,' said Alistair.

'Then why couldn't you catch it?' said Richard.

'Whoever it was knew the backstage area like the back of their hand,' said Alistair.

There was a pause as everyone considered the implications of that.

'Maybe it was the theatre ghost!' Chris said excitedly.

Richard winced. 'Really not helping, Chris.'

'But what if it's some sort of Phantom of the Opera?' Chris said excitedly. 'A survivor from one of the old theatre companies, still haunting the building, brought to life again by our arrival . . .'

The cast turned on each other, as competing conspiracy theories fought it out. Interestingly, out of everyone present, the two producers seemed the least upset. They looked happily about them, revelling in the drama of the situation, all part of their dream of life backstage at the theatre. The clamour gradually died down as people got tired or just didn't want to argue any more.

'It's time we were going!' Micah said finally. 'Come along, David, we have business to be about that can't wait.'

'But not to worry, everyone!' David said cheerfully. 'We're leaving you in the safe hands of the Holy Terrors.'

Richard hurried forward to escort the two producers off the

stage and back through the auditorium. Cast and crew watched them go, and Alistair had no problem reading the expressions on their faces. The producers could leave, but they couldn't. They still had to carry on working in a building with a bad reputation, with someone at large who might or might not be a witch, but had just made it clear they could raise rings of fire at will. Richard came back to the stage and glared around him.

'All right, people, break time is over! Everyone back to work!'

'But what are we supposed to do about these circles of fire?' said Paul.

'Don't stand inside one,' said Richard.

He gestured for the backstage people to join him, and the cast broke up, moving slowly off in small groups. Because nobody wanted to be on their own.

Diana looked at Alistair. 'We can't concentrate on the investigation if we're having to constantly protect ourselves from black magic and death by fire.'

'I don't think we have anything to worry about there,' said Alistair. 'Our saboteur won't repeat an old trick, because they know we'll be looking for it.'

'So what do we do?' said Diana.

'Talk to people, learn their secrets – and wait for someone to give themselves away,' said Alistair.

'Ah,' said Diana. 'The usual.'

'Go with what works,' said Alistair.

THREE

What the Actress and the Bishop Didn't Hear Because They Were Just a Bit Busy at the Time

On an old stage in an old theatre, cast and crew came together to meet the people who were paying for it all. David and Micah couldn't talk to everyone at once, so a great many subsidiary conversations grew up around them. The roar of raised voices filled the stage as people discussed many things Alistair and Diana would probably have profited greatly from overhearing.

Jenny hung on to David's arm so tightly it was a wonder she didn't cut off the circulation, determined not to be separated from him while she was doing her best to vamp the man. She'd already tried all the main tricks in her armoury, including smiling seductively, making suggestive comments and pressing the whole length of her body against his. But so far none of it had produced any noticeable effect. David was polite and occasionally attentive, but apparently entirely unmoved by what she had to offer. What she was in fact handing to him on a plate, wrapped in a ribbon and personally autographed. Jenny wasn't used to that. So she kept on chattering cheerfully, while she struggled to find some stratagem that would open him up and make him vulnerable to her.

'Are you married, David?' she said brightly, pretending she hadn't already noticed the lack of a ring.

'No,' said David. 'I suppose I'm just not the marrying kind.'

'Don't be so silly, sweetie,' Jenny said quickly. 'A good-looking man like you? You're not shy, are you? There's no need to be shy with me.'

She hit him with her most alluring smile, but he just smiled calmly back at her.

'I think you need looking after,' she said, pressing her breast against his arm.

'Perhaps,' said David. 'But not by you, my dear.'

Jenny pouted at him. 'Why not?'

David allowed himself a small sigh. 'Because I'm really not interested in women.'

Jenny carefully disengaged herself from his arm and took a step back. Their eyes met, and neither of them blinked.

'Not at all?' Jenny said finally.

'I'm a middle-aged man who never married and loves musicals,' said David. 'It's not like I'm hiding anything.'

'We could still be friends,' Jenny said hopefully.

'I have enough friends,' said David.

Jenny shrugged and smiled brightly. 'Then I'll just have to try my charms on someone else.'

'You leave Micah alone,' David said sternly. 'He is very happily married, to a woman who could drop-kick you through a wall.'

Jenny looked at him carefully. He didn't appear to be joking. So she just nodded and moved on. There had to be someone who would prove vulnerable to her predatory charms. There was always someone.

Sarah watched Jenny walk away from David and moved quickly to intercept her. Jenny did her best not to see the older actress, but she had no choice when Sarah planted herself right in front of her.

'This is supposed to be a civilized social gathering,' Sarah said sternly. 'Not a hunting ground.'

'It's always the right time to be looking out for number one,' Jenny said calmly. 'Especially in a production as precarious as this one. If it should end up going to hell in a handcart, and our revered angels kick us into the gutter, I'm going to need a new sugar daddy to help me get over the shock. I shall, after all, be inconsolable at the lost opportunity, and in need of some very expensive comforting.' She sighed sadly. 'David would have been so perfect for that . . .'

'I could have told you not to waste your time on that one,' said Sarah.

'I didn't pick up any vibes,' Jenny said defensively. 'I call it cheating, to seem so available while keeping your fingers crossed behind your back. And unfortunately, it would appear Micah is happily and very dangerously married . . .' She looked restlessly around her, her gaze drifting from one face to another, like a hunter putting prey in the crossfire. 'So, who does that leave to protect poor little me from the troubles of this world, while I consider how best to rebuild my career? Todd, Paul . . . Richard? I don't think so; there's no room for anyone in their lives but them.'

'You stick with me,' said Sarah, dropping an arm lightly across her shoulders. 'I'll take care of you.'

Jenny produced something very like a real smile. 'Oh, Sarah, sweetie, what would I do without you?'

'You're my girl,' said Sarah. 'And don't you forget it.'

'For now,' said Jenny.

Richard talked steadily at Micah, doing his best to tell him what he thought the producer wanted to hear, but the producer was too busy gushing enthusiastically over the play to realize he was being played.

'I love what you've done with the material,' said Micah. 'The new aesthetic, the attention to detail, the inspired way you've solved problems with the text and the new setting.'

'While being very careful to keep the expenses under control,' Richard said quickly. 'It may seem like I'm being extravagant sometimes, but it's always to achieve something that matters.'

Micah smiled at him crookedly. 'We appear to be talking at cross purposes. I am interested in art, while all you want to talk about is money. Shouldn't it be the other way round?'

'I just wanted to make it clear we both speak the same language,' said Richard.

'David and I are perfectly happy with the way you're running things,' Micah said firmly. 'Trust me, you'll be the first to know when we're not.'

'Our present troubles are only temporary,' said Richard.

'Of course they are,' said Micah. 'You have the Holy Terrors to protect you now.'

'You have faith in them?' said Richard.

Micah raised an eyebrow. 'Don't you?'

'The problems plaguing this production are very real,' said Richard. 'I can't see them being solved by two attention-seekers running around searching for clues. I'm still not convinced we're experiencing anything more than a longer than usual run of bad luck.'

'Let us hope so,' said Micah.

The sheer press of bodies prevented Chris from getting close enough to hear what Richard and Micah were saying, and it frustrated him that he couldn't work out whether Richard was being complimented, threatened or in danger of being fired. And if the latter, whether a young actor with excellent prospects might be better off switching his allegiance to someone else. Chris had suspected for some time that Richard's control over the play was slipping, and there was no way Chris was going to just stand by and let the production fall apart.

Because Seyton was the best role Chris had ever lucked into.

He had no doubt the producers would prune the play and cast in a moment if they found it necessary to assume control. Chris had already decided he was ready to do whatever it took to make sure he was too important to the play to risk losing. But who else could he depend on to support him? Once the axe started falling, it would be every actor for themselves, and the devil take those who didn't ring their agent fast enough.

None of the leads had any time for Chris, despite his best attempts to ingratiate himself with all of them. Todd was too up himself, Paul was too loyal to Todd, and Diana only had eyes for her bishop. Chris frowned. He wasn't sure what to make of the Holy Terrors. He'd read all about them online and immersed himself in the more sensational magazine accounts, but it all seemed very unlikely. The Actress and the Bishop . . . solve murders? Chris scowled and rubbed a knuckle against his chin as he searched the crowd for a likely prospect. There had to be someone . . .

And then he smiled slowly as he took in three familiar faces. Richard had made the witches so central to his play that if he were to attach himself to one of them, it could help make his position in the company so much more secure.

It probably wasn't going to be Jenny, unfortunately. He'd seen her flirting with David, and he couldn't compete with that. And almost certainly not Sarah; Chris had a sneaking suspicion she could see right through him. But Angela . . . Chris could see real possibilities there. An established actress, with all kinds of connections in the business – and older women had always found Chris's charms very acceptable. He eased through the packed crowd to join Angela, and she fixed him with a look that was far too understanding.

'What do you want, Chris?'

He made a quick decision that honesty was probably the best policy, for the moment, and met her gaze squarely.

'I'm looking for an ally,' he said. 'To help me survive what's happening to this play. I thought you might be interested in finding someone like that. We could watch each other's back and work together on tactics of mutual interest.'

'But what is it you want?' said Angela.

'I want to be really good in this play,' said Chris. 'So good that I'm indispensable. But it's become increasingly obvious I can't manage that on my own. I'm getting damn all support from Todd, because he sees anyone who distracts the audience's attention from him as a threat, and Richard is too busy with all his many problems to listen to my ideas.'

'What do you think I can do?' said Angela.

'I thought we could combine our tactics,' Chris said carefully. 'Swap background information and defend each other against mutual enemies.'

'You think I need your help with any of that?' said Angela.

'Have you seen the state of this production?' said Chris. 'Everyone's so freaked out that no one trusts anyone. If this cast hangs together long enough to reach the West End, it'll be a miracle.' He glanced dismissively around him. 'Look at them . . . like cattle huddled together because they sense a storm is coming. Come on, Angela, there are lots of good reasons why we should work together, most definitely including enlightened self-interest.'

Angela nodded slowly, acknowledging the point. 'I've spent so long in television that I'd forgotten how much personal politics goes on in the theatre.'

'I could be just what you need, to help you fight your corner,' said Chris.

'You have no idea what I need,' said Angela. 'But I could use someone to watch my back. If only to intercept the occasional knife.'

They looked at each other appraisingly.

Todd and Paul stood off to one side and kept a careful eye on the producers as cast and crew lined up to talk to them. Out of the entire production, Todd and Paul were the only ones not prepared to suck up to David and Micah: because they were leads and wouldn't lower themselves, and because they knew it wouldn't do them any good. They recognized hard-hearted businessmen when they saw them, even if they did like to present themselves as starry-eyed fanboys.

Todd and Paul weren't at all surprised to see Jenny throw herself at David, though they were both a little surprised to see her fail so abjectly. They watched her walk away from the producer and exchanged a look.

'You do know she tried it on with me?' said Todd.

'Of course,' said Paul. 'I think pretty much everyone in the company has been exposed to Jenny's very practised charms, at one time or another.'

'That girl is going places,' said Todd. 'And it has nothing to do with talent.'

'Saucer of milk for little miss cat,' said Paul. He looked thoughtfully at Todd. 'Did she get anywhere with you?'

'I like to believe that at least some part of a seduction is my idea,' said Todd. 'Or I'd never be able to respect myself in the morning.'

'She always seemed a bit too . . . obvious, for me,' said Paul.

Todd's attention had already returned to the producers.

'Don't frown at them,' Paul said quietly. 'They might notice.'

'They shouldn't be here,' Todd said flatly. 'They're just dilettantes. Amateur night, with money.'

'But we can't put the play on without them,' said Paul. 'So if you can't find it in you to bow and scrape, just stand back and incline your head politely from a distance. Look at Richard . . .

Playing politics for all he's worth, smiling and nodding like he's actually interested in anything David and Micah have to say. Sometimes I think that man is a better actor than both of us put together.'

Todd sniffed. 'Money talks, directors listen.'

'I don't know what you're so worried about,' said Paul. 'This whole production is built around your performance. Backed up by me, of course. And Diana, as Lady M.'

'Stunt casting,' Todd said sniffily.

'Diana is doing good work,' Paul said firmly. 'Your scenes together blow the bloody doors off.'

Todd nodded reluctantly. 'You're doing good work too. Don't think I haven't noticed.'

'You've been like this in every play we've done together,' said Paul. 'Always convinced you're about to be fired. And it never happens.'

'If I was to go to the producers,' Todd said slowly, 'and tell them I wouldn't work with Richard any more – that it's either him or me – what do you think they'd say?'

Paul looked at him carefully. 'Does that feel like something you might do? Because I would advise very strongly against it.'

'But if I did draw a line in the sand . . .' said Todd.

'You might end up tripping over it,' said Paul. 'Richard is a proven money-maker, and that makes him bullet-proof.'

Todd shrugged. 'I have a horrible suspicion you might be right. I just hate the way things are going.'

'We've survived more chaotic productions than this,' said Paul. 'And we did it by holding our nerve.'

Todd growled under his breath. 'It's just . . . all those rumours about witchcraft are starting to freak me out.'

'None of that's real!' said Paul.

'I'm not so sure,' Todd said darkly.

They stood together, not looking at anything in particular.

'So,' Paul said finally, 'am I forgiven?'

Todd looked at him. 'For what?'

'We could have had big parts and big profits in that *Swiss Family Robinson* musical,' said Paul. 'If I hadn't talked you into walking away.'

'But you were right,' said Todd. 'They weren't our kind of

roles, and the script was a mess. Who knew that piece of shit would catch on the way it did?'

Paul shook his head. 'If we'd stayed, we could have made some serious money.'

'More likely the whole thing would have died the death with us in it,' said Todd. 'No, we're better off here, doing work that suits us.'

'So you don't feel even a little bit cheated over what might have been?' said Paul.

'No,' said Todd. 'Do you?'

'Sometimes,' said Paul. 'When I think of how close we got . . .'

'Let it go,' Todd said wisely. 'You have to live in the future, not the past. Or you'll end up like Mark.'

Mark advanced ponderously on Jenny and Sarah, and they moved quickly to stand shoulder to shoulder to receive him.

'Well met, a long way from moonlight,' boomed Mark. 'You bless me with your presence, ladies.'

'Even I know that's from the wrong play,' said Jenny.

She walked away. Mark looked reproachfully at Sarah.

'Have you been warning her off me?'

'Didn't need to,' said Sarah. 'She's smart as a whip, that one.'

'I see you're running the same old game,' said Mark. 'Teaching a young dog old tricks. Though I would have thought dear little Jenny was a bit young, even for you.'

'Didn't stop you giving her the full force of what you like to think of as your charm,' said Sarah.

'I knew I wasn't going to get anywhere,' said Mark. 'I was just defending my reputation. I have to play the larger-than-life figure that people expect of me.'

'Because your reputation is all you have left?' said Sarah.

'I believe I still have one great performance left in me,' said Mark. He looked narrowly at Sarah. 'Would I be right in thinking you're genuinely attached to that girl?'

'We fit well together,' said Sarah.

Mark smiled. 'Now, there's a mental image I wasn't expecting to be taking away with me.'

Sarah slapped his arm. 'Behave yourself, old bear.'

They stood together for a while, looking at the bustling crowd and then out across the empty auditorium.

'All the things we were going to do . . .' said Mark. 'And we ended up here.'

'Spending all our time being other people,' said Sarah, 'because who we really are isn't worth looking at.'

'You're too hard on yourself,' said Mark.

'Someone has to be,' said Sarah. 'One of those American life coaches once told me, *You need to take a big swim in lake you.* And I told her, *My lake has sharks in it.*'

'We've come a long way to be here,' said Mark. 'So many parts, in so many plays and movies. When you look back at all the lost opportunities, and the projects that weren't worthy of us . . . do you think it was worth it?'

'Stop that,' said Sarah. 'I don't do nostalgia. The past is gone; let it go.'

'But what else is left for us?' Mark said heavily. 'When you realize your best work is in the past?'

'Why do you keep asking me questions when you already know the answers?' said Sarah.

'What else are friends for?' said Mark.

'Friends?' said Sarah. 'Is that what we are?'

'Aren't we?' said Mark. 'Who else has seen and done the things we have?'

'Friends . . .' said Sarah, as though the thought had honestly never occurred to her. 'I suppose we are.'

'I was there,' said Mark, 'when you decided to give up the baby for adoption.'

'There was never room for a baby in my life,' said Sarah. 'Wasn't room for anyone but me.'

'Do you ever regret . . .?'

'Don't go there,' said Sarah.

Mark nodded slowly. 'I can't help thinking about the career I should have had. The work I might have done. I wasn't supposed to end up an aged Falstaff, crying into his mug because there's no more cakes and ale.'

'Don't think you can lean on me,' said Sarah, not unkindly. 'It's all I can do to support myself.'

* * *

Tom McIntire, playing the Thane Lennox, was a large stocky figure fighting middle age with everything he had. He approached Richard, left abandoned by the producers so they could bask in the presence of the far more glamorous cast members.

'What's the word from our beloved money men?' said Tom.

'They're still keen to back the play,' said Richard. 'And they say they still have faith in me.'

'Do you?' said Tom.

'Sometimes,' said Richard.

'But word of your genius precedes you,' said Tom. 'Banging loudly on a big bass drum while playing jazz trombone.'

'I'm no genius,' said Richard. 'I'm not convinced anyone is. There's just talent and hard work, and being in the right place at the right time.' He looked thoughtfully at Tom. 'What's your take on all the crazy stuff that's been plaguing us? Does any of it bother you?'

'I haven't seen anything weird or wonderful,' said Tom, just a bit wistfully. 'And nothing even remotely witchy. I haven't even had a glimpse of the theatre ghost. We're all under so much pressure that it's no wonder we keep losing track of things, or thinking we see and hear things that aren't actually there. Everyone will settle down once we've left this shithole behind us and established ourselves in our very own West End theatre.' He looked steadily at Richard. 'Be honest. Have you seen anything you would accept as out of the ordinary?'

'Not a damned thing,' said Richard. 'Sometimes, when I hear what other people are saying, I feel a bit left out. But there is definitely an atmosphere . . .'

'Of course there is,' said Tom. 'We're putting on *Macbeth*.'

Sometime later, David and Micah reluctantly tore themselves away from their wonderful new friends and headed back to the real world. Everyone shouted their goodbyes and waved enthusiastically as David and Micah made their way through the auditorium, but the sound cut off quickly once the door had closed behind them. Micah immediately put a staying hand on David's arm, and David looked at him in surprise.

'I thought we were in a hurry?'

'We are,' said Micah. 'But I think we need to make a firm

decision before we leave. Are we going to continue funding this play?'

David stared at him, aghast. 'What are you talking about? Putting on a play like this has been our dream for as long as I can remember!'

'But we never anticipated these kinds of problems,' said Micah. 'The endless accidents and drawbacks are eating up money faster than we can shovel it in. And given some of the things people have been talking about . . . I mean . . . *witchcraft*?'

'I don't believe in any of that nonsense,' said David. 'And neither do you.'

'But I get the feeling a lot of the people here do,' said Micah. 'And now they've called in the Holy Terrors . . .'

David brightened immediately. 'Yes! I would have loved to spend more time with them! I never thought I'd be in the same building as two living legends!' He realized he was babbling and made an effort to rein in his enthusiasm. 'Just their presence here will raise a lot of interest in the media and ensure maximum publicity for the show.'

'Contrary to what you may have heard,' said Micah, 'not all publicity is good publicity. We want the kind that will bring people in, not scare them away. The Holy Terrors are only good for us if they solve the mystery of what's going on.'

'They do have an excellent track record,' said David.

'On two cases!' said Micah. 'If they fail us . . .'

David shrugged. 'Let the Actress and the Bishop wander around looking for clues, while the media writes it all up in excited prose, and we'll laugh all the way to the box office.' He looked steadily at Micah. 'Do you still believe in Richard?'

'Of course,' said Micah. 'Don't you?'

'Of course,' said David.

They shared a smile. It wasn't a very nice smile.

David paused and looked around the lobby. 'You know, for a moment there I thought I heard footsteps . . . But there's no one around.'

Micah didn't even glance back as he headed for the front door. 'I'm not hearing anything. You mustn't let the cast's imaginations get to you. Come on, I'm taking you out of here before you start having close encounters with the theatre ghost.'

'I think I'd quite like that,' David said wistfully. 'Just think of all the great stories he could tell . . .'

'Out!' said Micah.

Somewhat to her surprise, Jenny found herself talking to Chris. He'd just appeared out of nowhere and started talking excitedly about all the strange things that had been going on, and she simply didn't have the heart to walk away. It would have felt too much like kicking a puppy. Not that she had anything against that, when she was in the right mood. She let Chris prattle on for a while, but finally had to stop him with a look.

'Why are you telling me all of this, Chris?' Jenny said sharply. 'We are not close, and we are never going to be. I am only ever interested in people who can advance my career.'

'Like Sarah?' said Chris.

'Exactly,' said Jenny.

'Does she know that?'

'I think it would be fair to say we support each other for our own purposes,' said Jenny.

'But are they the same purposes?' said Chris.

Jenny nodded approvingly. 'You're not as dumb as you appear. Mind you, that would be difficult. What do you want from me, Chris?'

He smiled cheerfully. Jenny shook her head.

'Apart from that.'

'You have to admit, something way off the map is taking place in this theatre,' said Chris. 'Maybe witchcraft, more likely sabotage, but either way, it's got to be threatening not just our safety but also our career prospects. I thought perhaps the two of us could start our own investigation into what's really going on.'

'I saw you talking with Angela,' said Jenny.

'You don't miss much, do you?' said Chris.

'Not if I can help it,' said Jenny. 'It looked like the two of you had come to some kind of agreement.'

'Angela may think that,' said Chris. 'I couldn't possibly comment.'

'So what are you doing here with me?' said Jenny.

'I'm going to need all the help I can muster if I'm to get

to the bottom of what's really going on in this place,' said Chris.

'The Holy Terrors already have that covered,' said Jenny.

'But they are not on our side,' said Chris. 'We need an answer, and a solution to all our problems, that won't threaten the future of this production.'

Jenny nodded slowly. 'I can see some situations where it might not be in our best interests for the whole truth to come to the surface. But if we do work together on this, Chris, our partnership is not going to be in any way personal. Got it?'

Chris smiled brightly. 'Of course.'

Jenny walked away. Chris watched her go.

'But it might become personal,' he said softly. 'If I play my cards right. There's nothing like shared danger, and shared accomplishments, to bring people together. And you can never have too many strings to your bow.'

Mark made his way through the packed crowd, smiling and nodding, but no one seemed interested in talking to him. They were all too caught up in their own conversations and their own problems. Mark finally spotted Tom McIntire standing alone and moved over to join him. They'd worked together in the past, but then Mark had worked with pretty much anyone, back in his golden days.

'Just wanted to say sorry for nearly crushing you with my throne,' said Mark. 'And my not inconsiderable bulk.'

'Not your fault,' said Tom. 'We all got out of the way in time because we were half expecting something like that to happen.'

'Do you think there's a saboteur?' said Mark.

'Makes more sense than a witch,' said Tom. 'They'll be blaming gremlins next.'

'But does the threat come from outside,' said Mark, 'or from one of us?'

Tom looked at him thoughtfully. 'Why would anyone in the cast want to undermine the show?'

'That's the question, isn't it?' said Mark. 'Someone with a grudge, perhaps, or someone with a vested interest in the play failing. I've been away from the theatrical scene for some time. I don't even recognize most of these people. Do you?'

'I've at least heard of most of them,' said Tom. 'I'd hate to think anyone in this production could be vindictive or petty enough to wage a war of nerves like we've been enduring . . .'

'But if one of us should turn out to be behind it all?' said Mark.

'Then someone is going to get a good kicking,' said Tom. He looked steadily at Mark. 'Do you have a problem with that?'

Mark laughed richly. 'Hell, no. I'll just wait till you're through with him and then sit on the bastard.'

The props and costumes mistresses stood off to one side, feeling more than a little left out of things. Richard had insisted they attend the gathering, because he wanted them on hand if he had to explain the extent of the play's problems. But in the end, the two women never even got a chance to speak to the producers, who were only interested in soaking up reflected glamour from the cast.

Josie and Caitlin couldn't have given less of a damn.

'I've done everything short of sewing tracking devices into my costumes,' said Josie, peering glumly over her sunglasses at the milling crowd. 'But I only have to take my eyes off something and it disappears. Even though I'd swear on a stack of *Vogues* there was no one near it. All right, the costumes usually turn up again later, but that's not the point!'

'I've done everything short of barricading myself in my workroom,' said Caitlin. 'But Richard will keep summoning me to the stage so he can find fault and shout at me. I am *this* close to striking him down with a blunt instrument I just happen to have about my person, and then walking out on this whole damned mess. I don't need this job that badly.'

'But I do,' said Josie. 'I've already left two productions over the way I was treated. I can't keep doing that, or word will get around that I'm impossible to work with. And a reputation like that is easy to acquire but hard to shake off.'

Caitlin nodded. 'And no one wants to be thought of as rats deserting a sinking ship.'

'So what do we do?' said Josie.

'Keep our heads down and do our jobs, and make sure that

whatever happens, none of the blame sticks to us,' said Caitlin.

They stood together for a while, arms folded, thinking their own thoughts. Until finally Caitlin looked at Josie.

'Is there anyone on this stage you haven't slept with?'

Josie let out a harsh bark of laughter. 'I haven't had the time or the energy to get through half of them.'

'Maybe I should aim you at the producers,' said Caitlin. 'We could use them on our side.'

Josie shook her head firmly. 'One isn't interested and the other is too scared of his wife.'

Caitlin grinned broadly. 'You've already tried?'

'Let's just say I opened some lines of communication,' said Josie. 'Only to find no one was on my frequency.'

'Pity,' said Caitlin. She shot the costumes mistress a sly sideways glance. 'What about the bishop?'

'He only has eyes for Diana,' said Josie. 'I think that's very sweet.'

'They're from extremely different worlds,' said Caitlin. 'I can't help thinking one of them is in for a very upsetting surprise.'

'What about you?' said Josie.

'What about me?' said Caitlin.

'Has anyone special caught your eye?' Josie said patiently. 'Have you pried open anyone's knees, so far?'

'Not as such. Though I suppose there is someone I'm interested in . . .'

'Who? Who?' said Josie, bouncing up and down on her toes.

'Maybe . . . Richard.'

Josie stopped bouncing. 'Are you kidding? Really? *Richard* . . .'

Caitlin grinned. 'Why do you think I keep going out of my way to give him a hard time? Treat them mean to keep them keen. I think that man could have untapped depths of passion, if I could just get his attention.'

'Do us all a favour,' Josie said firmly. 'Back him up against a wall and knock out his back teeth with your tongue until he gets the message. I'm sure he'd mellow out big time if he just woke up in the morning with a big grin on his face.'

'I'll think about it,' said Caitlin.

* * *

Richard walked up to Todd and planted himself directly in front of the actor.

'Are you thinking of leaving the show?' he said bluntly.

Todd stared at him. 'Are you out of your mind? I'm more committed to this show than you are!'

'But you've been fighting me right from the beginning,' said Richard.

'That's my job,' said Todd. 'To make sure you know what you're doing.'

'And do I?' said Richard.

'So far,' said Todd. 'Look, I don't know about you, but I am in this for the duration. And Paul will stick it out as long as I'm here. As for the rest of the cast, or at least the ones who matter . . . Mark doesn't have anywhere else to go, and we all know Diana doesn't scare easily.'

Richard nodded slowly. 'What do you make of the bishop?'

Todd shrugged. 'The whole Holy Terrors thing makes for great headlines, but whether they'll be any use . . . Hopefully, just having them around will make people feel more secure. If someone has been messing us about, just the threat of a proper investigation could be enough to put an end to all this nonsense.'

'That would be a help,' said Richard.

'And if it should turn out that there is some form of witchcraft involved,' Todd said slowly, 'I can't think of anyone more qualified to get to the bottom of it. Of course . . . if it is witchery, there are three very obvious suspects.'

It took Richard a moment to get the point, and then he looked genuinely startled.

'You mean the three witches? That's a bit on the nose, isn't it?'

'They've all been boasting about the extensive research they did on the subject,' said Todd. 'Who else would know so much about the appearance of witchcraft than three women who'd steeped themselves in the stuff?'

'But what possible reason could they have to destroy this production?' said Richard. 'They need this show to be a success if they're to make money.'

'Unless they're already being very highly paid to put the boot in,' said Todd. 'You must know this show has enemies. Other productions with falling attendances, afraid of being pushed aside by a new success. Now, I'm not ready to point the finger at any witch in particular, but I do think it might be wise to keep an eye on them.'

'I'm keeping an eye on everyone,' said Richard.

Chris took his time approaching Sarah, while she just stood her ground and scowled at him. She waited till he was almost upon her and then got her opening in before he could.

'You have got to be joking if you think you're going to get anywhere with me. You think I haven't seen you wagging your little tail at Angela and Jenny? Are you so desperate to complete the set?'

Chris kept his face and his voice carefully calm. 'Like everyone else in the company, I'm feeling very under threat. From all the weird stuff that's been stalking us, and what the producers might do if they get cold feet. Is it really so strange that I should be looking for allies? I went to Angela because she's spent a lifetime in this job and knows all the ins and outs of protecting herself. I went to Jenny because she knows more about putting other people between her and trouble than anyone I know.'

'And you've come to me because . . .?' said Sarah.

'Because you don't let anything get in the way of you getting what you want,' said Chris.

Sarah smiled slowly. 'You have been paying attention. But what is it you think I can do for you?'

'I need help working out some ideas, to deal with anyone who might be prepared to throw us to the wolves to protect themselves,' said Chris. 'Like Todd, or Paul, or Richard . . . And very definitely David and Micah. I need advice from someone who won't quibble when it comes to doing what's necessary to save ourselves.'

'All right,' said Sarah. 'Let's talk.'

Mark stood alone in the wings, enjoying the quiet and the cool of the shadows inside the heavy drape curtains. He ached all over and wished he had gone back to his dressing room for a lie down, but this was more important. He had to be seen waving the flag in a confident manner. He sensed a presence at his side and looked round to see one of the backstage people had moved in beside him. The balding, middle-aged type smiled pleasantly at Mark, and he smiled back automatically, even though he didn't recognize the man. He felt a bit guilty about that. He really should have made more of an effort to get to know everyone's name, because you never knew when you might have to rely on them at some point. The man nodded, as though he knew what Mark was thinking.

'I'm Griffin,' he said easily. 'It's my job to make sure things run smoothly around here.'

'You must have your work cut out for you at the moment,' said Mark.

Griffin nodded solemnly. 'You don't need to worry about all the bad stuff that's been happening. I don't see it lasting much longer.'

'That's good to know,' said Mark.

'I started out in this theatre, back in the old days,' Griffin said comfortably. 'I've seen them come and I've seen them go. The great triumphs and the legendary disasters – it's all grist to my mill. But it is good to see the old place coming alive again.'

Mark hesitated. 'Do you think there's anything to the rumours . . .'

'About witchcraft?' Griffin shook his head firmly. 'Trust me, there is nothing supernatural going on here. I'd know. Now, you look tired. I'll walk you back to your dressing room, so you can put your feet up.'

'That sounds like a good idea,' said Mark.

He made a point of not leaning on Griffin as they walked away. Just in case anyone was watching.

Richard stood on his own, ignoring the slowly dispersing crowd as he stared out over the auditorium, remembering the great dream that had set him on the path to doing this play. He felt in danger of losing that sometimes, drowned in the mess of details and derailed by all the little disasters.

He needed to make this show something he could be proud

of, to prove to everyone that he did know what he was doing. And no one and nothing was going to stop him. He smiled slowly. He would make this show one to remember, despite everything a saboteur or a witch or the whole unfriendly universe could do to stop him.

FOUR

Where's the Best Place to Look for a Witch?

Alistair and Diana decided they might as well check out the entire backstage area while they had it all to themselves. It turned out to be mostly empty corridors and firmly closed doors, along with a great many surfaces that clearly hadn't had any acquaintance with cleaning products in far too long. Alistair strode up and down the narrow passageways, determined not to overlook any nook or cranny that seemed in the least interesting, while Diana wandered along in his wake and did her best not to appear too obviously bored.

'I'm back here all the time,' she said finally. 'If there was anything out of the ordinary going on, I'd know. I mean, I've seen unwise assignations, hair-pulling fights and temper tantrums over someone not coming on stage when they should have, and that's just the men. Think about it, Bish: if there is a real witch, they're hardly going to leave a broomstick or cauldron just lying around, are they?'

She tried to make it sound like a joke, but Alistair could hear the tension in her voice. He was careful to keep his answer calm and to the point.

'You said the props mistress provided a cauldron for the three witches.'

'It got thrown out, right after the business with the nasty chemicals,' said Diana. 'No one trusted it after that.'

Alistair stopped and looked at her. 'You said no one was hurt.'

'Not for want of trying,' said Diana.

Alistair nodded thoughtfully. 'A failed attack against all three witches, in full view of the entire company, would be a good way to shake off suspicion.'

'You're not still thinking one of our witches could be the real thing, are you?' said Diana.

'The best place to hide is in plain sight,' said Alistair.

'But would our saboteur really put themselves at risk?' said Diana.

'They might, if they were a professional,' said Alistair.

'I don't like the idea of pointing an accusing finger at any of the people I work with,' said Diana. 'Show a little compassion, Bish; they're having to cope with an actual reign of terror.'

'And the best way to put a stop to that is to see things as they are, and not as we would wish them to be,' said Alistair. 'In my experience, anyone will do anything for the right motivation or the right price. No, the only answer that makes sense is that someone in this production has been hired to use the appearance of witchcraft to terrorize the cast.'

'I'm not seeing any evidence to back that up,' said Diana.

'Because we haven't finished looking yet,' said Alistair.

Diana heaved her best dramatic sigh. 'I'll give it another half hour, Bish. And then I'm out of here.'

'Oh, I'm sure we'll find something long before that,' said Alistair.

Diana gave him a hard look. 'You sound very sure.'

'The ring of fire in the wings was just the opening shot,' said Alistair. 'Whoever we're pursuing is desperate to scare us off, and now that their simple magician's trick has failed so abysmally, they know they need to up their game and hit us with something really impressive.'

'Something worse than a ring of blazing fire?' said Diana.

'Well,' said Alistair, 'that goes without saying.'

They arrived back at the dressing rooms. Alistair considered the long row of closed doors and smiled suddenly.

'Do you think your fellow cast members would be really upset if we were to ever-so-slightly search their dressing rooms and rummage through their things?'

'They would hit the roof big time,' said Diana. 'This is the only part of the theatre the cast can call their own. More important, it's where everyone keeps their good luck charms. If you move the wrong thing even an inch out of place, you can be sure the actor will notice, and come after you with a chainsaw in each hand. If word gets out that we've messed with their good luck, the entire cast will walk.'

'Really?' said Alistair.

'Definitely,' said Diana. 'And make an official complaint to Equity, who would shut this entire production down in a moment, as a warning to others.'

'Would you walk out?'

'Too right I would,' said Diana. 'You mess with my lucky support gonk at your peril.'

'Then we'll just have to be extremely careful to look and not touch,' said Alistair.

Diana raised her eyes to the ceiling. 'I know I'm talking because I can feel my lips moving, so why isn't he listening?'

'Because we have a job to do,' said Alistair. 'And please don't address the heavens in that way; that's my job.'

Diana scowled at the long line of dressing rooms. 'It's all hypothetical anyway, because everyone locks their door these days.'

'Every lock in the theatre must open to a basic skeleton key,' Alistair said cheerfully. 'In case of fire. I contacted the building's owners before I came here and acquired their duplicate.'

Diana had to smile. 'You are one seriously sneaky bishop.'

'All part of the job skills,' said Alistair.

He produced his pass key with a flourish, unlocked the first door and stepped inside. Diana followed after him, shaking her head.

'This can only go well . . .'

Alistair shook his head disbelievingly. The dressing room before him was barely eight feet long by six feet wide, with an intimidatingly low ceiling. Furniture and fittings were so basic that they were cheap without the cheerful, with most room given over to the makeup table and mirror.

'Maybe I should have started with one of the star dressing rooms,' said Alistair.

'You have,' said Diana. 'This is Todd's room. They're all much of a muchness – designed for privacy, not comfort.'

Alistair moved slowly forward, careful to keep his arms tucked in at his sides to make sure he didn't nudge anything.

'I suppose you could call this cosy,' he said. 'All you'd have to do is plant your chair right in the middle and everything would be within arm's reach.'

'At least Todd has a room to himself,' said Diana. 'Anyone who's not a featured player has to share. When it gets down to the extras, they're crammed in like sardines, and they have to learn to all breathe in at the same moment if someone wants to get up to put on their makeup.'

'I can't believe people put up with this,' said Alistair. 'Veal on its way to the slaughterhouse is legally guaranteed more room than I'm seeing here.'

'It does help to encourage a sense of community spirit,' said Diana. 'When it isn't setting people at each other's throats. I have seen actresses go for each other with heated hair tongs and broken perfume bottles over who gets to the makeup mirror first. These things matter . . .'

Alistair stopped in the middle of the dressing room, because there was nowhere else to go, and studied the photos and good luck messages attached to the makeup mirror with Blu Tack. Bits of discarded costume lay scattered across the floor, while Todd's street clothes hung from a single hook on the wall. Empty pizza boxes had been piled up haphazardly under the makeup table.

'I was going to turn the place over,' said Alistair. 'But there doesn't seem to be anywhere to look. I'm thinking of battery hens, and not in a good way.'

'You always get the best results from a pressure cooker,' said Diana.

They made their way from one dressing room to the next, carefully relocking each door behind them. Diana pointed out a few of the more usual hiding places, where they found the occasional item of interest. An impressively large bag of weed, a rather impressive sex toy and a box of chocolates with all the soft centres missing . . . but nothing that pointed to a witch or a saboteur. Out in the corridor again, Alistair and Diana looked at each other and shrugged pretty much simultaneously.

'Well, that was a waste of time,' said Diana. 'Though the sex toy was a bit of an eye-opener.'

'I was hoping to find a few insights into people's characters,' said Alistair.

'Then you should have asked me,' said Diana. 'I am up on all the latest gossip. How else would I know what people are saying about me? So . . . what do we do now?'

'We go back to the auditorium and talk to people some more,' said Alistair. 'After you've given me some idea of what to talk to them about. Unless you'd feel guilty about sharing their secrets.'

'Don't be silly, darling,' Diana said briskly. 'The whole point of gossip is to share it with others. What does bother me, though, is that we still haven't got a firm grip on what we're dealing with here.' She looked steadily at Alistair. 'That ring of fire in the wings wasn't any kind of trick or illusion. My skin is still smarting from the heat . . .'

'Just because the flames were real, it doesn't mean it wasn't a trick,' said Alistair. 'It was a trap – rigged in advance and left for us to walk into. The saboteur needed to hit us with something dramatic, because they knew we'd be harder to scare than the regular cast. So they came up with something devilish enough to strike fear into our hearts.'

Diana looked at him sharply. 'Are you talking black magic?'

Alistair surprised Diana by taking her question seriously. 'Not necessarily . . .'

'I was really hoping you were going to say *No of course not*, in an extremely reassuring tone of voice,' said Diana.

'I read extensively on the subject, when I was studying at the seminary,' said Alistair. 'And I have to tell you that the real thing is a lot rarer than popular media would have you believe.'

Diana raised an eyebrow. 'You mean Hollywood lies to us?'

'I know – shocking, isn't it?' said Alistair. 'But I'm pretty sure we can put the ring of fire down to a magician's trick – the kind where quickness of the mind deceives the eye. I've already worked out a dozen ways it could have been faked.'

'Bish!' said Diana. 'We're not alone . . .'

A dark figure was standing motionless at the far end of the corridor, half hidden in shadows. It wore a long dark robe, with the hood pulled forward to hide the face. Something about the figure's almost unnatural stillness raised all the hackles on the back of Alistair's neck, and his hand rose immediately to the crucifix at his neck. Diana leaned in close and lowered her voice.

'It wasn't that dark down there just a moment ago. All the lights at that end of the corridor have been turned off.'

'It's just another attempt to mess with our heads,' said Alistair. 'They're trying to manipulate our emotions.'

'If you mean scare the hell out of us, it's working,' said Diana. 'How can anybody stand that still? I'm not even sure they're breathing . . . This is not natural, Bish! If I was any more freaked out, I would be standing in a puddle of something.'

'Don't let it get to you,' said Alistair. 'I would never let anything bad happen to you.'

'You know I have faith in you, Bish,' said Diana. 'But every instinct I've got is yelling at me to get the hell out of here while I still can.'

'Stand your ground,' said Alistair. 'Running is what they want.'

'But what are we going to do?' said Diana.

'Face it down,' said Alistair. 'Show it we're not scared.'

Diana glared at the motionless figure. '*Piss off!*'

Alistair smiled, in spite of himself. 'I think it's going to take just a bit more than that . . .'

'All right, you think of something,' said Diana. 'You're the spiritual authority; put the hard word of Heaven on him.'

Alistair raised his voice and addressed the unmoving figure.

'Identify yourself! Don't make me have to come over there.'

The figure didn't react in any way. Its utter stillness was becoming seriously disturbing. As though it was just waiting for the right moment to do something awful. Alistair made a point of showing the figure his most casual smile.

'It's up to you,' he said. 'Either you talk to me or I am going to find something suitably heavy and bounce it off your forehead.'

Diana let out a sudden bark of laughter. 'Way to go, Bish!'

The figure still didn't respond in any way. Diana lowered her voice again.

'There's something very wrong with whoever that is . . .'

The figure burst into flames. Supernaturally bright fires surrounded it in a moment, the roaring flames rising high enough to scorch the ceiling. The figure didn't flinch or make the slightest sound. And yet despite everything that was happening right in front of him, Alistair still couldn't bring himself to believe that he was witnessing anything supernatural. Perhaps because it was all so on the nose, so determinedly dramatic . . . As though the whole spectacle had been staged just for them.

He started forward to try to put out the flames, just in case there was someone who needed saving, but Diana grabbed his arm with both hands and held him back.

'You stay right where you are! Feel the heat on the air! There's nothing you can do . . . Whoever that is, if they weren't dead before, they sure as hell are now.'

Alistair stared at the fiercely burning shape and nodded slowly. 'I don't think that thing was ever alive.'

'What?' said Diana.

'It never made a sound when the flames first rose up,' said Alistair. 'It didn't make any move to protect itself. And with a fire that fierce, anything living would have collapsed on the floor by now from lack of oxygen. I don't believe we were ever looking at anything human.'

'OK . . .' said Diana. 'You are seriously creeping me out now, Bish.'

'I was pretty spooked, for a while,' said Alistair. 'Which was almost certainly the intention.'

They stood close together and watched the motionless figure burn. The heat was so intense it made the air ripple like a mirage and beat against Alistair and Diana's faces.

'They burned witches, didn't they?' said Diana.

'Actually, they hanged most of them,' said Alistair.

'We're going to have to have a serious talk with someone about fire extinguishers,' said Diana, trying hard for a moment of normality. 'Because I'm not seeing one anywhere.'

'Probably best not to say why we're asking,' said Alistair. 'Not until we're sure what's going on.'

The flames suddenly erupted in a sharp blaze of light, blinding Alistair and Diana and forcing them to turn their heads away. When they finally looked back, all signs of the fire and the figure were gone, with not even a trace of smoke left on the air. Where the burning figure had been, the end of the corridor was completely empty. Alistair moved cautiously down the corridor, with Diana tucked in close beside him. She glared at the spot where the figure used to be.

'Someone thinks they can frighten us off,' she said loudly. 'They don't know us very well, do they?'

Alistair smiled briefly. 'We have seen worse . . .'

Diana winced as they drew nearer. 'Whatever we just saw was quite definitely real. I can still feel the heat hanging on the air.'

'The flames were real enough,' said Alistair. 'They left scorch marks on the floor and the ceiling.'

'Did we just watch somebody die?' Diana said quietly. 'Did the saboteur murder someone right in front of us?'

'No one died here,' said Alistair. 'There was never anyone here who could die.'

'That probably sounded a lot more reassuring before you said it,' said Diana.

They finally reached the spot where the figure had been, and all the lights snapped back on. Diana jumped just a little, despite herself, and then scowled at Alistair when he didn't.

'This is getting so obvious it's practically insulting,' she said very loudly.

'Someone must have rigged an override for the lights,' Alistair said absently. 'So they could trigger them from a distance. They want us to get a good look at the scene and be properly impressed.'

'You don't believe any of this, do you?' said Diana.

'Our saboteur is repeating himself,' said Alistair. 'This is, after all, his second attempt at a supernatural fire.'

'But what happened to the body?' said Diana. 'There should have been something left behind, but I'm not even seeing any ashes!'

'I don't believe anyone was actually set on fire,' said Alistair. 'Because nothing human could have stood that still. Think about it, Diana; see what was there, not what you expected to be there. What kind of human shape would never move or react, no matter what you did to it? Only one thing comes to mind: the kind of figure I saw in a tailor's shop window on my way here.'

'A tailor's dummy!' said Diana. 'Josie made a whole bunch of mannequins for Richard, so they could be dressed up and used to bulk out the crowd scenes!'

'Just another spooky conjuring trick,' said Alistair.

'Nice going, Bish!' said Diana. 'But wait a minute . . . Even the kind of fire we just witnessed wouldn't have been enough to consume an entire mannequin in just a few moments.'

'Remember the flash of light at the end?' said Alistair. 'So bright we had to look away? Perfect cover for a disappearing act.'

'So he's not just a saboteur; he's a master magician?' said Diana.

Alistair smiled briefly. 'We can ask them how they did it when we catch them. What matters is, if they're trying this hard to scare us off, we must be getting really close to the truth.'

'Be nice if we had some idea who we were getting close to,' said Diana.

'You can't have everything,' said Alistair. 'I mean, where would you put it?'

'Very deep, Bish.'

Alistair knelt down and examined the scorch marks on the floor. He tested them gently with his fingertips.

'More of the accelerant grease I found at the ring of fire.'

And then he broke off as he spotted something lying on the floor just a few feet away. He picked up the small brown object and studied it carefully.

'What have you got there?' said Diana, leaning in to peer over his shoulder.

'Damned if I know,' said Alistair, rubbing the tiny shape between his fingertips. 'I think it's plastic, but apart from that . . .'

Diana straightened up and shook her head. 'Could be anything. All kinds of junk turn up backstage.'

Alistair slipped the small object into his pocket and got to his feet. Diana brushed absently at his clothes in case he'd picked up a few ashes.

'Typical of our luck,' she said. 'We finally find a clue, and it's no damn use at all.'

'It'll mean something later,' Alistair said confidently.

He looked around him, and the empty corridor stared silently back.

'Whoever it was, they're long gone by now,' said Diana.

'Not necessarily,' Alistair said quietly. 'The lights coming back on just in time to be helpful suggest someone is still watching us.'

Diana lowered her voice. 'I'm not seeing anyone. I can't even see where someone could be hiding themselves.'

'I think it's fair to assume our saboteur studied the layout of this theatre before they arrived,' said Alistair. 'Arming themselves with a good working knowledge of all its hidden ins and outs.' He thought for a moment. 'I think we should leave. Before our hidden enemy can think of something else to throw at us.'

Diana scowled unhappily. 'I don't normally believe in backing down to anyone. But given that there's nothing even remotely normal about this situation, I say we get the hell out of here and worry about our pride later.'

Alistair nodded. 'Sounds like a plan to me.'

They moved quickly back through the corridors, constantly alert for any new sign of enemy action, but everything seemed perfectly still and quiet. They finally ended up back in the auditorium, next to the raised stage, and stopped for a moment to regain their composure.

'Now what?' said Diana.

'We question the cast some more,' said Alistair. 'Hit them with a few probing questions.'

'I'm all for a good probe,' said Diana. 'But don't forget, Bish, you'll be talking to actors. Every single one of them trained to lie convincingly every night of the week and twice on Saturdays.'

'I hear a lot of lies in my line of work,' said Alistair. 'You'd think I'd be better at recognizing them by now, but I always want to see the best in people. It doesn't matter. Sooner or later, we'll catch someone in a contradiction, and that's when our saboteur will give themselves away.'

'Actors are different,' said Diana. 'Most of them would cheerfully lie, exaggerate or drop someone else in it just to hear themselves talk.'

'You should know,' said Alistair.

Diana smiled sweetly. 'Play to your strengths – that's what I always say.'

They went up on to the stage. The cast and the producers had long since departed, leaving only Richard standing by the wings, lost in his own thoughts. Alistair and Diana headed straight for him, but even though their footsteps echoed loudly on the quiet, he refused to admit their existence until they were right on top of him. Richard finally turned to face them, giving Alistair his best *You are wasting my time* glare. Alistair smiled back at him, entirely unmoved.

'What?' said Richard.

'Is there any reason you can think of,' said Alistair, 'why someone would want to take revenge on you, the company or the show?'

Richard sighed heavily, just to make it clear how much he objected to Alistair's presence when he was already burdened with so many problems. Alistair was impressed the director could pack so much information into one sigh, but didn't let that affect his remorseless smile. Richard reluctantly gave the question his full attention, frowning hard as he considered the matter.

'All I can think,' he said finally, 'is that it must be to do with the musical. When something makes that much money, someone is bound to think they were cheated out of their fair share.'

'Did you cut any corners?' said Alistair. 'Disappoint anybody?'

'No to the first; maybe to the second,' said Richard. 'I had to give most of my attention to holding the show together, so if I did upset anyone, it wasn't deliberate. Most actors would know better than to take it personally.'

'What sort of things are we talking about?' said Alistair.

'And who got hurt?' said Diana.

Richard thought some more, scowling less as he became genuinely interested in the question.

'Once I started working on the mess that was the original script, it became clear I was going to have to make some major cuts so we could fit in more songs. I had to let some actors go because their roles didn't exist any more.'

'That would be a good reason to get mad,' said Diana. 'Dropped from the show just before the big payout.'

'Particularly if they believed someone else deserved it more,' said Alistair.

'I did make certain promises, to some of the actors, that I couldn't keep,' Richard admitted reluctantly. 'I assured them that their roles were safe, and they had nothing to worry about . . . But in the end, I had no choice! The show had to come first!'

'So there could be people out there who bear you a grudge,' said Alistair.

'It's possible,' said Richard.

'Give me their names,' said Diana. 'I'll reach out to people I know, see if anyone's been raising a stink lately, or dropped out of sight.'

'Every success comes with a price,' said Richard.

He broke off as Diana suddenly stepped forward and fixed him with a hard stare.

'You made a lot of promises to the people in this play,' she said coldly. 'Not least that we're cut in for some serious profit participation if the play is a success. That's what's kept a lot of the cast here, despite everything that's been happening.'

'But this time I'll be able to keep my promises,' said Richard. He turned quickly to Alistair. 'You've been hanging around for a while now, Bishop. Have you experienced anything out of the ordinary?'

Alistair and Diana exchanged a look. Richard caught them doing it, but Alistair just shook his head firmly. Diana took her cue from him and hit Richard with a stare sharp enough to keep him from challenging either of them.

'So far, it's all just been shadows and atmosphere,' said Alistair. 'There are some aspects to this case I don't fully understand yet, but give me time and I will get to the bottom of what's going on.'

'He really will,' Diana said proudly. 'It's what he does.'

'He'd better,' said Richard.

He started to turn away, but Alistair moved quickly to intercept him.

'We need to speak to Macbeth and Banquo.'

'Don't let me stop you,' said Richard.

'I think he wants you to go and find them,' Diana said sweetly. 'And send them here.'

'When did I become your errand boy?' said Richard.

'Since you're most likely to know where they are,' said Alistair.

Richard started to say something heated, caught Alistair's steady gaze and thought better of it. He stomped off stage, muttering to himself. Diana looked at Alistair.

'Why do you need to speak to Todd and Paul?'

'As leads, they must have the most contact with the other actors,' said Alistair. 'I'm hoping they might have noticed changes in behaviour that we ought to know about.'

'I'm afraid you're going to be disappointed,' said Diana. 'Leads don't normally chum around with anyone who isn't a lead. It's that whole feudal thing again.'

'So you don't know much about the cast either?' said Alistair.

'Ah, but I am famously addicted to the gossip, darling,' said Diana. 'Which means I get to hear all kinds of things I'm not supposed to know.'

'That could make you a threat to our guilty party,' said Alistair. 'Someone who might need to be taken care of . . .'

Diana sighed. 'I'm going to end up as bait in a trap, aren't I?'

'Very attractive bait,' said Alistair.

They waited, but neither Todd nor Paul showed up.

'I get the feeling Richard could be taking his time, just to spite us,' said Alistair.

'Wouldn't surprise me in the least,' said Diana.

Two sets of footsteps finally made themselves heard in the wings. Very clearly not hurrying themselves.

'It would appear Todd and Paul have their own point to make,' said Alistair. 'Is everyone in this place so childish?'

'Of course,' said Diana. 'They're actors.'

Alistair grinned suddenly. 'You think they're bad; try attending a parish meeting, and listen to them argue over what kind of biscuits to have with their tea. I've seen civil disturbances break out over the bourbons and brandy snaps.'

Todd and Paul finally emerged from the wings and strolled imperiously over to join them. Todd looked belligerent, Paul as though he'd rather be anywhere else. Todd fixed Alistair with his best defiant scowl.

'What is so important that we had to be dragged away from our rehearsal time?'

'Lose the attitude, darling,' said Diana. 'Richard's too preoccupied right now to give a damn about rehearsals. You're just marking time, like the rest of us.'

Paul smiled at Todd. 'She's got you there.'

Todd stared at him. 'Whose side are you on?'

'Oh, yours, always,' said Paul. 'Now answer the nice bishop's questions, so we can get back to doing nothing.'

Todd nodded stiffly to Alistair. 'What do you want to know?'

'In your opinion,' Alistair said carefully, 'has anyone in the cast been acting strangely or out of character?'

Todd's head rose as he picked up on the implications of the question.

'You think the saboteur is one of us?'

'Don't you?' said Diana.

Paul was already nodding. 'It would make sense.'

Todd frowned so hard the others could all but see the thoughts moving back and forth in his head.

'Our enemy has to be someone who knows this production inside and out, so they can target our weak spots.'

'But why would anyone want to?' said Paul.

Todd smiled coldly. 'The usual. Money, revenge, ambition . . .'

'Those are good reasons,' said Paul.

'Would either of you care to point a finger at any particular individual?' said Alistair.

'I wouldn't trust anyone in this cast further than I could throw a wet camel,' said Todd.

Diana drew herself up to her not inconsiderable height, the better to look down her nose at him.

'Are you including me in your suspicions?'

Todd looked at her coldly. 'Why not? What better cover could there be for a saboteur than to make herself part of the investigation?'

Diana started to say something heated, but Paul talked right over her until she gave up.

'Sabotage makes a kind of sense, but I don't believe in any of this talk about witchcraft. It's all just cheap theatrics, designed to make an impression on the not-too-tightly wrapped.'

'We've been thinking along the same lines,' said Alistair. 'Our saboteur has put a lot of time and effort into putting on their own show, with all of us as the audience.'

'Trying to scare the wits out of everyone, so they'll quit,' said Paul. 'Good thing we have our very own Scooby crew to set on their trail.'

'Are you sure you haven't seen anything weird?' said Diana.

'Not a thing,' Paul said firmly.

He turned to Todd to back him up, but his friend hesitated. Everyone looked at him, caught off guard. Paul seemed the most surprised. Todd nodded to him in an apologetic sort of way.

'I didn't want to worry you . . .'

'Whatever it is, I need to hear it,' said Alistair.

'Tell the man,' Paul said sternly.

'Sometimes,' Todd said reluctantly, 'I've seen shadows moving backstage, with no one around to cast them. I've heard people talking in empty corridors. And once I found a dead bat nailed upside down on the inside of my dressing-room door, even though I'm sure I locked the door after I left, and I have the only key.'

'What did you do with the bat?' said Alistair.

'Tore it off the door and flushed it,' said Todd. 'Why?'

'It could have been evidence,' said Alistair.

'I wasn't having that nasty thing in my dressing room,' said Todd. 'I do have standards.'

Paul moved in close beside him, to show his support. 'You could have told me about this. You didn't have to carry all the weight on your own.'

'What could you have done?' said Todd. 'I didn't see any reason for both of us to have nightmares.'

He broke off as Paul suddenly stared right past him. Everyone turned, to take in a dark figure standing at the opposite wings. Alistair's hands clenched into fists as he realized the figure looked just like the one that had burned, right down to the same robe and pulled-forward hood.

It raised an arm and pointed a grey gloved hand at Todd. He cried out in shock and collapsed to one knee. Paul tried to help him up, but it was like trying to shift dead weight. Paul let him go and placed himself squarely between the stricken Todd and the pointing figure. Paul glared at it defiantly.

'You'll have to go through me to get to him!'

The figure took a step forward, and Alistair moved quickly into position beside Paul. He raised his voice, letting it ring out across the open stage.

'Begone, powers of darkness! Stand down, all creatures of the night. God has authority in this place, so avaunt, dark spirits!'

The figure slipped back into the shadows and disappeared.

Alistair went after it, with Diana right behind him, but by the time they got to the wings, there was no trace of anyone ever having been there. Alistair and Diana glared into the shadows and then turned reluctantly away.

'Nice words, Bish,' said Diana.

'I was just ad-libbing,' said Alistair. 'Fortunately, whoever it was didn't seem to know that.'

'What was it trying to do?' said Diana.

'Put on another dramatic scene,' said Alistair. 'With a definite witchy feel.'

'It certainly got to Todd,' said Diana. 'He went down like someone had hit him over the head with a two by four. At least now we can rule him out as one of the main suspects.'

'It would seem so,' said Alistair. He glowered into the wings. 'I'm starting to think we should tear this whole theatre apart, so we can search for hidden trapdoors and secret passages.'

'Wouldn't do you any good,' Diana said briskly. 'If there were any trapdoors left over from the bad old days, they would have been nailed shut and made safe before we were ever let in here, because of health and safety. And this building doesn't look old enough to have hidden passageways.'

Alistair nodded reluctantly. 'There's no point in trying to find the figure, because all they'd have to do is take off their robe, and then they could just blend in with everyone else.'

'Oh, well done, Bish,' said Diana. 'Because I really needed something else to worry about.'

'That's what I'm here for,' said Alistair.

They went back on to the stage, to find Paul helping Todd on to his feet. Todd's face was pale, and his hands were shaking.

'It felt like someone cut my strings,' he said. 'All the strength went out of me.'

'Probably just the power of suggestion,' said Alistair.

'No,' said Todd, his eyes far away. 'Whatever that was, it was real.'

'I'm taking Todd back to his dressing room,' Paul said firmly. 'He needs a sit down, a stiff drink and a timeout.'

Some life came back into Todd's face as he smiled briefly at his friend.

'You've got some of the good stuff? You've been holding out on me.'

'How else was I going to keep it for myself?' said Paul. 'Besides, it's strictly medicinal. I know I always feel better after I've had some.'

'Lead me to it,' said Todd. 'Only promise you'll check my dressing-room door for dead bats before we go in.'

'Of course,' said Paul.

They moved away, with Todd leaning heavily on Paul as his friend kept up a constant stream of cheerful chatter.

'I know a really good recipe for bat soup.'

'You haven't started another of those exotic cooking courses, have you?' said Todd.

'Live the dream,' said Paul.

'My bowels still haven't forgotten that chickpea surprise . . .'

'I'm almost certain I know what went wrong there,' said Paul.

They finally disappeared into the wings. Diana looked at Alistair, who was frowning thoughtfully.

'What's on your mind, Bish?'

'I'm not sure what just happened,' Alistair said slowly. 'Except that I'm certain it wasn't what it appeared to be.'

Diana shrugged. 'Par for the course, so far.'

Alistair nodded. 'Our unknown saboteur is really piling on the pressure.'

'So what do we do?' said Diana.

'Keep digging,' said Alistair. 'And I think we need to start by talking to the actresses playing the three witches.'

'Oh, come on, darling,' said Diana. 'They're too obvious to be real suspects.'

'Nothing's obvious in this case,' said Alistair. 'Any idea where they might be hiding themselves?'

'They have their own private little hidey-hole out back,' said Diana. 'It used to be some kind of storage room, back in the day.'

'What's it used for now?' said Alistair.

'It isn't,' said Diana. 'That's why they were able to commandeer it so easily. So they'd have somewhere to hide when they didn't want Richard to be able to find them.'

'But you know where it is,' said Alistair.

'Of course! Because I am Gossip Queen! Do you want to know who's sleeping with whom, or wishes they were?'

'Maybe later,' said Alistair.

Back through the maze of backstage corridors they went, until they came at last to a door that looked no different from any of the others, except it was a little more off the beaten track. Diana shouldered the door open and strode right in.

'Knock knock, ladies!'

The three actresses looked round, startled, as Alistair strolled in after Diana. The three women were sitting bent over a Ouija board, with their extended hands resting on an upturned glass. They jerked their hands away quickly and sat up straight. Alistair raised an eyebrow.

'Have we been communing with the not entirely departed?' he murmured. 'Or diving into the deeper recesses of the subconscious?'

'It's just a bit of fun!' Jenny said loudly.

'We thought we might try to get some answers from the spirits,' said Angela. 'Since you're always too busy to tell us anything.'

'And it does help pass the time,' said Sarah.

'We've been getting some very interesting results,' said Angela.

'To what questions?' Alistair said politely.

'Who or what is haunting this theatre!' said Jenny. 'Who's responsible for all the bad stuff that's been happening!'

'And what did the board have to say for itself?' said Diana.

'Gibberish, for the most part,' said Sarah. 'But . . . Well, see for yourself.'

She nodded to the other two, and they all pressed a single fingertip to the upturned glass. It immediately started skidding round and round in circles. The three actresses leaned back from the glass, keeping themselves at arm's length to show they weren't applying any pressure. Alistair watched closely. The actresses actually seemed to be having trouble maintaining contact with the glass, it was moving so quickly. And part of Alistair couldn't help but wonder if the glass would keep on moving if the actresses took their hands away.

Diana watched the glass with fascinated concentration as it skidded back and forth between the individual letters on the board, and rapidly spelt out a name: *Hecate*. The actresses snatched their hands back, and the glass stopped moving. It trembled slightly as it settled, like a horse after a race.

'It's done it again,' said Jenny, her voice barely a whisper.

'The same name,' said Angela.

'Three times in a row,' said Sarah.

'Hecate,' said Diana. 'Queen of the witches.'

'In a theatre plagued by witchcraft,' said Sarah.

'A character that Richard cut entirely from the play,' said Alistair. 'Meaning a complete loss of work and income for one particular actress. Good reason for a grudge, and maybe even revenge.'

'Elspeth?' said Angela. 'You can't blame her for what's been happening! She was only with us for a few days. Hardly had a chance to get her feet under the table before Richard decided she was surplus to requirements, and she was out of here so fast her feet barely touched the ground.'

'I talked to her before she left,' said Angela. 'She didn't seem that upset. She said she had other work to go to.'

'And yet the glass spelt out that particular name,' said Diana. 'It could have come from your subconscious minds, if one of you thought of her as a suspect.'

'You saw for yourselves!' said Sarah. 'It was all we could do to keep up with the glass's movements!'

'I was barely touching it at the end,' said Jenny. She shuddered suddenly. 'I don't think I want to do this any more. It's stopped being fun . . .'

Sarah glared at Alistair and Diana. 'What are you doing here anyway, barging into our private retreat?'

'Yes,' said Angela. 'Why come looking for us?'

Diana smiled easily. 'When you're looking for a witch, where better to start than with three women pretending to be witches?'

'But we're just playing at being bad!' said Jenny.

'What she said,' said Angela. 'Only more convincingly.'

'No real witch would be caught dead saying some of the nonsense we have to,' said Sarah.

'The results we've been getting with the board don't really mean anything,' said Angela, shooting a reproving glance at Sarah. 'It's just our subconscious impulses, acting out through the glass. Between the three of us, even the slightest contact could be enough to send it in the right direction.'

'But I wasn't thinking about Elspeth,' said Sarah. 'Or Hecate.'

'I didn't even know her!' said Jenny. 'She was let go before I'd even been introduced to everyone!'

'Have the three of you been in this room long?' said Alistair.

The actresses looked at each other uncertainly.

'It's been a while,' said Angela. 'Couldn't tell you how long, exactly. There's no clock on the wall, and time does get away from you when you're involved in something interesting.'

'More than interesting,' said Jenny. 'Look, I've got goose-bumps . . .'

'Did any of you leave the room at any time?' said Alistair.

'All of us, I should think,' said Sarah. 'The bathroom is just down the corridor. Why? Has something happened?'

'Todd had a bad turn,' said Diana. 'Something scared the crap out of him.'

'Wish I could have seen that,' said Angela. 'But it seems none of us have alibis. Of course, we didn't know we'd be needing one.'

'Don't you dare accuse me of anything!' said Jenny.

'No one has,' said Diana. 'Yet.'

'You're just a big bully,' said Jenny, and her lower lip jutted out.

Sarah patted her arm comfortingly and fixed Alistair with a hard look.

'Do you honestly believe one of us could be an actual witch? All spells and curses and bad intent?'

'There is no witch in this theatre,' Angela said sharply. 'Just some mean-minded practical joker. And when I finally work out who it is, I will jam a broomstick so far up their arse it will come out of their eye.'

Jenny snorted suddenly and dissolved into giggles.

'Now, if you'll excuse us,' Sarah said pointedly to Alistair and Diana, 'we'd like to get back to the board while we're still getting results.'

Jenny shook her head stubbornly. 'This was supposed to be a bit of fun, not something that would actually attract ghosts.'

'What makes you think it has?' said Angela.

Jenny's gaze dropped, and her voice was suddenly very small.

'Ever since we started, I keep getting this feeling that there's someone else in the room with us, peering over my shoulder.'

Sarah patted her arm again, but Jenny didn't even seem to notice. Diana shot a glance at Alistair to make sure he'd picked up on that, and he nodded briefly.

'I think the mood's been broken,' said Angela.

She gave the upturned glass a nudge with her fingertip and it barely moved. Alistair and Diana nodded to the three witches, turned and left.

FIVE
The Spectre at the Feast

Alistair and Diana were on their way back to the auditorium when they heard hurried footsteps approaching them. They stopped and braced themselves, only to relax immediately as a familiar face came skidding round the corner and smiled ingratiatingly at them.

'Chris?' said Diana. 'What are you doing back here?'

The young actor had to take a moment to recover his breath before he could answer.

'Richard sent me to find you. He wants everyone back on stage, right now, no excuses. And yes, he did mention you specifically. Now, if you'll excuse me, I have a great many other people on my list who need a nudge.'

And off he went again, sprinting down the narrow corridor with no regard at all for anyone who might be coming in the opposite direction, or any unnoticed inanimate object that might interrupt his progress.

'You have to admire his enthusiasm,' Alistair said solemnly.

Diana shook her head. 'Give some people a moment's power and it goes straight to their egos. Mind you, that one didn't have far to go. Director's little pet . . . He'd curl up in Richard's lap if he let him.'

'It's to the director's credit that he doesn't,' said Alistair. 'What do you suppose Richard wants us for, that's so urgent?'

'Hopefully, it means our revered director has finally come out of his funk and remembered where he left his mojo,' said Diana. 'We don't have that much time left before the play transfers to the West End theatre. And we're not nearly ready for that.'

'I have to ask,' said Alistair. 'Are you sure you still want to be a part of this production, after everything that's been happening?'

Diana stared at him as though he'd just asked whether the sky was still blue. 'Of course! I'm not giving up on this play while it still has every chance of being a major success!'

'But why is that so important to you?' said Alistair. 'You've had a successful career . . .'

'I've had a good career,' Diana said steadily. 'Worked almost constantly, when a great many others haven't, made a living and a name for myself . . . But I've never enjoyed a major West End success. Never been celebrated and adored by the best audiences in the world, and envied by all my peers who matter. And I want that.'

'Why?' Alistair said bluntly. 'So you can prove to all the right people that you really are the great actress they should have known you were?'

'To prove it to myself,' said Diana.

'You have nothing to prove to me,' said Alistair.

Diana smiled. 'I know that, darling. But you don't buy tickets. Now, come along; we'd better not keep Richard waiting. He might lose his nerve again.'

'Maybe if we look really hard, we can help him find it,' Alistair said cheerfully.

'Maybe we could hit him over the head with it,' growled Diana.

By the time they got back to the auditorium and strolled unhurriedly on to the stage, most of the cast and backstage crew had already assembled. They hung around muttering to each other in small groups and shooting Richard expectant looks as he strode up and down, studying his script and scowling heavily enough to discourage anyone from asking questions.

The costumes and props mistresses stood side by side with their arms tightly folded, glowering at the director and sharpening their defiance, ready to throw it in his face if he dared make any new problems for them. The backstage people stood around in their brown coats with their hands thrust deep into their pockets, talking quietly about everything but Richard. Just to make it clear they weren't taking any of this too seriously.

A few people sneaked glances at Alistair and Diana, but no one seemed interested in asking them where they'd been or what they'd been doing.

'All right, listen up!' Richard said finally. 'We've a lot to do, and not much time to do it in.'

Everyone shut up and studied the director carefully, if only to help themselves work out which way to jump, if necessary. Alistair got the impression most of them were simply relieved that Richard had finally decided he knew what he was doing again. The director looked to Josie and Caitlin, and they showed him their most determined faces. Richard just nodded briskly in their general direction and moved on. He took a deep breath and addressed the waiting crowd like a general mustering his forces.

'We're going to rehearse the appearance of Banquo's ghost at the banquet. Josie, don't bother with the latest costume changes. We'll go with what we've got for the moment. Anything we need that isn't already being worn, go fetch it, but don't take too long or I'll start without you. Caitlin, I want every prop the scene calls for, on stage, right now!'

Josie and Caitlin nodded quickly, acknowledging the director's returned powers of decision-making, and disappeared into the wings. The actors murmured among themselves at the choice of scene, not all that keen on playing a supernatural encounter in such a disturbed setting. Alistair took the opportunity to look them over. Todd and Paul were standing side by side, eager to get to work. Mark held himself proudly erect, a fine Falstaffian figure ready for anything, but fatigue showed clearly in the dark smudges under his eyes. The actors playing the Thanes started some simple stretching exercises, every inch the professional and entirely unmoved by all the fuss.

The backstage crew just ambled unhurriedly offstage, to be about their business.

Diana scowled fiercely as she realized Richard hadn't even glanced at her, and made a point of trying to catch his eye, but he just nodded vaguely in her direction and moved on.

'Is that a good sign?' said Alistair.

'Hard to tell,' said Diana.

Chris was bouncing up and down on his toes in his eagerness to do whatever it was Richard wanted. The extras muttered excitedly together, pleased at the chance to be in a major crowd scene. They gathered together at one side of the stage and tried hard to look as though what they did mattered. Alistair noticed that the three actors who'd played the murderers earlier on were standing a little apart. He drew Diana's attention to them.

'They're just making the point that they're not extras,' she said. 'Because they have lines. It's all about status and the pecking order, darling.'

The three actresses playing the witches appeared suddenly on stage, each of them breathless from having to run all the way from their latest Ouija session. Richard looked up from his script and glared at them coldly.

'Nice of you to join us, ladies, but I don't need you for this scene.'

'We'll stick around,' said Sarah.

'Just in case you find a use for us,' said Angela.

'And because we're always an adornment to any scene,' Jenny said sweetly.

Richard had already gone back to scowling over his script.

Alistair leaned in beside Diana and lowered his voice. 'Why are the witches suddenly being so pleasant?'

'They just want to remind Richard how important their characters are,' said Diana. 'The appearance of Banquo's ghost is one of the play's showcases. So watch the witches try every trick in the book to shoehorn themselves into it.'

'So far, it's been the important scenes that have attracted the saboteur's attention,' Alistair said thoughtfully. 'The poisoned cauldron, the collapsing throne, the injured Banquo . . .'

'Well, you're just going to have to cope without me for a while,' Diana said briskly. 'I have to concentrate on being Lady M. But while I'm working . . . don't you dare take your eyes off me, darling.'

Alistair smiled. 'I never do.'

Richard raised his voice. 'If I could have everyone's attention, please! This scene is all about Banquo's ghost crashing the great celebration banquet, after Macbeth has been declared king. So if your character's not a part of that, go find a seat in the auditorium and practise being patient, because we have a lot of work to get through today. I will get to everyone, in time.'

There was a certain amount of muttering and grumbling as some of the actors left the stage, but most seemed happy enough that at least something was happening. Alistair moved to the wings and stood there with his arms firmly folded, to make it clear he wasn't going anywhere. Richard glared at him, and Alistair stared calmly back. Richard decided he was too busy to argue.

Caitlin emerged from the opposite wings, followed by half a dozen men in brown coats carrying a long wooden table. They set it down carefully in the middle of the stage, so it could dominate the proceedings, and then hurried back into the wings. They returned with a collection of heavy ornate chairs to place around the table. Caitlin then organized the setting out of plates and goblets, and platters of food, and several elegant cut-glass decanters full of something that looked very like wine.

The director barked out a series of orders, and the actors moved quickly to take up their positions. Todd seated himself at the end of the table, in the place of power. Chris as Seyton sat down beside Todd, who did everything in his power to ignore him. The Thanes seated themselves all along one side of the table, facing the audience, as Richard called out their names and positions, allowing the audience an uninterrupted view. Richard called to Diana, but she was already settling herself elegantly at the far end of the table, facing Todd. She smiled graciously on her most royal husband, but he just nodded, barely acknowledging her presence. Diana's smile became just a little more forced.

Josie hurried out of the wings with her own men in brown coats, who carried on a small crowd of full-sized mannequins – all fully costumed so they could bulk out the crowd watching the banquet. It only took Alistair a moment to work out that a big crowd was necessary to make it clear to the audience just what an important occasion this was. But he still got a chill as he took in the unmoving artificial figures and remembered the burning figure backstage. The extras slipped quickly in and around the mannequins, leaning on the dummies' shoulders or miming conversation with them – and just like that, the whole thing had the appearance of an actual crowd.

Alistair wondered if Josie had noticed one of her figures was missing.

And that was when the three witches moved purposefully forward to confront Richard.

'We should be part of this scene,' Sarah said firmly.

'I know we're not written in,' said Angela, 'but this is one of the most important moments in the play, where everyone gets to see Macbeth lose his mind.'

'And since the scene is based around a ghost, that means magic,' said Jenny. 'So we should be here too.'

'To imply we're behind the ghost's appearance,' said Sarah.

Richard shook his head. 'I don't have time for this.'

'Make time,' said Angela.

'I can't have you on stage,' Richard said sharply. 'I will not have the audience wondering what you're doing there, when they should be giving all their attention to the main players.'

'We could dress up as ladies of the court, rather than in our usual witchy outfits,' said Sarah.

'Be nice to wear something decent for a change,' said Angela.

'We could play down the makeup, lose the fake warts,' said Sarah.

'I never thought they were necessary anyway,' said Jenny.

'I will not have the three witches distracting the audience!' Richard said loudly. 'Now, please leave the stage so I can concentrate on what matters!'

The three actresses exchanged a look, but seemed to accept they'd pushed the director as far as they could. They withdrew with dignity and took up positions in the auditorium seats. Richard made a point of not noticing them. He turned away and suddenly seemed to see Mark hovering hopefully at the edge of the scene.

'Ten out of ten for enthusiasm,' Richard said briskly, 'but I can't use you in this scene either. Duncan is dead, and I can't have two ghosts haunting Macbeth. But don't go anywhere, Mark. Take a seat in the audience. I've got something in mind for you later.'

Mark nodded and left the stage. Alistair could tell this was more attention than Mark had expected. He'd just wanted to make it clear that his accident hadn't affected his enthusiasm for the play. Alistair followed Mark down into the auditorium, and they sat together near the front. Mark nodded cheerfully to Alistair.

'Now you'll see something. This is one of the most powerful scenes in the play, and Richard is always at his best when emotions are running wild.'

Up on the stage, the director was giving Todd and Diana the benefit of his best hard stares.

'Todd, remember you only see Paul when he's manifesting as Banquo's ghost. When he comes on, it'll be as one of the crowd of servants, so the audience shouldn't notice him.' He turned to Diana. 'You never see Banquo. Concentrate on reacting to Macbeth apparently going crazy.' He frowned suddenly and looked around the stage. 'Paul, where are you?'

Josie stepped out of the wings. 'I gave him his ghostly face mask and he went off to search for a mirror, so he could check out how he looked. I told him he'd be needed soon, but . . .'

Richard looked very much as though he wanted to say *Actors . . .* but didn't.

'Will you please go and find him, Josie. Tell him I need him on stage – right now, if not sooner!'

Josie quickly disappeared back into the wings. Richard turned to the patiently sitting Thanes, looked them over critically and nodded to one in the middle.

'Tom . . . I want Lennox sitting right next to Macbeth. Chris, stir yourself and stand behind Macbeth.'

Chris looked as though he wanted to object, but didn't. He reluctantly adopted the less dominant position, while Tom eased into the chair at Macbeth's left hand. Josie hurried back on stage, peering worriedly over her sunglasses because she knew she was going to have to tell Richard something he wasn't going to be happy hearing.

'I'm sorry, but there's no sign of Paul anywhere!'

'He'll turn up,' Todd said quickly. 'Paul never misses an entrance.'

Josie quickly removed herself from the director's gaze and busied herself with the crowd of extras, tugging and adjusting their clothes and arranging the mannequins to their best advantage. Someone yelled from the wings that Banquo was back and ready to go, and Richard gestured violently for Josie and the hovering Caitlin to leave the stage. He yelled for the waiting servants to make their entrance, and suddenly crowds of them came flooding forward from both wings at once, to surround the table in a bustling flurry of movement. Alistair was impressed by the sheer spectacle of the scene. He searched the servants for some sign of Paul, but the actor had concealed himself very successfully in the crowd. Richard left the stage and went to stand with the audience, to see things as they would.

Once again, Alistair's imagination kicked in. Instead of an open stage with a painted backdrop, he saw a great medieval hall of rough stone walls and a high raftered ceiling, with straw scattered across the floor and torches flaring in iron wall-brackets. King Macbeth and his court sat at their feast, a wild and raucous assembly in their barbaric finery. And yet it seemed to Alistair that the shadows were unusually deep and dark, and that there was a real sense of evil on the air. A feeling of something awful about to happen.

He forced himself out of his reverie, and, just like that, he was looking at people in costumes sitting around a table, trying to pretend the food on their plates was real. As always, he looked to Diana first, and smiled as he saw she was completely in character, all her attention fixed on Todd as Macbeth. And then Richard raised his voice again, and everyone turned to look.

'Remember, everyone! Banquo's ghost will seem to appear out of nowhere. As long as he looks like everyone else, Paul can move among the servants without being noticed, but once he puts his mask on, that marks him as the ghost. But only to Macbeth! No one else! Paul, where the hell . . . Oh, there you are. Just do the accusation bit, take off the mask and then leave with the other servants when it's time.'

Alistair finally spotted Paul, standing at the back in his torn and bloodstained jacket from the murder scene. His features were completely hidden behind a palely glowing silver mask. Elegantly stylized, the blank face had no eye or mouth holes, giving it a suitably eerie look. Alistair couldn't help but wonder how Paul could see out of it. He also couldn't help but consider the possibility that the saboteur might also be hiding in plain sight among the servants. With so much going on, and so many people in one place, it wouldn't be that difficult for one man to hide his presence and bad intentions until it was too late.

Alistair was concentrating so hard he actually jumped a little when Richard shouted for everyone to shut the hell up and pay attention.

'If everyone has quite finished contributing their entirely

unasked-for opinions . . . Paul will be mingling with the servants, just another face in the crowd. And because no one ever pays attention to servants, no one in the audience will spot his presence. But you can all help support the illusion by *not seeing him*. I don't mean don't look at him – that would be a giveaway in itself; just don't see him as anyone important. Only Macbeth ever sees the ghost.'

Richard scowled around at his cast. His expression did not encourage questions or comment, and everyone kept their mouths sensibly shut. The director checked that all the servants were where they were supposed to be, holding food and drink and ready to spring into action, and nodded brusquely.

'All right. Let's do this. Banquet scene is go!'

The servants immediately surged forward to bustle around the long table, dispensing food and filling goblets, while being careful not to do anything that might distract from the main characters' dialogue. Macbeth, Lady Macbeth and the various Thanes all had important and interesting things to say, and woe betide any mere servant whose improvised bit of business got in the way. If the director didn't club them down, the leads would. Most definitely including Diana. Alistair couldn't take his eyes off her, fascinated by the poise and authority she brought to her role.

Anyone not actually speaking kept up a cheerful murmur at the table and among the watching crowd – enough to make a convivial sound without distracting from the drama. Everyone sitting at the table drank thirstily from their goblets, and the servants were kept busy refilling them from the cut-glass decanters. Alistair thought he spotted a few veiled expressions of distaste on the Thanes' faces over a lack of quality in the wine, which might or might not have been acting. He was so caught up in the drama of the scene that it actually came as something of a shock when Banquo's ghost suddenly appeared, blank-faced and menacing, right at Macbeth's shoulder. Alistair flinched·back a little, and some of the actors on stage looked as though they wanted to. It really did feel like the figure had appeared out of nowhere.

Banquo's ghost stood supernaturally still, reminding Alistair uncomfortably of the unmoving figure backstage. He quickly counted the mannequins in the crowd, to make sure one of them hadn't been swapped for Banquo. He wouldn't have put it past Richard to pull a fast one, just to see everyone's reaction. But all the dummies were still where they should be. Paul's face was entirely concealed behind the palely glowing mask, making him genuinely disturbing. Alistair felt like applauding but didn't want to break the cast's concentration, as they all did their best not to react to the spectre at the feast.

The ghost stood between Macbeth and Thane Lennox, though only Macbeth was shrinking back in horror. He lurched to his feet and railed loudly at the dead man only he could see, and everyone else at the table stared at Macbeth, astonished and then disturbed as they watched their new king lose his mind right in front of them. Lennox took a deep gulp from his goblet, rather than look at his king, and then pulled a face. He looked surprised and lurched suddenly to his feet. Macbeth broke off as Lennox stood swaying, staring at Banquo's ghost, his face a mask of pure terror.

Todd forgot all about his big speech and reached out a hand to Tom, who suddenly fell forward, crashed face first on to the table and didn't move again.

For a long moment no one reacted, caught completely off guard by the unexpected turn of events. The nearest Thanes quickly got their act together, took hold of Tom and turned him over, only to cry out in shock and back away when they saw his dead face and wildly staring eyes. Todd hurried forward and elbowed the Thanes out of the way so he could check for a pulse, and then shook his head slowly.

'He's dead . . .'

Diana was quickly on her feet. 'It could be a heart attack! Does anyone know how to do chest compressions?'

'Tom didn't have any heart problems!' said Todd. 'He passed the same insurance medical we all did! He just looked at the ghost . . . and died of fright.'

Everyone was on their feet by now, backing away from the dead man at the table.

Alistair raced down the aisle and vaulted up on to the stage. The cast took one look at his determined face and got out of his way. Alistair bent over Tom, tried both wrist and neck for a pulse, and finally took off his glasses and held them in front of the man's mouth, to see if even the slightest trace of breath would fog the lenses. But there was nothing. Alistair put his glasses back on, made the sign of the cross and murmured a brief prayer for the dead. And then he stopped and looked quickly round the table.

'Where's the goblet Tom was drinking from?'

'What difference does that make?' said Todd.

'I saw him drink from his goblet and then pull a face, right before he collapsed,' said Alistair. 'Someone could have dropped something in his wine. Now, what happened to the goblet? Because I can't see it anywhere!'

Everyone looked round the table, but no one had anything to say. Alistair turned to the servants, huddled together for comfort.

'Did any of you have orders to remove the goblet?'

They all shook their heads quickly.

'Who placed it on the table in the first place?' said Alistair.

The servants paused, looked at each other and conferred in a series of increasingly urgent murmurs. Finally, one of them stepped forward reluctantly.

'We all just placed a goblet in front of each seat, like we were told. It didn't matter who got which goblet, or what happened to them afterwards.'

'It did to someone,' said Alistair.

'Richard ordered Tom to change his seat at the last moment,' said Diana.

'I didn't decide that until I saw how the scene looked!' said Richard. 'And I had no way of knowing which goblet he'd drink from!'

'Hold everything!' said Alistair, so loudly that everyone's head snapped round to look at him. 'Where's Paul?'

The stage fell silent as everyone looked around them, and then a low murmur of disbelief rose up as people realized Banquo's ghost was nowhere to be seen. Alistair turned to the audience in the auditorium, but they were already raising their voices and shaking their heads.

'He didn't come down here!' Mark said loudly from his seat at the front. 'We would have noticed. So he couldn't have made it to the lobby.'

'Paul!' Todd shouted. 'Where are you?'

There was no response. Todd seemed to crumble a little, his usual assurance abandoning him. 'Maybe he went to find the theatre ghost . . .'

Richard came up on to the stage to join the scene, looking lost and confused.

'The only way Paul could have left the stage without being noticed was as we planned: with the other servants. And they're all still here.'

'He could have just slipped into the wings,' said Alistair. 'While we were all preoccupied with Tom.' He looked quickly around him. 'Did anyone see anything?'

There was a general shaking of heads. Alistair turned back to Richard.

'We have to find Paul.'

'You think the killer could have got to him too?' said Todd.

'It's possible,' said Alistair. He gave Richard a hard look. 'Have your backstage people search the theatre. Everyone else, stay where you are! You're all witnesses to Tom's murder.'

'Murder?' said Richard. 'Couldn't it have been some kind of accident?'

He was clutching at straws, and everyone knew it. Alistair moved in close to the director.

'This was no accident,' he said sharply. 'Someone must have put poison in Tom's wine. And the only person close enough to drop it in the goblet and not be noticed . . . was Paul.'

'It couldn't have been him!' Todd said loudly. 'Paul wouldn't do something like that!'

'Then why isn't he here?' said Diana. 'Why did he run away?'

'Paul had no reason to kill Tom,' Todd said stubbornly.

'Whoever's behind all of the bad stuff that's been happening has finally crossed the line,' said Alistair. 'From sabotage to murder. We have to find Paul.'

'If only to make sure he's safe,' Diana said quickly. 'He could have drunk from that goblet too.'

'No,' said Alistair. 'He was wearing a full-face mask, remember?'

Richard yelled at the wings. 'Josie, Caitlin! Get your people together and organize a full search backstage. Check everywhere. Find Paul! No . . . Wait a minute . . .'

He fished in his pockets and finally produced a key. Alistair recognized it as a duplicate of the skeleton pass key he'd been given, and wondered how many other copies there might be. Richard strode over to the wings, and Caitlin stepped out on to the stage to receive the key.

'The producers assured me this would open any lock in the place,' said the director. 'Now, get your people moving. I want every room in this building searched.'

Caitlin nodded quickly and hurried off into the wings to shout at people. Richard looked to Alistair.

'Maybe we should all join in the search. We might locate Paul more quickly that way.'

'None of us are going anywhere,' Alistair said steadily. 'The police are going to want to talk to all of us.'

Everyone was suddenly very quiet. One by one, heads turned to look at Tom's dead body, sprawled across the table.

'You want to call the police?' said Richard, his voice rising. 'Are you insane? If we bring in the authorities, they could shut us down!'

'They definitely will if they think you've tried to conceal something,' said Alistair. 'We have no choice, Richard. Someone just killed a man, right in front of us. Cooperate fully, and the police should let you get back to work as soon as possible. You could justify keeping quiet about your previous problems, as long as everyone thought it was just things going wrong, but Tom's murder changes everything.'

'We are not calling in anyone until we've found Paul,' said Todd. 'And heard his side of things.'

'That's not your call to make,' said Alistair.

'I'm the lead,' Todd said flatly.

'Not any more,' said Alistair, nodding to Tom's dead body. 'It's all about him now. But there's no point in calling anyone until the backstage people have finished their search.'

'You don't think they're going to find Paul, do you?' said Diana.

'I have a feeling he isn't around any more,' said Alistair. 'The police will want to know that.' He looked steadily around him. 'Everyone is to stay exactly where they are. That goes for the rest of you too, out in the auditorium. Mark, keep an eye on them. We don't want any runners to confuse the situation.'

And then they all looked round sharply as Caitlin emerged from the wings, shaking her head.

'None of the backstage people have been able to find a trace of Paul anywhere.'

'You can't have searched the whole theatre this quickly!' said Todd.

Caitlin met his gaze unflinchingly. 'It's not that big a building. We have more people than there are rooms. Of course, if Paul knows some secret hiding place . . .'

Alistair looked to Todd. 'Is that possible?'

'We haven't had time to go exploring,' said Todd. He sat down suddenly, as though all the strength had gone out of him. 'None of this makes any sense . . .'

'Only because we don't have all the facts yet,' said Alistair.

'Why would the saboteur finally decide to kill someone?' said Diana.

'To make an example?' said Alistair. 'Or to throw a real scare into us, because the weird tactics weren't working . . .'

'But why kill Tom?' said Richard.

Alistair thought about it, frowning hard. Everyone else watched silently. In the end, he just shrugged.

'It's always possible that by changing his seat at the last moment, Tom was simply in the wrong place at the wrong time.'

'Paul would never kill anyone!' Todd said loudly.

'I have to say, I really don't see Paul as a killer,' said Diana.

'You did say he was a very good actor,' said Alistair. 'And right now, his not being here is not looking good for him.'

Todd shook his head slowly, like a man taken down by a blow he never saw coming.

'We have to find Paul. He could be hurt or in trouble! He can't just have vanished into thin air . . .'

Sarah came striding down the main aisle of the auditorium with a determined look on her face. Mark started to heave himself up out of his seat to intercept her, but shifting his weight took so long that by the time he was on his feet, Sarah was already up on stage and glaring at Alistair.

'What makes you so sure the ghost didn't just disappear?'

'Because it wasn't a real ghost,' said Diana.

'Are you sure about that?' said Sarah. 'We can't be certain

that what we saw on stage was actually Paul! We never saw his face – only that awful mask. Remember Tom's expression when he died. He was looking right at the ghost and he was scared out of his mind . . .'

There was a long pause as everyone thought about that.

'It can't have been the theatre ghost,' Richard said finally. 'He's been around for ages and never hurt anyone.'

'That was before the theatre was shut down,' said Sarah. 'Maybe our coming here disturbed something, and it woke up angry.'

'You can't really believe that,' said Diana.

Sarah smiled coldly. The possibility of a genuine supernatural event seemed to have given her new authority.

'Think about all the strange things that have been happening, that none of us can explain. Is an actual ghost really so hard to accept?'

'Yes,' said Alistair firmly. 'A saboteur who's escalated to murder is one thing; a ghost who can kill people just by looking at them is something else.'

'You have so little faith, Bishop,' said Sarah. 'Remember the results we were getting from our Ouija board sessions.'

'Where are Jenny and Angela?' Alistair said politely. 'Only I can't help noticing they're not getting involved with this.'

'They moved away to sit on their own somewhere,' said Sarah, gesturing vaguely at the seats. 'What matters is that we heard voices from beyond, warning us to beware!'

'Be sure to tell the police that, when they get here,' said Diana. 'I'm sure they'll be very interested.'

Sarah folded her arms stubbornly. 'You'll see. This isn't over yet.'

Everyone was looking at everyone else, but no one had anything to say. They were all thinking too hard. If Tom's death was murder, that meant his killer was probably still in the theatre with them. He might even be one of them. And if Paul couldn't be found, that could mean two victims rather than one. People looked around with growing suspicion and started to edge away from each other. Suspicious glances were already leading to angry words.

Witches, sabotage, murder . . . The ghost . . .

Alistair quickly raised his voice. 'Ghosts don't poison people!'

'We all saw Tom's face!' said Todd. 'Nothing natural could have scared him that much. Maybe the ghost lowered its mask for a moment and showed Tom what was underneath.'

'I know you don't want Paul to be responsible for Tom's death,' Alistair said steadily, 'but that's no reason to abandon reason.'

'We can't put off calling the police any longer,' said Diana. 'We need professional investigators, if this really is murder.'

'I thought that was you and the bishop,' said Richard.

'We're just gifted amateurs,' said Alistair. 'The police have more resources.' He nodded to Richard. 'They're going to need access to the crime scene while the evidence is still fresh.'

'How do you know so much about what the police will want?' said Todd.

Alistair smiled. 'I'm the Bishop of All Souls Hollow.'

Some impressed murmuring broke out among the cast as they took in the name of London's most notorious parish.

'While I have appeared in any number of crime shows on television,' Diana said proudly.

'We can't let the police shut down the production!' said Richard. His voice was strained, almost shrill. 'We could lose everything!'

Alistair looked round at the cast. 'Could you really continue working here, knowing one of you could be a murderer, just waiting to strike again?'

No one had an answer to that. Richard sighed heavily, and all the fight suddenly went out of him.

'Call them.'

Alistair took out his mobile phone and dialled the emergency number.

Everything moved surprisingly quickly once he set things in motion. It was barely half an hour before Detective Inspector Forbes, Detective Sergeant Hill and a small army of uniformed officers arrived to take control of the situation. None of them seemed at all impressed by their surroundings, or the actors. Inspector Forbes marched straight through the auditorium and up on to the stage, while the uniforms spread out to cover all the exits, in a calm but very firm way. The actors moved closer together, presenting a unified front to a possible enemy.

The inspector took up a position at the front of the stage and looked the cast over. A tall, dark-skinned man in his late twenties, he wore a smart three-piece suit that couldn't have looked newer if it still had a price tag dangling down the back. He projected a cold, focused air and looked perfectly ready to get to the truth by walking over anyone who got in his way. He considered the assembled cast and backstage crew with a calculating gaze, as though just hoping for a chance to catch someone being evasive so he could accuse them of wasting police time.

'I am Detective Inspector Forbes,' he said heavily, holding his ID out in front of him like a weapon. 'Which means I'm in charge here. Do as you're told, answer all questions put to you and, above all, don't try to be clever.' He called over his shoulder without looking back. 'Sergeant Hill! Where are you?'

An older man, with silver-grey hair, handsome features and an elegant if somewhat vacant aristocratic air, moved unhurriedly across the stage to stand beside Forbes. He was wearing what had probably once been a very expensive suit, but now looked as if it had been sent to the cleaners a few times too often. His old school tie was so faded it was impossible to make out the design. He already looked quietly resigned, as though preparing himself for difficult times ahead.

'Here I am, sir, ready for anything and eager to hunt crime to its lair. Would you like to give me some orders? You know that always makes you feel better.'

Forbes didn't take his eyes off the cast for a moment. 'No one is to leave the theatre without my express permission. I want names, contact details and full statements from everybody – no exceptions. Anyone gives you any trouble, feel free to drag them down to the station, throw them in a cell and leave them there until I feel like talking to them.'

'Well, of course, sir,' said Hill. 'That goes without saying. Shall I arrange for some shackles and chains?'

Forbes raised his voice, still not even glancing at Hill. 'Once we have everything we need, I want every single one of these people out of here, and the door locked behind them. This entire theatre is our crime scene, until I say otherwise.'

Richard raised his hand, like a child at school. 'Do you have to close down the whole building? Couldn't we stay on and rehearse somewhere else, so we won't lose our momentum?'

Forbes looked at Richard until he stopped talking. 'Anywhere could hold useful evidence, until the science team assure me to the contrary.' He looked directly at Hill for the first time. 'Don't let the nerds get pushy. Just tell them to lift the prints and cover the scene, and keep their stupid theories to themselves. They've all watched too much television.' He turned back to Richard. 'You're all suspects until I say otherwise. Anyone who drags their feet instead of cooperating fully will be arrested on the spot. For perverting the cause of justice in a murder investigation.'

Richard looked to Alistair. 'Can he do that?'

'If he wants,' said Alistair.

Forbes took in the dog collar and gave Alistair his best hard look.

'They told me you'd be here. The sky pilot who thinks he's Sherlock Holmes. Let us have a clear understanding, Bishop: you have no official standing on this case. As far as I'm concerned, you're just another suspect. And that includes your actress friend.'

'That would be me!' Diana said brightly, bouncing up and down on her toes and waving cheerfully at the inspector. 'Star of stage, screen and television. Don't be afraid to ask for an autograph.'

Forbes shook his head slowly. 'Did I shoot an albatross and no one told me?' He looked from Diana to Alistair, as though trying to decide which of them annoyed him least. 'This is an official warning. There is no place for amateurs in a police investigation. I do not need, want or require any assistance from unauthorized individuals.'

'I feel much the same way when it comes to religion,' Alistair said easily. 'It's always best to leave the real thing to the professionals.'

Forbes blinked, caught off guard, but quickly rallied. 'What business do you have being here anyway?'

'I was called in by the show's producers,' Alistair said easily. 'To look into some rather unusual things that had been happening here. I could tell you all about them, if you're interested.'

Forbes increased the intensity of his glare. 'What did I say earlier, about not interfering?'

Alistair shrugged. 'For what it's worth, I am the one who called you in.'

'Am I supposed to be grateful?' said Forbes.

'I wouldn't presume,' said Alistair. 'But I have to ask: is this really a crime scene? We don't know that the deceased – that's Tom McIntire, by the way – was actually murdered. Because of the suddenness of his death, we've all been assuming some kind of poison, but it could have been natural causes. Heart attack, stroke or some unknown medical condition.'

Forbes shook his head. 'Please tell me you don't have a theory. I hate it when people have theories.'

'Perish the thought, Inspector,' said Alistair.

'It's a crime scene because I'm here,' Forbes said heavily. 'And I will decide what kind of crime.'

Alistair cleared his throat very politely. 'I've attended enough fatalities in my parish to know that in situations like this, an autopsy is mandatory. That should give you cause of death.'

Forbes moved in close, so he could push his face right into Alistair's.

'Get in my way, just once, and all those tabloids who love you so much will be running front-page photos of you behind bars. Understand?'

'Of course, Inspector,' said Alistair, meeting the inspector's gaze entirely steadily. 'You're making yourself perfectly clear.'

Forbes could tell he was being quietly but firmly defied. He turned abruptly to glare at his patiently waiting sergeant.

'Get to work, Hill. The sooner we can collect everyone's stories and boot them out the door, the better.'

'Of course, sir,' said Hill, not even trying to hide the resignation in his voice. 'Can I just ask what will you be doing, while I am running things?'

'Detecting,' Forbes growled. He turned to Richard. 'You. Come with me.'

He led the director off to one side, backed him up against the painted backcloth and fired question after question at him. Richard struggled to hang on to his calm and answered everything as best he could. Hill went to the front of the stage, clapped his hands politely to get the uniforms' attention and then addressed them cheerfully.

'Come along, boys and girls, time to work for a living. I want you to spread out and check every room, nook and cranny in this theatre. Do try to be careful; our missing person might turn out to be injured, or even a second body . . . But he could also be a person of interest in the murder. And vicious with it. Either way, if he does turn up alive, do your very best to bring him back more or less intact and able to answer questions. Or at least nod in a useful way. All right, that's it – off you go! Hop like bunnies!'

The uniforms exchanged meaningful glances and set off into the depths of the theatre. Alistair couldn't help but notice that most of them already had their truncheons at the ready. Diana moved in beside him.

'I hate to say it, darling, but I can't help feeling the inspector is going to be more of a hindrance than a help.'

'Give the man time,' said Alistair. 'He's probably just trying to find his feet in unfamiliar circumstances.'

'You really do try to see the best in everyone, don't you?' said Diana.

'It's my job,' said Alistair.

Diana looked across the stage at Forbes, still struggling to get something useful out of Richard, who had recovered enough of his dignity to be mildly sarcastic.

'The inspector won't get anything out of Richard by bullying him. He's used to dealing with producers.'

'They'll probably end up shouting each other into submission,' said Alistair. He looked Diana over carefully. 'Are you all right?'

'Of course,' Diana said quickly. 'It's not the first time someone has been murdered right in front of me.'

'But it never gets any easier,' said Alistair.

'No,' said Diana, 'it doesn't.'

'Were you and Tom close?'

'Barely knew the man,' said Diana. 'And before you ask, no, I haven't a single idea as to why anyone would want to kill him.'

'But you know all the gossip,' said Alistair.

Diana shrugged irritably. 'Tom was just another jobbing actor. Never happy unless he was working. He had a reputation as a safe pair of hands. Someone you could trust to handle whatever kind of role you threw at him.'

'But what was he like as a person?' said Alistair.

Diana thought hard. 'Quiet. Easy-going. Kept himself to himself, mostly.' She smiled quickly. 'Isn't that what they say about most serial killers?'

'Tom changing his seat at the last moment complicates things,' said Alistair. 'We can't be sure he was the intended target for the poison.'

'I have to wonder,' Diana said carefully, 'whether someone could have nudged Richard's elbow, to put the idea in his head.'

'Did you see anyone near Richard at the time?' said Alistair.

'No,' Diana admitted. She turned away, to look at the left- and right-hand wings. 'I'm still trying to work out how Paul could have got off stage without anyone noticing.'

'I don't believe the ghost we saw was Paul,' said Alistair. 'He didn't have any dialogue, so anyone could have put on the mask and taken his place on stage; then all he had to do was remove the mask to disappear among the servants. No, wait a minute . . . The ghost was wearing Banquo's bloodstained uniform.'

'Only the jacket,' said Diana.

'Well spotted,' said Alistair. 'All the fake ghost had to do was throw off the jacket in the confusion, while everyone was concentrating on Tom . . .'

'Easy enough for whoever it was to have another costume on underneath,' said Diana.

'And he'd be just another face in the crowd,' said Alistair. 'Like everything else our saboteur has done, this was all very carefully planned.'

'But why?' said Diana, just a bit desperately. 'What could matter so much about stopping this play that someone was prepared to kill a man in cold blood?'

'Once we've worked out the why, that should give us the who,' said Alistair. 'Or possibly vice versa.'

Diana glared at him. 'You can be a real pain sometimes, Bish.'

'It's a gift,' said Alistair.

Taking everyone's details and a statement took a long time. Several of the actors insisted on telling the police all about the supernatural elements of the murder, even though the uniforms clearly didn't want to know. Alistair and Diana kept their opinions to themselves. Sergeant Hill took their statements personally, and then asked Diana for her autograph – but as an actor, not a Holy Terror. Apparently, he spent a lot of his spare time at the theatre.

'You have to make allowances for Inspector Forbes,' he said quietly. 'He's new to the area, and he really didn't need a mess like this for his first big case.'

They looked across to where Forbes had finally given up on Richard. He dismissed the relieved director with a brusque jerk of the head, and Richard left the stage as quickly as his precarious dignity would allow. Forbes's head came up sharply as he spotted a dim figure standing in the shadows of the left-hand wings and bustled over to confront him. Alistair and Diana drifted quickly in the same direction and put their listening boots on. Hill just smiled and let them get on with it.

'Who are you?' Forbes said bluntly to the man in the wings. 'Part of the backstage crew?'

'I'm Griffin, sir,' said the balding middle-aged man. 'I work behind the scenes.'

'Were you here when the victim died?'

'Of course, sir,' said Griffin. 'I spend a lot of time in the wings, watching what goes on.'

'Were you close enough to see what happened?'

'Oh no, sir. The poor man's death occurred on the stage, and I'm not allowed on stage.'

'Not much use, then, are you?' said Forbes.

'I do what I can, sir. Now, if you'll excuse me . . .'

He disappeared back into the shadows, and Alistair and Diana moved quickly away before the inspector could realize they'd been earwigging. Sergeant Hill dropped them a discreet wink.

Eventually, the uniforms ran out of statements to take and questions to ask, and the sergeant politely but firmly escorted everyone to the lobby, the front door and the street, in quick order. The door was then slammed and locked behind them. Cast and crew milled uncertainly around in the empty street, not sure what to do next. Diana turned to Richard, but he seemed as lost as everyone else. So she took a deep breath and raised her voice, and everyone looked at her gratefully, glad someone was taking charge.

'I say we all retire to the Paradise Hotel next door,' she said loudly. 'It's where most of us are staying anyway. More importantly, there's a very well-stocked bar!'

She gestured grandly at the shabby hotel. Those without rooms at the Paradise weren't at all impressed by the grimy gothic exterior, but it didn't take long for everyone to decide that a bar was very definitely where they needed to be, and that any port in a storm would do. Richard moved in beside Diana.

'Thanks for taking the lead. After what happened to Tom, and then the inspector giving me the third degree, it's been hard for me to get my head together.' He looked back at the locked front door and scowled fiercely. 'I swear I will get my show back on, if only to spite that man.'

'You honestly think that's a real possibility?' said Diana, not even trying to keep the hope out of her voice.

'Of course,' said Richard. 'David and Micah are important men in the City. They have connections; they know people.'

Diana and Alistair exchanged a look, but said nothing. Diana drew herself up and yelled for everyone to follow her. She strode over to the hotel and hit the front doors like a gunslinger entering a saloon, and everyone else followed on behind.

It didn't take most people long to decide that, if anything, they were even less impressed by the interior than the exterior. The hotel lobby might have been luxurious once, but the bloom had long since faded from that particular rose. The smeared windows only reluctantly let in the light, the cracked plaster walls were stained and spotted with mould, and the parquet floor looked like generations of visitors had stamped it into submission. Packed with disgruntled thespians, the lobby seemed shabby and shadowy, and completely unwelcoming. Alistair folded his arms tightly, as though to make sure he wouldn't touch anything, and shook his head slowly.

'If this place was any more run-down, it would have tyre-marks on it. Why are you putting up with such sub-standard accommodation?'

'Because it's free, and it's handy,' Diana said briskly. 'Do you have any idea how much theatrical digs can cost in London? By the time you've found somewhere acceptable and reasonably priced, you're practically in another city. David and Micah might be happy to throw money at the production itself, but they've cut financial corners everywhere else they could. We were offered free board at this hotel as a *Take it or look out for yourselves* proposition, and we grabbed it with both hands.'

'There don't seem to be any staff on duty,' said Alistair, nodding at the unattended front desk.

'There aren't any staff at all,' said Diana. 'We have to do everything for ourselves, including make our own beds, run the bar and forage for food. Luckily, Mark was able to use his contacts in the hospitality trade to stock the bar, and Domino's delivers from just down the road. Look, the lights work and the toilets flush. I've stayed in worse digs. All actors have. It's not as bad here as it looks.'

'Methinks the lady doth protest too much,' Alistair said solemnly.

'Leave the dialogue to me, darling,' said Diana. 'Now, changing the subject! How long do you think it'll be before the police are gone and we can get back to work?'

'Hard to say,' said Alistair. 'Even if the producers can use their influence to hurry things along, it wouldn't surprise me if the inspector dragged his feet just to be bloody-minded. But he won't have any real excuse to stay once the science people have given the theatre the all-clear.'

Diana looked at him sharply. 'You don't think they'll find anything?'

'Our saboteur has proven himself a complete professional, and he's had lots of time to cover his tracks.'

'But are you sure Tom was poisoned?' Diana scowled unhappily. 'I can't help but remember the awful expression on his face when he looked at Banquo's ghost. Like he was seeing the real thing.'

'The man was dying,' Alistair said bluntly. 'Who knows what was going through his mind? Poison has to be the most likely explanation, and I'm certain the autopsy will back me up.'

'But what's happened to Paul?' said Diana. 'And where is he now?'

'I've no doubt the inspector's people are searching the theatre from top to bottom even as we speak,' said Alistair. 'But if

Richard's backstage crew couldn't find Paul, I don't see the police doing any better.'

'He can't have just disappeared!' said Diana.

Alistair sighed. 'So many questions, and not an answer in sight. We'll just have to be patient and see what the evidence throws up.'

Diana raised an eyebrow. 'You think the inspector will share what he finds? He doesn't approve of us.'

'He just doesn't know us yet,' said Alistair.

'You think that'll change anything?' said Diana.

'We'll just have to charm him,' said Alistair.

'Better leave that to me, dear,' said Diana.

'David and Micah will make sure they're kept in the loop by the inspector's superiors,' said Alistair. 'And then they'll pass on everything they're told to Richard, so they can feel they're part of the production.'

'Do you know why the inspector is being such a pain?' said Diana.

'I've met a lot of police, working my parish,' said Alistair. 'They find it hard to trust anyone, because they get lied to so much. I think Forbes just wanted to make it clear he was in charge of the situation. Unfortunately for him, I answer to a higher authority.'

'That's my Bish!' Diana said happily.

SIX
Secrets Come Out to Play

In the faded elegance of a forgotten hotel lobby, cast and crew milled this way and that, talking at and over each other until Mark raised his great booming voice.

'Everyone, follow me to the bar! All drinks are on David and Micah . . . even if they don't know it yet!'

A great cheer went up, and Mark led them in a grand procession to the adjoining bar. Diana started to follow along with everyone else, but Alistair put a staying hand on her arm. She looked at him questioningly, but he refrained from saying anything until they were the only ones left in the lobby. Diana glowered at Alistair.

'There had better be a good reason for this. I am missing out on free drinks, and I have a hell of a thirst on.'

'Never knew you when you didn't,' said Alistair. 'We need to talk about the hotel. I familiarized myself with the layout of the theatre before I arrived, and that has given me some insights as to how our saboteur could be appearing and disappearing so easily, but if everyone has been using this place as well . . .'

Diana smiled suddenly, as she made the connection.

'You think there might be some old hidden ways, connecting the hotel to the theatre?'

'I'm starting to think so, given the age of both buildings,' said Alistair. 'And it would explain a lot.'

Diana smiled sourly. 'All you really need to know about this dump is that it's cheap but characterless, a hovel away from home. Basically, just somewhere warm and dry where we can all collapse when we're not working. I doubt there's anyone who'll admit to actually liking it here, but the bar is always well stocked, and that helps. The rooms are . . . acceptable. Only the rooms on the first two floors are in use; everything above that has been officially condemned as unsafe.'

'In what way?' said Alistair.

'Pretty much every way you can think of,' said Diana. 'The upper floors are where rising damp meets descending mould, the floors are not just unsafe but actually treacherous, and the ceilings slump in worrying places. Don't even ask about the health hazards. And no, no one has ever gone exploring, because you can only get to the third floor through a single door that's always locked.'

Alistair smiled briefly. 'We already know there are skeleton keys for the theatre; it seems likely the producers would have similar keys for this place. And a whole bunch of rooms that most people can't get to strike me as the perfect base for our saboteur to hide things.'

'What kind of things?' said Diana.

'Props, to help stage his apparently witchy actions,' said Alistair. 'Maybe a changing room, with costumes and makeup, to help him keep up unnatural appearances.' He thought for a moment. 'Tell me more about the rooms the cast are staying in.'

'The walls stand upright and the doors stay closed,' said Diana. 'Which is all we have any right to expect from a hotel this decrepit. A local service provides us with clean linen, when reminded. There's no en-suite, and the bathrooms are unreliable, so we have to rely on a china receptacle under the bed, which is harder to hit than you might think when you're still half asleep.' She stopped and frowned. 'We at least thought our rooms were secure, but if we can't trust the locks, none of us are safe. From now on, I'm jamming a chair up against my door before I go to sleep.' She grinned at Alistair. 'Want to come up and see me do it?'

'Maybe later,' said Alistair.

'The producers never stop talking about their grand plans to rebuild and refurbish the hotel, but apparently getting planning permission takes time. Technically, we shouldn't be staying here at all, but, as usual, David and Micah know people . . .'

'So none of you have experienced any problems in the hotel?' said Alistair.

'I wouldn't say that,' said Diana. 'The whole building creaks and groans like it's dying, it's really not a good idea to drink the water from the taps, and most of the cast are having to bunk together because there are so few rooms suitable for sleeping in.'

Alistair raised an eyebrow. 'So who are you sharing with?'

'I do not do the sharing thing, darling. I am a star. Of course, now that you're here . . .'

'Stick to the point,' said Alistair. 'There could be any number of secret passageways, and maybe even underground tunnels, connecting the hotel to the theatre . . .'

Diana smiled dazzlingly. 'I love the way your mind works, Bish.'

'My thoughts move in mysterious ways,' said Alistair.

'You know, we could go and do a little exploring while everyone else is occupied,' said Diana. 'I don't think anyone will be leaving the bar for some time.'

'That can wait,' said Alistair. 'I'm more interested in hearing what people might have to say once liquor has loosened their lips.'

Diana grinned. 'These are actors, darling. They don't need the excuse of booze to speak whatever's on their minds.'

'But the sudden death of one of their own might encourage them to open up about things they would normally keep to themselves,' said Alistair.

'That's a bit cold, Bish,' Diana said reproachfully.

'Just being practical,' said Alistair.

Diana looked wistfully in the direction of the bar, where the roar of raised voices was reaching extraordinary levels.

'Listen to the children at their play . . . Do you really believe the killer is one of us?'

'What better place for our saboteur to hide in plain sight?' said Alistair.

'And you honestly think you can trick them into giving themselves away through simple questioning?' said Diana.

'A lot of my job involves getting people to open themselves up to me,' said Alistair. 'So, let us join the revels.'

'I'm always up for some revels,' said Diana.

* * *

The moment they entered the bar, the noise hit Alistair like a tidal wave, though he couldn't help noticing Diana took it in her stride. The bar was packed from wall to wall, with cast and crew crammed in shoulder to shoulder, and it was all they could do to force their way past the door. There were no tables or chairs, but everyone had a drink in their hand, and wherever Alistair looked, a sea of flushed faces shouted happy confidences at each other. Mark ranged back and forth behind the long bar, serving one and all with practised skill, though Alistair noticed everything came in bottles, presumably because the bar pumps weren't working. Mark was doing his best to be the cheerful host and take people's minds off everything that had happened, and perhaps only Alistair could see how much the effort was taking out of him.

The bar had no windows, and only some of the lights were working, so the general gloom had a character all its own. The cracked plaster walls were completely lacking in decoration, with only a faded mosaic on the floor to add a touch of colour. Cast and crew didn't appear to give a damn; they were there for the drink, not the atmosphere. Mark spotted Alistair and Diana standing trapped by the doors, and once again his great booming voice smashed through the general uproar.

'Make room, you heathens! The Actress and the Bishop are here, and no doubt in need of a great many drinks!'

People fell back, as much as they could, so Alistair and Diana could squeeze their way through the crowd and belly up to the bar. She ordered a large brandy, Alistair a diet coke. Mark gave him a disapproving look.

'Never trust a man who doesn't drink.'

'Never trust a bishop who does,' said Alistair. 'Has Paul turned up yet?'

'Not a sign of the man anywhere,' said Mark. 'Todd is out of his mind with worry. Twice now I've had to talk him out of trying to con or charm his way back into the theatre, so he could join in the search. He's worried Paul might have been locked up or left lying injured somewhere, so someone else could take his place on stage. And I'm not so sure he's wrong.'

Alistair nodded slowly. 'Is there anyone else who isn't here, who should be?'

Mark looked out over the crowded bar. 'Not as far as I can tell. And I'm pretty sure someone would have said something by now . . .'

'Alistair believes we'll be back in the theatre before nightfall,' said Diana. 'That the police won't be able to keep us out.'

'The sooner that can happen, the better,' said Mark. 'These people need work, not booze, to take their minds off what's happened. And I don't know how much longer they can keep up this level of drinking without serious consequences. Apart from the damage they're doing to themselves, they've already made such inroads into the bar stock that I'll have to put in another order.'

'Will the producers OK that?' said Diana. 'They've been cheap enough about everything else to do with this hotel.'

Mark shrugged. 'They haven't challenged any of my bills so far. They must know actors don't run on talent alone.' He looked out across the determinedly hard-drinking crowd. 'But I'm starting to suspect that there's not enough booze in the bar to put this cast back in the proper frame of mind. The saboteur's done his job; all enthusiasm for this play is gone. After what happened to Tom, the play is as dead as he is.'

'Is this hotel haunted?' said Alistair.

Mark stared at him. 'Where did that come from?'

'He's changing the subject,' said Diana. 'He thinks he's being subtle.'

Alistair shrugged. 'The theatre came with its own built-in ghost story, so it seemed likely an adjoining building of the same age might have its own resident spooks. Hotels do tend to accumulate ghosts, because more people die in a hotel than in a theatre.'

Diana snorted into her brandy. 'I've been in shows where we died on stage every night, darling.'

Mark nodded solemnly. 'Happens to the best of us. Afraid I can't tell you anything about the history of this place. The Paradise has been shut down for so long that all its old stories died with it. Certainly, David and Micah never said anything when they moved us in.'

'Well, they wouldn't, would they?' said Diana. 'But when I

got my letter telling me I'd be expected to live here, I made a point of doing some online research . . . And I turned up several interesting stories from the Paradise's past.'

'Of course you did,' said Alistair.

Diana shot him a cutting look and pressed on. 'A travelling salesman killed himself in his room, back in the 1920s. Cut his throat with his own shaving razor. There are reports of guests shaving themselves who said they saw the man's face peering over their shoulder, smiling and nodding as he tried to encourage them to do what he did. Then there was a woman abandoned by her lover, who was supposed to be still waiting in her room for him to come back to her. People would just walk through the door and see her sitting on the bed, smiling at them hopefully. And' – she paused, to stare meaningfully at Alistair – 'a number of people swore they saw the ghost of an actor who'd been cast as Banquo in a previous production of *Macbeth*, who was fired before he ever got a chance to be on stage. He was found hanged, inside his closet. But his ghost still wandered the hotel corridors at night, trying to get back to the theatre . . .'

'It's quite possible that our saboteur learned of this story in the same way you did,' said Alistair. 'And decided to put it to good use.'

'Well, thanks a bunch, the pair of you,' said Mark. 'I just know I'm not going to get a moment's sleep tonight.'

'They're only stories,' said Diana.

'The problem with ghosts,' said Mark, 'is that they don't care whether you believe in them or not. What do you suppose Tom saw when he looked Banquo's ghost in the face?'

He didn't wait for an answer, just moved away to serve a bunch of actors hammering their empty glasses on the bar top.

'You're looking thoughtful, Bish,' said Diana.

'There's a lot to think about,' said Alistair. 'This whole case seems soaked in the supernatural, but it's never anything you can get a grip on. I can't help feeling that whether it's witchcraft or ghosts, it's all just grist to the mill for our saboteur. He's happy to use whatever material he can get his hands on, that he thinks will terrorize people.'

'So you don't believe any of the weird stuff that's been happening is real?' Diana said carefully.

'Of course not,' said Alistair. 'I know a cover story when I see one, and so should you.'

'One thing the theatre teaches you is that stories can have a power of their own,' said Diana.

Alistair smiled. 'What do you think my religion is based on?'

Diana grinned and toasted him. Alistair toasted her back, and they both drained their glasses and set them down on the bar, before turning away to look out over the packed room.

'No one seems in any hurry to leave,' said Alistair. 'I would have expected most of the cast to be exhausted after everything they've been through.'

'They probably think there's safety in numbers,' said Diana. 'Or perhaps they just like being able to keep an eye on each other.'

'It must be very difficult for a company as tightly knit as this one, when they suddenly discover they can't trust anyone around them,' said Alistair.

'Don't you believe it,' said Diana. 'Any troupe worth its salt runs on backstabbing and paranoia, as well as support and comradeship. That's what keeps us sharp and on our toes. We're all just overgrown children who never got over the need to play at being someone else. Not that you'll get anyone here to admit it, of course.'

'Let's go ask them,' said Alistair.

He set off through the crowd, smiling and nodding and throwing charm in all directions, while Diana tucked herself in at his side and did her best to be supportive. Alistair asked everyone calm and cheerful questions about the play, and received the general impression that everything had been going well enough until the bad stuff started happening. Now people couldn't think about the play without dwelling on everything that had gone wrong.

Alistair tried a few quietly probing questions about whether they had any bad feelings about anyone in particular . . . but it turned out most of them had never even met before rehearsals started. They were all strangers, with nothing in common but their talent. Most had at least heard of the more important players, like Todd and Diana and sometimes Mark. But whatever opinions they might have about the high and mighty leads, they were careful to keep to themselves. There was a lot of glancing around to check who might be listening.

Eventually, Alistair and Diana ran out of anyone useful to talk to, and so they set their sights on the director, who was propping up the far end of the bar and scowling into a large whiskey. He saw them head in his direction and looked around for some way to avoid them, but the sheer press of bodies held him where he was long enough for Alistair and Diana to reach him.

'What do you want?' he said bluntly.

'Why did you cast Tom as Lennox?' said Alistair, just as bluntly.

The question seemed to catch Richard by surprise, and he took a moment to consider his answer.

'I asked around, and he had a reputation for being reliable. And he did give the best audition by far.'

'So there was never any pressure on you to cast him?' said Alistair. 'From David or Micah?'

'I would never have put up with that,' Richard said flatly. 'Making the play work is my business, not theirs. Tom was just another photo and a résumé when he came to me.' He paused, staring into his drink. 'And now I have to wonder . . . if I hadn't cast him, would he still be alive?'

'You can't let yourself think like that,' said Diana.

'But I do,' said Richard.

Alistair and Diana left the director to his drink and whatever dark things he saw in it, and moved on. Alistair tried another round of questions, looking to get a feel for the people as well as the play. On the whole, the cast seemed guardedly optimistic, the crew less so. Some had found being questioned by the police a disturbing experience; others thought it intriguing. Many said it felt like being cast in a television police procedural. A surprising number had appeared in such shows, as a suspect, a witness or friend of the family. Never as the murderer, though. That was always reserved for the big-name guest artists.

'If you want to know who did it, just look for who cost the most money,' Diana said wisely.

No one had a good word to say about Inspector Forbes. *Too obvious casting* was the general consensus: the grumpy old-fashioned copper who inevitably comes good in the end.

'Hard-arsed detectives are so passé,' said Todd. 'These days you need a good quirk, or a gimmick, to help you stand out.' He smiled knowingly at Diana. 'Like you two. The Actress and the Bishop . . . solve murders. That's such good drama the bouncer is outside chucking them in. And playing the Holy Terrors helps hide the fact that you're actually pretty good at what you do. I made a point of studying your previous cases. You do seem to have a gift for finding the truth in a haystack of lies and misdirection.'

Diana raised an eyebrow. 'I hadn't realized you knew so much about us. I wouldn't have thought you read that kind of magazine.'

'I read up on you when I learned we'd be working together,' said Todd. He smiled briefly. 'Know your enemy . . .'

'What do you think has happened to Paul?' said Alistair.

'My friend is dead,' Todd said dully. 'He must be, or he'd be here. Someone murdered him, just so they could replace him on stage.' He shuddered briefly. 'I can still see the look on Tom's face when he stared at Banquo's ghost like it was the real thing. What could he have seen that was so terrible it scared him to death?'

'I think he saw his killer,' said Alistair. 'And recognized the person who'd put poison in his wine.'

Todd met Alistair's gaze steadily. 'I know you don't believe there's any actual witchcraft going on, but I'm starting to think whoever is behind all of this does. And that means they're ready to do whatever it takes to get the job done. So you have to be ready to do the same to stop them.'

'That is the plan,' said Alistair.

Todd nodded brusquely and turned away so he could give his full attention to his drink. People shot Todd sympathetic glances, while giving him as much space as they could. Several female extras looked perfectly ready to provide a comforting shoulder or bosom, given the opportunity, but Todd showed no interest in anything but his drink and his own private thoughts. Diana led Alistair away.

'As far as Todd is concerned, all of this is just a wake for his lost friend,' she said sadly.

'Come on,' said Alistair. 'We still have people to talk to.'

'I don't think they want to talk to us,' said Diana.

'Then it's time for you to unleash your noted charm,' said Alistair.

'You mean take a deep breath and point my bosom at people?'

'That would be a good start.'

Diana took the lead and moved cheerfully through the crowd, smiling brightly at one and all and not so much displaying her charm as clubbing people over the head with it. Alistair trailed along in her wake, carefully watching and paying attention. And almost to a man and a woman, the cast and crew turned out to be surprisingly open in their answers. Alistair had taken it for granted there would be secrets, but everyone Diana talked to seemed perfectly happy to discuss not only their own little failings but also the much bigger motes to be found in the eyes all around them. They cheerfully recounted so many tales of backstage romances and unwise assignations, and things glimpsed through hotel doors that kept opening and closing all through the night, that Alistair just knew he was going to have a hard time scrubbing some of the images out of his head. Diana shot him a smug smile.

'Told you, darling.'

It soon became clear to Alistair that the cast were only telling such stories to avoid talking about things they didn't want to discuss. Like whether or not the supernatural elements in the weird happenings were real. Alistair listened patiently to back histories, feuds and bitcheries, and any number of battles for attention on stage, while Diana quietly murmured in his ear that all of it was just standard behaviour for any theatre company.

Absolutely no one seemed to want to talk directly about witchcraft, ghosts . . . or murder. Instead, people put pressure on Alistair to provide comfort and reassurance. He couldn't help but be affected by the dread and disquiet he saw in so many eyes, and found himself falling back on the usual inspiring platitudes. That if everyone would just stick together, they'd be safe. That they were all stronger than they thought they were. And that faith was always the best answer against dark forces.

'Well, you would say that, wouldn't you?' said Diana, after she and the bishop had moved away and they had a moment to themselves.

'It's usually true,' said Alistair. He sighed, just a little grimly. 'But these aren't usual circumstances.'

He moved on through the hard-drinking crowd, soaking up bits and pieces of conversations and using them to put together a sense of the company as a whole. It didn't take Alistair long to realize they were acting like any group under threat, looking for comfort and security in company, even as they distrusted everyone around them. They hadn't yet reached the point of open insinuations and accusations, but given the sheer amount of drink being knocked back, it was only a matter of time.

Alistair spotted the props and costumes mistresses leaning against the far wall, passing a bottle of cherry brandy back and forth between them. They had their heads close together and seemed to be discussing something of great importance, so Alistair headed straight for them. Josie and Caitlin looked up as he and Diana approached, and immediately stopped talking. Diana flashed them her most disarming smile.

'Calm down, ladies, no need for shyness among friends.' She twitched an eyebrow at Josie. 'And you do have so many friends in this company . . .'

Josie smirked. 'Everyone needs a hobby.'

Caitlin snorted into her drink. 'Not so much a hobby, more like a life's work. Is there anyone in this bar you haven't climbed all over?'

'There are still a few holdouts,' Josie said airily. 'But I'm working on them.'

'Then you must hear a lot of pillow talk,' said Alistair.

Josie pulled her sunglasses down her nose so she could stare at him.

'I'm not much of a one for listening.'

'Anything you might have heard could be very helpful,' said Diana.

'It might even save lives,' said Alistair.

Josie sighed heavily. 'There are those who will insist on talking, even when all I want to do is doze and cuddle. Mark had a lot to say, but it was mostly about himself.'

Caitlin stared at her. 'You slept with Mark?'

'It did feel a bit like mountain climbing,' said Josie. 'And Jenny said . . .'

'You've had sweet little Jenny?' said Caitlin.

Josie smirked again. 'Not so sweet in private. All teeth and nails. I don't think she had a good word to say about anyone. Except as people she could use on her rise to inevitable stardom. No shortage of ambition in that one. I think she only slept with me to make sure her costume repairs would always go to the front of the queue.'

Caitlin shook her head. 'It's always the quiet ones . . .'

Diana smiled at Alistair. 'Feeling shocked yet, Bish?'

Alistair smiled back at her. 'You won't get far as a shrinking violet in All Souls Hollow.' He looked thoughtfully at Josie. 'Has anyone said anything that struck you as unusual or out of place?'

'Nothing you'd be interested in,' said Josie. 'I have no idea what's going on with this production, except that it freaks the hell out of me.'

'I keep telling you,' Caitlin said harshly, 'there's no such thing as witchcraft.'

'Then why did I find one of the small costume dolls in my dressing room, with a pin thrust through its heart?' said Diana.

Caitlin stared at her. 'I never heard anything about that . . .'

'Or me!' said Josie. 'And I thought people told me everything.' She smiled suddenly at Diana. 'Of course, I haven't got around to everyone.'

'This lady is spoken for,' said Alistair.

Caitlin snorted into her drink again. 'Like that's ever stopped her!'

'Anyone could have taken the doll from my workroom,' said Josie. 'There isn't enough security backstage to keep a mouse out. I didn't even know one of my dolls had gone missing.'

'It's all just mind games!' Caitlin said fiercely. She glared at Alistair and Diana. 'So when are you going to do something about it?'

'We're working on it,' said Alistair.

'Damn right,' said Diana.

They made their goodbyes to Josie and Caitlin, and moved off into the crowd with a certain sense of relief.

'I'm not sure whether that was a useful conversation or not,' said Diana.

'I've been feeling that way ever since I got here,' said Alistair.

Next, they bumped into Jenny, who didn't seem at all pleased to see them.

'There's no point in talking to me,' she said loudly. 'I don't know anything.'

'Tell us about your Ouija board sessions with Angela and Sarah,' said Alistair. 'What did all those spirits from the vasty deeps have to say to you, exactly?'

'None of that was real,' Jenny said quickly. 'It was all just a bit of fun, something to pass the time.'

'So none of you took it seriously?' said Diana.

Jenny hesitated. 'I think we all paid more attention once the glass started spelling out messages of bad things to come, about ghosts and horrors and dead men walking . . .'

'Did you ask the spirits who was behind all of that?' said Diana.

'Of course! And the board said Hecate . . . a witch.' Jenny shuddered suddenly. 'Look, it was just a game! Quick thrills and cheap laughs, to keep us from thinking about all the genuinely scary stuff that's been happening.'

'Do you believe there could be an actual witch, somewhere in the theatre?' said Alistair.

Jenny stared at the floor, like a small child who'd just been told she had to walk home through the dark alone. Alistair wasn't entirely sure he believed that, after everything he'd heard from Josie.

'You don't have to talk to us if you don't want to,' said Diana. 'But it might make you feel better . . .'

Jenny's head came up immediately. 'No, it won't! Why do you have to keep poking your noses into things that are none of your business! Of course there's a witch! Everyone knows it. After everything we've seen and heard . . .'

'You're keeping something from us,' said Alistair.

'Yes!' said Jenny. 'I'm sleeping with Sarah! We're an item! There – are you satisfied now?' She broke off and looked around quickly, in case anyone had overheard her raised voice, but even those nearest her were too taken up with their own conversations. Jenny scowled at Alistair. 'I didn't want anyone else to know, in case they thought Sarah helped me get this part. But she didn't! I never even met her until after I'd been cast. Richard went out of his way to tell me how impressed he'd been by my television work, and how important a fresh young face could be for this production. I don't care what anyone says, I won my part through sheer talent!'

Sarah emerged suddenly from the packed crowd to join them. She moved in beside Jenny and scowled protectively at Alistair and Diana.

'Have you been bullying this poor girl?'

'Not really,' said Jenny, but she stared at the floor as she said it. Sarah fixed Alistair with her coldest stare.

'What have you been asking her?'

'The same questions I've been putting to everyone else,' Alistair said calmly. 'What's really going on? And is there any actual witchcraft involved?'

'How can you doubt it?' said Sarah. 'I know the real thing when it comes sniffing around me looking for blood. I've studied the old Wiccan ways, the book of shadows and the left-hand path.'

'Why would you want to do that?' said Diana.

'What do you care?'

'It can be a dangerous path to follow,' Alistair said carefully.

'It's also a recognized way to female empowerment,' said Sarah. 'And a guaranteed protection against outside threats. But most of all, I got involved because people like you don't want me to.' She realized she'd been lured off track and glared at Alistair. 'I still want to know why you were trying to intimidate Jenny!' She turned away before he could answer and gave all her attention to Jenny. 'Are you all right, dear?'

Jenny glanced at her, all wide eyes and trembling mouth, before staring guiltily at the floor again. Alistair had to admire the performance. Sarah nodded slowly and showed Alistair an openly defiant stare.

'So, now you know. I suppose you don't approve.'
'I have no problem with your relationship,' said Alistair.
'Your Church does.'
'We're working on that.'
'I don't care if you tell the whole company about us,' said Sarah. 'Jenny and I have nothing to be ashamed of. In fact, I can't see any reason why we shouldn't just tell everybody, right now!'
Jenny grabbed Sarah's arm. 'Please, don't!'
A slow realization filled Sarah's face. 'You're ashamed of me. Is it because I'm older than you?'
'Of course not!' said Jenny.
'Then why can't you be proud of us, the way I am?'
'There's more to it than that,' said Jenny.
'No,' said Sarah. 'There isn't.'
Alistair and Diana exchanged a look and moved away.
'I didn't mean to upset them,' said Alistair.
'If you keep pushing people to reveal their secrets,' said Diana, 'things are bound to emerge that you didn't expect. Why did you push Jenny so hard?'
'Because there's a lot more to that young lady than the innocent face she shows to the world,' said Alistair. 'Practically everything she says and does screams hidden agenda.'
'She's a young actress on the way up,' Diana said tiredly. 'Grabbing for every advantage she can see. You don't get anywhere in this business by playing Miss Goody Two Shoes.'
Alistair looked at her and considered an obvious response, but had more sense than to say it. Diana looked back at the two witches. Peace had broken out, and they were holding hands and staring into each other's eyes.
'You know, it is always possible that Sarah is using the relationship to give her control over a much younger woman,' Diana said slowly.
'Or Jenny is using Sarah,' said Alistair. 'For her own purposes.'
'But what does any of that have to do with the murder, or the witchcraft?'
'God knows,' said Alistair.
'Maybe you should ask,' said Diana.
'I'll see if she's in, later,' said Alistair. 'If not, I can always leave a message.'

Diana smiled, despite herself. 'I need another drink.'

They made their way back through the crush of bodies to the bar, where Diana caught Mark's eye with the ease of long practice and ordered another brandy.

'It might not be a good idea,' Alistair said carefully, 'to drink too much in a dangerous situation.'

'Don't fuss, Bish,' Diana said briskly. 'I came out of the womb two drinks down, and I've been trying to catch up ever since.'

'I'm never sure how seriously to take you,' said Alistair.

'Just as long as you remember to take me,' Diana said archly.

'Down, girl,' said Alistair.

Diana pouted. 'Loosen up, Bish. You'll have a lot more fun.'

'There's more to life than fun,' said Alistair.

'Don't blaspheme against my lifestyle,' said Diana.

Alistair decided it would probably be best to look away for a moment and spotted Angela standing alone and lost in her own thoughts. He went over to talk to her, and after a moment, Diana followed on behind. Angela saw them heading her way and glowered at them both.

'I don't know anything, and I don't want to know anything. I just need to keep my head down long enough for us to get to the West End theatre. Where, hopefully, all this nonsense will come to an abrupt halt, because by then it will be too late to stop the production. I've watched you circulating in what you clearly thought was an inconspicuous way. Why are you so determined to talk to everyone?'

'To find out what's really going on,' said Alistair. 'And uncover any secrets that might be significant.'

'People always have secrets,' said Angela. 'But I have no intention of discussing any of mine, because they're none of your business.'

'How can we tell unless we know what they are?' said Diana.

'That's your problem,' said Angela. 'I'm not saying a thing. And if that makes your job more difficult, I don't care and you can't make me.'

'We could always tell Richard that you're putting his production at risk by being uncooperative,' said Diana.

'Go ahead,' said Angela. 'See how far that gets you. Richard needs my talent and experience to hold this cast together, and he knows it. And if you're thinking about dropping a word to Inspector Forbes, I'll just spit in his eye like I am yours. None of what's been happening is anything to do with me, and I am not going to be dragged into it.'

'Even if keeping your mouth shut makes you look guilty?' said Diana.

'Guess if I give a damn,' said Angela. 'I could tell any number of tales out of school about you . . .'

Diana grinned back at her. 'I don't hide my past sins – I glory in them. And then sell them to the tabloids when I need the money or the publicity.'

'But now you're dating a bishop,' said Angela.

'He's very understanding,' said Diana.

'It's part of my job,' said Alistair.

Angela stared thoughtfully at Diana. 'I could always mention Brighton . . .'

Diana smiled sweetly. 'I could always punch you on the nose and tell Alistair anyway. I trust him.'

She slipped an arm through Alistair's and pressed it possessively against her side.

Angela's shoulders slumped, as most of the strength seemed to suddenly run out of her.

'There is nothing in my past or my present that you need to know about.'

'Your word is good enough for me,' said Alistair.

Angela shot him a grateful look, and he nodded briefly before moving away. Diana had no choice but to go with him, because her arm was still linked with his, but she looked at him incredulously.

'Her word is enough? Really?'

'Well, no,' said Alistair. 'But confrontation wasn't getting us anywhere, so I thought I'd try being nice. I'm a great believer in nice.'

'It's a mystery to me what we see in each other,' said Diana. She pulled her arm free of his and peered round the crowded bar. 'It feels like we've talked to everyone . . . Have we missed anyone important?'

'No,' said Alistair. 'But there is someone I think we should talk to again.'

He nodded at Todd, leaning heavily on the bar as Mark poured him another glass of wine. Mark went to take the bottle away, but Todd grabbed it first. Mark gave him an *It's your funeral and I will not be attending* look, and moved off down the bar.

'Can't we leave the man alone, Bish?' said Diana. 'He's worried sick that his best friend might be dead.'

'And yet . . . don't you think he seems just a little too calm and collected, for someone who's been through so much?' said Alistair.

'He's an actor, darling!' said Diana. 'You can't believe anything you see in an actor's face.'

'Even when they're not on stage?'

'Especially when they're offstage. Trust me, more acting goes into a backstage romance than you'll ever see under the spotlights.'

'I don't think I'll ask,' said Alistair.

'Best not to,' said Diana.

Alistair looked at her thoughtfully. 'Why are you so keen to defend Todd? I thought you couldn't stand the man.'

'Because sometimes I look at him and see myself,' said Diana. 'Or at least the kind of person I might have become if things had gone differently. If I hadn't found you . . .'

'You found yourself,' said Alistair. 'I just stood around and watched admiringly.'

'Quite right too,' said Diana.

Alistair headed for Todd. Diana sighed and went after him. Todd saw them coming but made no attempt to move away. He just swivelled slowly round on his bar stool, so he could show them a cold, disinterested face.

'There's something you're not telling us, Todd,' Alistair said bluntly. 'We need to know what it is.'

'You already know most of it,' said Todd. 'I was supposed to take the lead in Richard's *Swiss Family Robinson* musical, but Paul talked me out of it.' He shook his head. 'Paul still feels guilty that he persuaded me out of being rich. I wish I could have made him understand that how a career turns out has as much to do with luck as talent. That's why actors are so superstitious. All our little rituals and good luck charms are only there to give us some feeling of control over all the malign forces that shape our professional lives.'

'He's not wrong, Bish,' said Diana. 'The way things get decided in this business is so arbitrary it'll drive you crazy if you think about it too much.'

Todd looked down to the other end of the bar where Richard was sitting alone, ignored by everyone.

'Sometimes I think he only cast me as Macbeth because he felt guilty too. I might or might not have played on that a bit, to help me get cast. And to make sure he brought Paul on board as well. Because I needed to prove to my old friend that there were no hard feelings. I got him his part . . . and now he's dead. What else do you need to know?'

He looked steadily at Alistair, and his eyes were like open wounds. Diana tugged at Alistair's elbow, and he let her lead him away.

'Let's talk to Richard again,' he said.

'Haven't we done enough damage for one evening?' said Diana.

But when they got to the end of the bar, Richard wasn't there. They asked around and finally found him standing alone in the deserted lobby, holding an empty glass and staring at nothing.

'Richard, darling, what are you doing out here?' said Diana.

'Feeling like a fraud,' said Richard, not even glancing at her. 'I understand you've been busy digging out people's secrets. Well, mine's obvious enough. I'm the only person in the world who isn't convinced I'm a creative genius. I lucked into success with that stupid musical, and these days I live in constant fear of being found out. I don't know what I'm doing with *Macbeth*. I just keep hoping that if I throw enough ideas at the wall, some of them might stick.

'Now my production has been shut down by the police, I can't decide whether I should feel grateful or not. If *Macbeth* is over, then I won't have a chance to fail and prove how talentless I really am. But on the other hand . . . all those people in the bar are depending on me for employment. It's one thing for me to go under, but it's not fair to drag everyone else down with me. I'm hiding out here because I can't bear to look them in the eye . . .'

Alistair started to say something encouraging, but Diana quickly talked over him, because that wasn't what Richard needed to hear.

'We all feel that way at some point in our careers,' she said briskly. 'So just do what everyone else does. Put on a brave face and act like you know what you're doing. And we'll all muddle through this thing together.'

She shot Alistair a hard look, and he quickly picked up his cue.

'I have no doubt David and Micah are already piling on the pressure with certain well-placed personages. Odds are you'll be back in the theatre before it gets dark.'

'So start thinking about what you're going to do,' said Diana. 'It doesn't matter what it is, as long as it keeps everyone busy and buys you time to think.'

'But what about Tom?' said Richard. 'And what if Paul's dead as well?'

'Leave that to us,' said Alistair.

'Without meaning any disrespect to Tom's memory,' Diana said carefully, 'how soon can you get us another Lennox?'

'I've put the word out,' said Richard. 'I should have someone by tomorrow morning.'

'Someone good?' said Diana.

'As good as you can get by tomorrow morning,' said Richard.

Alistair and Diana went back into the bar, and the first thing they saw was Angela and Sarah talking animatedly together.

'That looks interesting,' said Alistair. 'Shall we ease on over and do a little discreet eavesdropping?'

'We'd be fools not to,' said Diana.

The two actresses were so taken up with themselves that they didn't even notice Alistair and Diana slipping quietly into position behind them, and then loitering and listening with intent.

'This is not the kind of life I expected to have, at my age,' said Sarah.

'And it's definitely not been the kind of career I wanted,' said Angela.

She started to raise her glass and found it was empty. Sarah kindly poured her some more wine from her bottle.

'I just wanted to work regularly,' said Sarah. 'Have a good time, make some decent money . . .'

'I honestly believed I was headed for greatness,' said Angela. 'But it didn't work out that way. I've been successful, even beloved in that never-ending soap . . . but never respected.'

'You did well enough offstage,' said Sarah. 'Three husbands, wasn't it?'

'Three of my own,' said Angela. 'And a few others I borrowed when no one was looking.' She gave Sarah a knowing look. 'How are you and Jenny getting on? Do you have to help her with her homework in the evening?'

'She's brighter than you think,' said Sarah.

'She'd have to be,' said Angela.

They suddenly spotted Alistair and Diana, and stopped talking. Alistair and Diana smiled and nodded as though they just happened to be passing by and went back to the bar. Todd was talking to Mark, who was doing his own polite smiling and nodding, like any experienced bartender.

'It does feel good to have a lead in a proper play,' said Todd, just a bit blearily. 'To be doing work that matters . . .'

'Enjoy it while you can,' said Mark. 'It won't last.'

'You'd know,' said Todd.

'Yes,' said Mark, 'I do.'

Todd seemed to realize he'd crossed a line. 'You know . . . you've been doing a really good job as Duncan. You'll make a big impression.'

'Once they can find a throne that'll hold together long enough to support me,' said Mark.

'That wasn't your fault.' Todd frowned hard, thinking. 'The stunt with the throne . . . That was the start of taking things to a whole new level. What happened before was all small, petty stuff. Now people are dropping dead in front of me, and Paul is missing.'

'They'll find him,' said Mark.

'Or what's left of him,' said Todd.

Slowly and undramatically, he began to cry. Mark brought him a new bottle of wine. Diana took Alistair by the arm and urged him further down the bar. She knocked back the last of her drink and scowled at the empty glass.

'I need another drink,' she said firmly.

Alistair looked at her, started to say something and then beckoned to Mark.

'You're a big girl.'

'Glad you noticed,' said Diana.

Mark poured Diana another brandy without comment and then nodded to Richard as he returned from his self-imposed exile in the lobby and planted himself firmly on a stool in front of Mark.

'I just wanted to make sure you know that I'm a big fan of your early work,' said Richard.

'Everybody is,' Mark said easily. 'Shame it was all such a long time ago.'

'I made a point of reaching out to your old agent, to make sure I could get you as Duncan,' said Richard.

'I suppose I should feel lucky he still remembered me,' said Mark. 'He hasn't been my agent for years. I'm actually a little surprised he knew where to find me.'

He offered Richard a refill, but the director shook his head.

'Why did you give up on the work?'

'It gave up on me,' said Mark. 'The drink didn't help, but really ... Acting styles changed and I didn't. Fortunately, Shakespeare never goes out of style.'

'It's good to be working with you,' said Richard.

'Let's just hope I'm up to it,' said Mark. 'It's been a long time since I trod the boards.'

'No one would know you'd ever been away,' said Richard.

'Now, we both know that's bullshit,' said Mark. 'But thanks anyway. Tell you what: I'll believe in you, if you'll believe in me.'

'Deal,' said Richard. And they shook hands solemnly.

And then everyone looked round sharply as a furious voice cut through the general noise. Conversations broke off as Todd backed Chris up against the bar and shouted right into his face.

'Stop upstaging me! No one is coming to this play to see you play Seyton!'

Chris glared right back at Todd but held on to his temper. 'I'm just following the director's instructions.'

'I'm the lead!' said Todd. 'And you'll do as you're told!'

Chris was trembling, more with repressed anger than anything else, but somehow kept his voice steady.

'I only take orders from Richard!'

Todd drew back a fist, and suddenly Alistair was there to grab Todd by the wrist and stop the blow before it could happen. He hauled Todd away from Chris and placed himself between the two of them. Todd struggled to pull his arm free, but couldn't break Alistair's grip.

'Let go of me!' said Todd.

'As soon as you calm down,' said Alistair.

Todd raised his other fist. Alistair piled on the pressure, and the fierce pain in Todd's wrist drove him down on one knee.

'All right!' he said loudly. 'I'm sorry, OK? Now ease off before you break something!'

Alistair let go of Todd's wrist and took a cautious step back. Todd rose slowly to his feet and nodded curtly to Chris.

'Sorry. It wasn't about you. I'm just worried about Paul.'

'I understand,' said Chris. He backed carefully away and disappeared into the crowd, which swallowed him up protectively. Mark came out from behind the bar, put an arm around Todd's shoulders and led him away. Animated conversations broke out all over the bar, because actors love a good drama. Alistair went back to Diana, and she toasted him with what was left of her brandy.

'That was truly impressive, Bish.'

'You learn useful moves like that, working in a parish like All Souls Hollow,' said Alistair.

'Todd will be fine by tomorrow,' said Diana. 'And probably shouting at someone else. There's a lot of pressure that comes from being the lead, and it has to get out somehow. We all know better than to take these little spats seriously.'

'Including Chris?' said Alistair.

'He'll act like it's nothing,' said Diana. 'Because Todd is the lead.'

'Todd was right about Paul,' said Alistair. 'If he was going to show up again, he would have by now. It's looking more and more likely that we have another dead body on our hands.'

'Do you think there's any chance the inspector and his people will find it?' said Diana.

'No,' said Alistair. 'Whoever our killer is, he's really good at hiding things. We'll just have to wait for David and Micah to get us back inside the theatre, so we can turn the place upside down.'

Diana looked at him sharply. 'Do you have an idea where Paul's body might be?'

'I might have a suspicion,' said Alistair.

Diana sniffed. 'That puts you one up on the inspector.'

And then they both looked round, just a little tiredly, as yet more angry voices filled the bar.

'What now?' said Diana.

A bunch of actors had surrounded Richard and were taking it in turns to shout questions at him, demanding answers he didn't have, while Richard did his best to hang on to his calm and his authority.

'What happens if the police won't allow the theatre to reopen?'

'Can the producers get the play going again somewhere else?'

'Can you hold them to their promises?'

'What if we don't have jobs this time tomorrow? Without them, we won't even have somewhere to stay!'

'That's *enough*!' said Richard, with sufficient volume to shut them all down. He glared about him. 'Given how much of their own money the producers have invested in this production, they can't afford to back out. And they have more enthusiasm for this play than all of you put together, so show a little faith and back off!'

Perhaps only Alistair and Diana understood what a great performance of certainty Richard was putting on. The complaining actors weren't entirely convinced, but they were hearing what they wanted to hear, so one by one they turned on their heels and walked away. Richard turned his back on the watching crowd and leaned both elbows on the bar. Mark was quickly there to pour a glass of whiskey and push it across the bar top to Richard.

'Lions nil, Christian one,' said Mark.

'They'll be back,' said Richard. 'When they get hungry enough.'

And then a sudden hush fell across the bar as the door swung open and Detective Sergeant Hill appeared. He looked calmly round the room, entirely unmoved by the impact of so many distrustful eyes.

'Well, well,' he murmured. 'Such a convivial gathering. How convenient to discover all of you gathered together in one place. I'm just here to inform you that Inspector Forbes has finished his preliminary investigation and released the crime scene. You are now free to return to the theatre.'

Richard rose to the occasion and nodded easily to the sergeant, doing his best to give the impression he'd never expected any other outcome. He cleared his throat carefully.

'Would I be right in thinking that our revered producers were finally able to contact their friends in high places?'

'I'm sure I wouldn't know anything about that, sir,' said Hill.

Alistair raised his voice, and the crowd around him fell back a little to give him a clear shot at the sergeant.

'Has the inspector determined whether there was an actual crime or not?'

'He doesn't share information like that with me, sir,' said Hill. 'But Mr McIntire's body has been removed and sent for autopsy. I'm sure we'll all have a much better understanding of the situation once the results come in.'

'But is it safe at the theatre?' said Diana. 'Would we be in any danger if we went back?'

'We searched the entire building very thoroughly, ma'am,' said Hill. 'We didn't find anyone or anything of a threatening nature. In fact, it all seemed very quiet and peaceful.'

'But did you find Paul?' said Todd.

'Not a trace, sir,' said Hill. 'It is the inspector's belief that your friend must have left the building. We do have people out looking for him.'

'More likely he's been spirited away,' Sarah said loudly.

A low murmur moved through the packed bar as everyone

considered that idea and decided they really didn't like it. Hill cleared his throat in a distinct sort of way, to draw everyone's attention.

'I'm sure you'll all be perfectly fine, but you have our number if anything should happen. We just love being called out to mysterious murders that make no sense at all.'

He showed everyone a polite smile that meant absolutely nothing and left the bar. The actors looked at each other, but no one moved.

'You heard the man!' Richard said loudly. 'The theatre is open again! Rehearsals will recommence immediately!'

'After everyone's had such a shock?' said Diana.

'Work is the best cure,' said Richard.

'After everyone's had so many drinks?' said Alistair.

'They look pretty sober now,' said Richard.

'But we still don't know what's happened to Paul!' said Todd.

'Face facts!' said Richard. 'Your friend just had enough and quit. If he shows his face by first thing tomorrow morning, the part's still his. If not, I'll recast. And don't say you won't work without him! I know how badly you need this role.'

Todd looked as though he wanted to say something cutting but couldn't find the words. Richard looked around the bar, taking in the open rebellion on the air.

'You can all have one hour to put yourselves back together,' he said. 'But that's all I can spare. After that, I expect to see every single one of you back in the theatre and ready to work. We're a long way from where we need to be. And if anyone feels like complaining, remember it wasn't that long ago you were shouting at me about whether or not you still had a job.'

He strode out of the bar. People fell back to let him pass, and then lined up to place their glasses on the bar top before filing out into the lobby, murmuring quietly among themselves. Soon only Diana and Alistair were left.

'I should feel happy that the play is back on track again,' said Diana. 'That we're all headed for the West End and imminent stardom and our own yachts . . . But going back into that theatre feels like walking into a minefield.'

'I would never let anything happen to you,' said Alistair.

Diana looked at him. 'Seems like everyone else is going to their rooms to freshen up. Would you like to take a look at mine?'

'Why not?' said Alistair. 'I can keep you company, while you get ready.'

They climbed the stairs together, companionably close. Diana led Alistair down a narrow corridor on the first floor. The walls were bare plaster, the colour of a recent bruise, while the carpet was so faded it was practically colourless. All of it illuminated by bare bulbs so old their light was a poisonous yellow. Diana stopped before a door halfway along and opened it with a heavy metal key. She ushered Alistair in with a grand gesture and then had to fumble around inside the door until she found the light switch. Alistair kept his face carefully empty as he took in the very basic bed, with its crumpled bedclothes that clearly hadn't been touched since Diana crawled out of them that morning. There was just the one chair, which Alistair knew would never support his weight, and a narrow window hidden behind grubby curtains. Everything smelled of damp and dust, and too many years left abandoned to Time's mercy.

Alistair turned to Diana, and suddenly she was standing right in front of him. She smiled happily and threw her arms around his neck. She tried to pull Alistair closer, but he stood very still. He could feel the whole length of her body pressed against his and smell the brandy on her breath.

'I don't think you're in any condition to be making important decisions,' he said steadily.

'I know what I want,' she said.

'But this isn't what I do,' said Alistair.

'It's what I do,' said Diana. 'Come on, we've got a whole hour. And later on you could spend the night.'

'No,' said Alistair. 'I couldn't.'

'Why not?' said Diana. 'Don't you want me?'

'You know how much I care for you.'

'Then what's stopping you?'

'My beliefs,' said Alistair. 'They make me who and what I am. My Church still believes in no sex outside of marriage. I can't just put some beliefs to one side when it suits me, no matter how much I might want to.'

Diana looked into his eyes and saw that he meant it. She pushed him away from her, and Alistair let her do it. He stood very still as she glared at him, breathing harshly.

'I spent so long looking forward to this moment,' she said. 'Rehearsing all the things I was going to say to you . . .'

'I'm amazed I let myself get this close,' said Alistair. 'Because saying no to you hurt me more than anything I've ever known.'

'So why did you say it!' said Diana, her voice heavy with pain and loss.

He managed a small smile. 'I could not love thee half so much, loved I not honour more . . .'

'Then what good are you?' Diana said. 'Get out of here. I have to get ready for work.'

Alistair nodded, not trusting himself to say any more. He walked out of the room, shutting the door carefully behind him because he wanted so badly to slam it. He stood alone in the bitter yellow light, head bowed and hands clenched into fists. He finally looked up again . . . to see Banquo's ghost staring back at him from the end of the corridor.

The silent figure stood perfectly still, like a bad dream that had fought its way into the waking world. Alistair's heart lurched as he remembered the story of the ghost condemned to wander endlessly through the deserted hotel. And then he took in the familiar torn and bloodstained military jacket, and the blank and palely glowing mask that covered the entire face.

'Paul?' said Alistair. 'Is that you?'

The ghost cocked its head a little to one side and raised a gloved hand, as though reaching out to him. Blood dripped steadily from the fingertips. Alistair started forward, and the ghost turned abruptly and darted round the bend at the end of the corridor. Alistair chased after the silent figure, but by the time he'd rounded the corner, the corridor in front of him was completely empty. Alistair stumbled to a halt.

For a moment, he thought the ghost must have vanished, and then he understood all it had to do was let itself into any of the rooms. Alistair scowled as he realized he couldn't just make his way down the corridor, banging on every door and demanding to be let in, because the mysterious figure just had to remove its jacket and mask, and it could be anyone at all.

Alistair's first impulse was to go back to Diana's room and tell her what he'd seen, but then he remembered he couldn't do that. He straightened his back, squared his shoulders and walked back down the corridor, heading for the stairs. He didn't even glance at Diana's door as he passed it.

SEVEN
Hidden in Plain Sight

Back on stage, the whole cast went at each other with really big swords. Steel slammed against steel as savage warriors surged back and forth, intent on blood and slaughter. Alistair joined Richard in the auditorium and watched the carefully orchestrated mayhem with great interest.

'We were supposed to have the services of a fight expert,' said Richard. 'But that turned out to be just another of the many promises David and Micah never got around to following through on. Fortunately, I have a little experience in that area, so I worked out some basic choreography for the final battle.'

Alistair couldn't suppress a wince as vicious swords whistled past ducking heads with only inches to spare.

'Do you really think this is a good idea,' he said carefully, 'given everything the cast has been through just recently?'

'Best way to get it out of their system,' Richard said briskly. 'Make them run the drills again and again, to get their heads back in the game. Carrying out action scenes in a completely safe and secure way should give everyone their confidence back. Make them feel like they're in control again.'

'What happens if a mistake is made and someone else gets hurt?' said Alistair.

'That's why we're running this over and over,' said Richard. 'To make sure that doesn't happen.'

Alistair nodded. 'Let's just hope and pray for the best.'

Richard snorted. 'Sometimes I swear my main job is to hold people's hands and tell them everything's going to be all right. It would be nice if there was someone to do that for me . . .'

'Everything's going to be all right,' Alistair said solemnly.

The two opposing forces hammered their heavy blades together, letting out savage cries and oaths. Alistair watched it all and never once saw it in a medieval setting. Perhaps because he was too busy looking out for real dangers to take his eye off the ball, even for a moment's fantasy.

'I am seeing some serious skill and self-control,' he said finally.

'It'll look more convincing when the moves aren't quite so obvious,' said Richard. 'They're all putting too much effort into it at the moment.' He looked briefly at Alistair. 'Where's Diana?'

'I'm sure she'll be along soon,' said Alistair.

'Have you two quarrelled?' said Richard.

Alistair stared straight ahead, giving all his attention to the battle on stage.

'What makes you say that?'

'Because you two have been joined at the hip ever since you got here.'

'Everything's going to be all right,' said Alistair.

'Will you please stop wincing!' said Richard. 'No one's in any real danger. Those are all prop swords, with no edges and no points.'

Alistair looked at him. 'Isn't that what Caitlin said about the dirk that cut Paul?'

'I checked every sword myself,' said Richard. 'They're all perfectly safe. Even the claymore that Todd insisted on having, because it was more *authentic*.' He sniffed loudly. 'He only wanted the ugly thing so his sword would be bigger than everyone else's.'

Alistair heard footsteps coming down the aisle behind him, but didn't turn around. Diana moved in beside him, but they didn't so much as glance at each other, pretending instead to take an interest in what was happening on stage. Richard looked from one to the other and headed immediately for the stage, calling loudly for everyone to stand down. The actors immediately backed away from each other and lowered their weapons, with every indication of relief.

'That went surprisingly well,' said Richard as he clambered up on to the stage. 'But you still need to tighten up some of those moves, and make sure you're in the right positions to show off the big set pieces. And yes, Todd, I know we still have to work on the big duel between you and Macduff. I haven't forgotten.'

He moved quickly among the cast, spelling out what was needed. Alistair and Diana concentrated on taking in his every word, rather than look at each other.

'Are we talking?' Diana said finally.

'I never stopped,' said Alistair.

'We're never going to change, are we?' said Diana.

'It's our differences that keep things interesting,' said Alistair.

'But if we can't find common ground . . .'

'We care for each other,' said Alistair. 'That's all the common ground we need.' He paused for a moment and then smiled briefly. 'You were supposed to agree with me there . . .'

'I missed my cue,' said Diana. 'How embarrassing.'

'We'll work something out,' said Alistair.

'How can we,' said Diana, 'when you'd rather cling to your antiquated rules than be happy?'

'I gave my life to a cause and a vocation without regret, because I believed in it,' said Alistair. 'If I did give up being who and what I am, would you still want me? It would be like my demanding you give up being an actress. And I would never do that.'

'Because you're better than me,' said Diana.

'Of course,' said Alistair. 'I'm a bishop.'

She smiled despite herself. 'So, Bish, what are we going to do?'

'It's just another problem,' said Alistair. 'And we're good at finding solutions to problems.' He looked at her for the first time. 'I'm assuming that's what you want?'

'Of course it is,' said Diana. 'But not every problem can be solved. Not when both sides are so far apart.'

'I have never believed that,' said Alistair.

Diana sighed. 'You're always so ready to see the best in people.'

'Somebody has to,' said Alistair.

There was a roar of raised voices, followed by a great clamour of clashing weapons, as open warfare broke out on stage again. Alistair and Diana watched in silence until one of the Thanes let out a startled cry as Todd's claymore passed so close to his face it all but gave him a shave. The Thane backed quickly away, but before he could get a word out, Todd was already shouting at him.

'You have to follow the choreography exactly! I have rehearsed exactly where to put my claymore; it's up to you to have your blade in the right place to parry it!'

'But your sword is twice as heavy as mine!' said the Thane. 'It's all I can do to slow it down!'

'Excuses, excuses,' said Todd.

'Oh . . . to hell with the battle and to hell with you!' said the Thane. 'I'm not doing this any more!'

He threw his sword on the stage and stomped off into the wings. Several actors called for him to come back, but he didn't even glance over his shoulder. Todd shook his head.

'If he was any more of a drama queen, he'd have to wear a tiara . . .'

'Your sword did get a bit close,' Richard said carefully.

'Because he wasn't in the right position!' said Todd. 'You have to commit fully to every blow or it's never going to look real! You told us that!'

Richard sighed. 'Everyone, take a break. We'll come back to this after you've had more time to practise your moves. For now, we'll move on to the big scene following Macbeth's death.'

Todd glared at him. 'But I'm not in that! I came here to work!'

'And you will,' Richard said flatly. 'But you're not the only one here. Go and sit down, and I'll call you when I need you.'

Todd looked as though he wanted to say something, but didn't. He stalked off stage, taking his claymore with him. Caitlin hurried after Todd, in hot pursuit of her prop.

'Macduff!' said Richard. 'Where are you?'

'Right here.' A tall, whip-thin fellow stepped out of the crowd. He had a narrow, gaunt face, accentuated by a jet-black and probably not-at-all-dyed goatee beard trimmed to within an inch of its life.

'You're going to need Macbeth's head,' said Richard.

'I'll get it, I'll get it!' said Caitlin, racing back across the stage. Without Todd's claymore, Alistair noted. The props mistress disappeared into the wings and came back out almost immediately, carrying a severed human head. It had been fashioned to look vaguely like Todd, but that was the best you could say for it. Caitlin handed the head to Macduff, who grabbed it by the hair and held it out at arm's length. Selected Thanes and warriors formed a respectful group in front of him, while everyone else filed off stage. Caitlin raced after them, quickly discovered they had no intention of giving up their weapons and retreated, sulking, to the wings.

'Here is the head of that ignoble traitor, Macbeth!' Macduff said loudly.

'Doesn't look a bit like me!' Todd said loudly from his seat in the front row.

'Keep the noise down, please,' said Richard. 'Let someone else speak, for a change. Peter, when you're ready . . .'

Diana nudged Alistair in the ribs. 'That's Peter Franke, playing Macduff. An old Shakespearean workhorse. Been everywhere, played everyone – and never lets you forget about it.'

'He has dyed his hair and his beard, hasn't he?' said Alistair.

'Repeatedly,' said Diana.

The scene progressed, with Macduff working steadily through his big victory speech. The crowd responded valiantly, and all seemed to be going well. Until Diana noticed Macduff was turning the head he was holding so it seemed to be looking at whoever in the crowd was talking. Diana snorted loudly.

'Gottle of gear!' she said loudly. 'I don't want to go gack in the gox!'

Everyone else immediately saw what she was seeing, and spluttered laughter broke out everywhere. Macduff had the grace to look a little ashamed.

'Knock that off!' said Richard, glaring about him. 'And Peter, one more unauthorized bit of business like that and I will recast you as a deaf mute, locked inside a steel box!'

He turned his glare on the people watching from the auditorium seats, but they were falling about with laughter. It had been a long, hard day, and this was the first chance they'd had to let loose. Richard shook his head despairingly.

'What I wouldn't give for a whip and an electric cattle prod . . . Caitlin! Get out here! That head is going to be a distraction. Put it in a canvas bag, with a little blood splashed across the bottom, and we'll go with that.'

Caitlin raced across the stage to grab the head away from

Macduff. Richard scowled at Diana, who had finally quietened down.

'If you can't control yourself, go and be somewhere else! I won't be needing you as Lady M for some time anyway. Bishop, can't you control her?'

'I wouldn't know where to start,' said Alistair. 'But I will take her away.'

'Good,' said Richard. 'Some of us have work to do.'

Diana sniffed loudly. 'I know when I'm not wanted. Come along, Bish.'

'Of course,' said Alistair.

As they moved along the front-row seats, on their way backstage, Sarah nodded knowingly at Diana.

'Seems there's more than one saboteur in this theatre . . .'

Diana smiled at her sweetly. 'Excuse me, but you still have one of those fake warts on your cheek . . . Oh, sorry, my mistake; it's real.'

She walked away with her head held high, and Alistair hurried after her.

They quickly found their way into the warren of backstage corridors. The moment the door swung shut behind them, it was suddenly very quiet. Most of the lights had been turned off, and the shadows were deep and dark. The corridors had the look of a maze that might have a Minotaur hiding in one of the dressing rooms. Diana looked at Alistair.

'We are going to have to establish a new rule for backstage,' she said sternly. 'All lights on, at all times, so no one can sneak up on anyone.'

'That would definitely help,' said Alistair.

'I like to feel I'm contributing something,' said Diana.

'I couldn't do this without you,' said Alistair.

Diana nodded slowly. 'It feels good . . . to be working together.'

'We'll always have that,' said Alistair.

'But is it enough?' said Diana.

'It's something we can build on.'

Diana shook her head. 'You are such an optimist.'

'Comes with the job,' said Alistair.

Diana looked determinedly around her. 'There must be somewhere we haven't checked before.'

'I thought we might have a quick but thorough rummage through the costumes department,' said Alistair. 'I have the beginnings of an idea . . .'

'And I'm just dying to hear it,' said Diana.

Alistair looked at her. 'No need to be quite so enthusiastic. I'm not mad at you.'

'But I might have been just a bit mad at you,' said Diana.

'You'll get over it,' said Alistair. 'Now, costumes . . .'

Diana led him to a door with a small sign that said *Costumes Department* in very neat handwriting. Diana knocked loudly.

'Open up, Josie; you have visitors! I promise one of them isn't Richard.'

There was no answer. Alistair tried the door. It wasn't locked, so he led the way in. The department turned out to be a large room half buried under all manner of costumes, in various states of repair and reimagining. Brightly coloured concept drawings had been tacked up on all four walls, crowding each other to the point of overlapping, along with a large Chippendales calendar showing someone called Big Steve flaunting his abs. Most of the days under the photo contained neatly written names and dates.

'How very organized,' Alistair said solemnly. 'Must be for fittings.'

'Or something very like that,' said Diana. 'She can't be as busy as she says; I would have noticed.'

They made their way carefully through mounds of discarded costumes and small tables covered with useful bits and pieces. At the back of the room, a crowd of costumed human mannequins stood in silent rows, like so many extras waiting for their big moment.

Diana shuddered. 'Now that . . . is spooky.'

'Especially when you consider some of them almost certainly witnessed Tom's death on stage,' said Alistair.

'Don't, Bish,' said Diana.

And then she stopped abruptly as she came across a collection of dolls laid out on one of the side tables. Barely a foot in height, they'd each been dressed in a costume from the play.

'I was going to ask if I could take mine home with me,' said Diana. 'But I went right off the idea after someone rammed a silver pin through its chest.'

'Understandable,' said Alistair, moving in beside her. 'I have to wonder why Josie needs so many disturbing little effigies. Particularly when you consider the role dolls have traditionally played in the dark arts.'

'Josie tries out her costume designs on the dolls and then shows them to Richard to approve,' Diana said patiently. 'If he does, then she makes the full-size costume. It saves wasting time and material.'

'But that isn't all that's going on here,' said Alistair. 'Take another look.'

He gestured at the doll wearing Macduff's costume. Silver pins had been thrust deep into its chest, forming a five-pointed star.

'Witchcraft?' said Diana.

'Or something meant to look like it,' said Alistair.

Diana looked at him sharply 'Do you think Josie . . .'

'No. She'd know better than to leave something like this out in the open. The door wasn't locked, so anyone could have got in here and left this poisonous little gift.'

Diana reached out to the doll.

'Don't,' Alistair said quietly. 'It's evidence.'

Diana carefully withdrew her hand. 'I just wanted to pull the pins out.'

'Best not to,' said Alistair. He frowned thoughtfully. 'The shape the pins form implies not witchcraft but black magic.'

'Isn't something like this a bit of a step down after openly poisoning someone on stage?' said Diana.

'It's all part of maintaining an atmosphere of dread and menace,' said Alistair. 'This little tableau was carefully thought out to intimidate whoever found it.'

'Could this be an actual threat?' said Diana.

'It's all just smoke and mirrors,' Alistair said firmly. 'None of this is real.'

'Those pins look pretty real,' said Diana. 'We have to find the witch, Bish. Before the whole cast lose their minds.'

'The only people who have admitted to an interest in such

beliefs are the actresses playing the three witches,' said Alistair. 'Sarah in particular told us she'd done extensive research in that area, and actually boasted about studying the left-hand path that leads inevitably to the dark arts.'

'Not something you'd expect a guilty person to admit to, under the circumstances,' said Diana.

'And I'm having trouble seeing any of them as a professional saboteur,' said Alistair. 'Could the real saboteur be trying to point us in their direction, to draw attention away from what's actually going on?'

'That makes sense,' said Diana.

'Unless that's what the killer wants us to think,' said Alistair.

Diana looked at him. 'Stop it . . .'

'We need to search this whole room from top to bottom,' said Alistair.

'I don't see anyone around to stop us,' said Diana.

They worked their way steadily through the jungle of hanging costumes and piles of materials, and carefully studied every item left out on the tables, until Diana came to an abrupt halt before the mannequins standing in rows at the back of the room. She made a low, shocked sound, and Alistair was quickly there beside her.

'What is it? Did one of them move?'

Diana shook her head. 'Look . . .'

Alistair's gaze swept quickly across the unmoving figures and then stopped when he saw Paul standing upright in the back row. The missing actor's face was slack, his eyes empty, and he didn't move at all. Diana's face hardened into harsh and unforgiving lines.

'He's dead, isn't he?'

'And has been for some time,' said Alistair. 'I'm not seeing any obvious signs of an injury. Nothing to suggest what killed him.'

'How can he just stand there like that?' said Diana, her voice rising. 'It's not natural.'

'Don't let this get to you,' said Alistair. 'It's just another trick, designed to upset whoever found him.'

'It's working,' said Diana.

Alistair stepped forward.

'Careful, Bish!' said Diana.

'Paul is no danger to us,' said Alistair.

He looked the body over carefully. 'He's not wearing his military jacket – the one we saw at the banquet.' He moved in closer and peered behind the upright figure. 'Ah . . . come and take a look at this.'

'You look,' Diana said firmly. 'I am not going anywhere near him. Just tell me what you've found.'

'He's being supported by a simple brace,' said Alistair. 'Holding him in position. No wonder the police never spotted him. He'd have been just another unmoving figure.'

'This is going to break Todd's heart,' said Diana. 'He and Paul have been friends forever. I can't believe anyone could be cold-blooded enough to just leave Paul standing here, like a scarecrow . . .' She stopped and looked at Alistair. 'Does Todd need to know about this? Couldn't we take the body down? Give Paul that much dignity?'

'We can't touch anything,' said Alistair. 'It's all evidence. We'll tell Todd . . . as much as he needs to know. Hold it. Wait a minute . . . There's a tear on Paul's left sleeve, from the scene with the three assassins. Remember all that fuss he made about being cut?'

He pushed the sleeve up to reveal a wound on the forearm. Dark against the pale skin, it stood out clearly. Diana wrinkled her nose and then leaned forward, intrigued in spite of herself.

'Could that be infected?'

'More likely a sign of poison,' said Alistair, letting the sleeve fall back. 'From the assassin's knife. We already know the saboteur got to it in advance, to make sure the blade couldn't retract into the hilt. It wouldn't have been difficult to also smear the blade with something deadly.'

'And slow-acting,' said Diana.

'Exactly,' said Alistair. 'The killer didn't want Paul to die immediately. He wanted him to walk away and then disappear. To add to the mystery and horror of what's happening.'

'But who could have hidden Paul here?' said Diana. 'Everyone in the play went to the hotel.'

'Did they?' said Alistair. 'With so many people packed into that bar, anyone could have sneaked out and back in again without being noticed. Particularly if there really are hidden ways linking the hotel to the theatre.'

He stopped and frowned.

'What?' Diana said immediately.

'After I left your room, I saw someone in the corridor,' he said slowly. 'Dressed like Banquo's ghost, right down to the face mask. I went after him, but the figure disappeared before I could catch whoever it was.'

'OK, that's it,' said Diana. 'I am not spending another night in that place.' And then it was her turn to stop and frown. 'If the poison affected Paul early enough, the killer could have taken his costume and mask and gone on stage in his place, as Banquo's ghost. Putting him in just the right position to drop poison in Tom's goblet!'

'I was thinking that,' said Alistair. 'You realize we're going to have to call the police back in?'

'Must we?' said Diana.

'A murder victim deserves a proper investigation,' said Alistair.

'Inspector Forbes is going to just love being called back,' said Diana. 'And poor Richard is going to lose his mind . . .'

The whole cast and crew had gathered together on the stage by the time the police showed up, determined to present a united front in the face of a common enemy. There had been a lot of discussion about Paul's death, and how he was found, but the main feeling was that the production couldn't survive another interruption. Todd's response to that had been simple and to the point.

'You selfish bastards. My friend is dead.'

No one had much to say after that.

Inspector Forbes came storming into the auditorium, followed by Sergeant Hill and all the usual uniforms. Richard tried to address the inspector from the stage, but Forbes talked right over him as he stomped down the aisle.

'I am seriously not happy about having to come back here, so soon after the last time. And even more so because it involves another corpse, which we somehow failed to spot.' He paused to glare at Hill. 'Your people are seriously underperforming. How could they have failed to find a second body?'

Hill faced him steadily. 'I really couldn't say, sir. It does seem rather odd, doesn't it? But these are very unusual circumstances. Very dramatic, in fact, as only befits a murder in a theatre. And according to the bishop, the body was extraordinarily well hidden, sir.'

Forbes turned his glare on Alistair, standing with Diana at the foot of the aisle.

'You found the body.'

'Diana spotted him first,' said Alistair. 'But I was there with her.'

Forbes shook his head slowly. 'I should have known you'd be involved. You're like my own personal albatross. I want to talk to you, Bishop.'

'Of course,' said Alistair. 'Diana and I are always ready to help . . .'

'Just you,' said Forbes. He turned to Hill. 'Take his little actress friend off to one side. I don't want them reinforcing each other's story.'

Diana looked ready to say something, but Alistair hushed her with a look. She nodded grudgingly and allowed the sergeant to lead her away. Alistair nodded easily to Forbes.

'How can I be of assistance, Inspector?'

'Walk with me.'

Forbes led Alistair to the back of the auditorium, right by the lobby door, and then glowered at him steadily for a long moment. Alistair smiled back, politely refusing to be intimidated. The inspector's mouth tightened into a thin line.

'Tell me what happened. And stick to the facts. No theories.'

Alistair ran through the story as succinctly as he could, while Forbes stared at him unblinkingly. Once Alistair had finished, the inspector just carried on staring at him, as though giving Alistair a chance to change his story and come up with something more plausible. Alistair kept up his polite smile. The inspector took a deep breath.

'So . . . your story is, you just happened to be visiting the costumes department, for no particular reason, and just happened to find the body?'

'Yes, Inspector.'

'And I'm supposed to believe you, because you're a bishop?'

'No, because I'm telling the truth.'

'I warned you not to interfere in my investigation!'

'Perish the thought, Inspector.'

'Do you really think your dog collar gives you permission to defy the proper authorities?'

For the first time, Alistair's gaze became cold and stern. 'I freely acknowledge that you are in charge of the official investigation, Inspector, but I answer to a higher authority, and I will not be diverted from my duty to help others.'

Forbes strode past Alistair and down the aisle to glare at Richard, who stood at the front of the stage.

'Get your people out of here! I will see this whole building torn apart until I can get to the truth. And this time not even your friends in high places will be able to get you back in again.'

'You can't do this to us!' said Richard. 'You're putting our whole production at risk!'

'Watch me,' said Forbes.

He moved away, gesturing sharply for Sergeant Hill to come and attend him. Diana hurried back to Alistair.

'What did you say to him, Bish?'

'I'm afraid I came very close to losing my temper,' said Alistair.

Diana smiled. 'I would have loved to see that.'

'Did the sergeant give you a hard time?' said Alistair.

'Oh no,' Diana said airily. 'He was a perfect sweetie. I just promised him tickets to our first night and he was as good as gold.'

Alistair shook his head. 'I was only trying to do the right thing, but I fear I've made things worse. I really should go after the inspector and apologize.'

'Do you honestly think that would make any difference?' said Diana.

'Not really, no. We'll never be able to persuade him to see our side of things now.'

And that was when the door to the lobby slammed open, and David and Micah came striding down the main aisle, accompanied by a distinguished-looking gentleman in a suit of such elegant cut and style it practically shouted money.

'Hello, everybody!' said David. 'Allow us to present our close personal friend, and renowned supporter of the arts, Hamilton Crane.'

'Police Commissioner Crane,' said Micah.

And perhaps only Alistair was close enough to see Inspector Forbes mouth the words *Oh shit* . . .

Crane beamed happily about him and nodded to Forbes, who stared coldly back.

'I have always been a great admirer of the theatre,' Crane said brightly. 'I've seen *The Swiss Family Robinson* eight times! What a marvellous show! So when my good friends David and Micah told me the director's latest production was in trouble, I just had to hurry over and see what I could do to help. Let me assure everyone involved with this production that the theatre will only remain closed for as long as is absolutely necessary. The moment the science people have done their job, you can all get back to work again.'

'Commissioner, I really must protest,' Forbes said doggedly. 'It is vital that we perform a thorough search of the building. Given that we somehow failed to discover a second body, there's no telling how much else might have been overlooked.'

'Then get on with it, Inspector,' said Crane, still smiling. 'And then let the actors back in, there's a good chap.'

Their eyes met and locked, and the inspector looked away first. He nodded shortly, not trusting himself to speak.

Crane shook hands with David and Micah, and then left. Still smiling. David and Micah exchanged a smile of their own and followed him out. Sergeant Hill quietly ordered the uniformed police to begin their search, and moved off after them. Forbes watched them go and then turned his back on the watching cast and crew, and went out into the lobby. Alistair gestured for Diana to stay where she was, and went after Forbes.

He found the inspector standing alone, staring at nothing. His head was down, and his shoulders were slumped, as though he was carrying some impossible weight. He had to have heard Alistair move in beside him, but didn't even glance at him.

'Have you come to confess?'

'No,' said Alistair.

'Then, what use are you? I should arrest you on general principles. But your friends in high places would make sure that didn't stick.'

'They're not my friends,' said Alistair. 'I never asked for their help. I'm the one who called you back in.'

Forbes growled under his breath. 'I knew I'd find something to blame you for.'

'Why are you letting this get to you, Inspector?' said Alistair.

Forbes spun round to face him. 'Because this was my first big case. My chance to make a name for myself! I have given my life to this job. It's all I've ever wanted to do. But thanks to all this witchcraft nonsense, and now interference from above, I can't see any way forward. None of them care who the murderer is, not when there's strings to be pulled and money to be made. Everything will end up being swept under the carpet, in the name of show business.' He sighed deeply. 'You want this case, Bishop? It's all yours. I don't care. I wash my hands of the whole affair.'

He walked out of the front door before Alistair could say anything. He heard someone approaching behind him and turned quickly to find Sergeant Hill looking at him with quiet understanding.

'I do beg your pardon, sir. I just wanted to say, you mustn't take any of that personally. The inspector isn't mad at you, just at a world that is never going to be as straightforward as he thinks it should be.'

'He said he doesn't want to know about this case,' said Alistair. 'So I suppose that means you're in charge now.'

'Well, yes . . . Bit of a poisoned chalice, though.' Hill pursed his lips thoughtfully. 'The commissioner wants this sorted out quickly, and doesn't seem to care how, as long as his friends are kept happy. Which means I am ready to accept all the help I can get. I understand that you and your associate have experience with the weird stuff, sir. Do you believe there could be an actual witch behind all these . . . unusual circumstances?'

'I think that's what someone wants us to think,' said Alistair.

Hill nodded slowly. 'You'd better make sure cast and crew vacate the building as quickly as possible, sir. The inspector was entirely correct that the whole building will have to be searched again. I will see that done properly, if nothing else.'

'Best of luck,' said Alistair.

Hill saluted him briefly. 'Evening, all . . .'

He went back into the theatre, and Alistair stood where he was for some time, thinking hard. He finally looked up to see a balding middle-aged man regarding him calmly.

'Sorry to disturb you, Bishop. I'm Griffin. I help out around here. You go ahead and escort everyone over to the hotel; I'll keep an eye on things until you get back.'

'Won't the police want you to leave as well?' said Alistair.

'Wouldn't doubt it for a moment, sir, but us old-timers are very hard to shift.' He smiled easily at Alistair. 'I have been observing you and the young lady, sir. You're getting very close to the truth now.'

Alistair looked at him steadily. 'Do you know who's behind this?'

'Of course, sir. And so do you.'

Griffin turned and walked away, disappearing back into the auditorium.

Not long after, the entire cast and crew were politely but firmly ushered out of the theatre and on to the street, and the door locked behind them – again. Everyone looked to Richard for their cue, but he had nothing to say.

'Maybe you should phone David or Micah?' said Diana. 'Make sure they're still in our corner?'

Richard shook his head. 'What's the point? One death might have been accidental, but two bodies, one of them very carefully concealed, means we have a serial killer on our hands. And probably hiding among us.'

Everyone looked at each other uncertainly.

'There must be something we can do,' said Todd.

But he didn't seem too sure what. Ever since Paul's death had been confirmed, all the strength had gone out of him. Alistair lowered his head to murmur to Diana.

'Since no one else seems to want to, I'd better take charge. Back me up as much as you can.'

Diana nodded quickly. 'Go for it, Bish.'

Alistair raised his voice, and everyone turned to stare at him.

'Let's go back to the hotel, everyone. We could all use a break and a chance to get our second wind.'

'If all else fails,' Diana said loudly, 'I have a great many contacts in the media. People who will be only too happy to hear what the Holy Terrors have to say about this situation.'

Richard looked at her with something that might have passed for hope.

'Do either of you have any idea who's behind all this madness?'

'We're working on it,' said Alistair.

He did his best to make that sound positive, but the watching crowd appeared distinctly unconvinced. Alistair gestured firmly in the direction of the hotel.

'If nothing else, I think we could all do with a few more drinks.'

'I always knew you were one of us, Bish,' said Diana.

But once everyone was back in the lobby, no one seemed to want to do anything. They just stood around, staring in the direction of the bar but making no move to go in. Alistair wondered if they were waiting for Mark to act the host again and dispense more free drinks. And then he frowned and looked around him.

'Where is Mark?' he said quietly to Diana.

'I don't see him anywhere,' said Diana. 'But I'm sure he'll join us when he's ready. He won't give up on the play; it means too much to him.' She glowered around her. 'What's the matter with you all? You look like a bunch of lost sheep!'

'It's shock,' Alistair said quietly. 'Shouting at them won't help.'

Diana sniffed. 'It's helping me.'

Alistair took a moment to listen to the dispirited conversations around him. Most of the cast were seriously upset over the second death and already discussing walking out on the play. Not just because they were scared there might be a murderer hiding among them, but because they were becoming increasingly convinced that there really might be a witch, after all. Some were already on the phone to their agents, trying to scare up replacement work and getting nowhere.

Alistair was still searching for the right thing to say when the front door slammed open and David and Micah walked in. They stopped and stared cheerfully about them, and everyone fell silent as David raised his voice.

'Your attention, please! I have important news. The play will most definitely go on.'

Cast and crew just stared at him, too beaten down by recent events even to react.

'David and I have talked things over with our good friend Hamilton,' said Micah, 'and he has agreed that the discovery of Paul's body doesn't change anything. Forensics have already been all over the building and turned up nothing, so now they've finished processing the costumes department, there's no need to preserve the entire building as a crime scene.'

'The police have left and the theatre is ours again!' said David.

He beamed around him, looking for a cheer and a round of applause in recognition, which didn't happen. Cast and crew were still trying to decide whether this was good news or not.

Alistair stepped forward to frown, just a little, at David and Micah.

'Detective Sergeant Hill didn't seem the type to give up that easily . . .'

David's smile widened a fraction. 'Our friend Commissioner Crane can be very persuasive.'

'Particularly when a certain sergeant is way overdue for promotion,' said Micah.

'Such power,' said Diana. 'If only we could harness it as a force for good.'

Todd emerged from the crowd. 'You really expect us to go back and work in a building where two of us have died?'

'It's either that or you have no play and no employment,' said David.

'We are still willing to back you,' said Micah. 'But you have to work with us on this.'

'Of course we'll go back,' said Richard. 'The play's the thing . . .'

Cast and crew looked at each other and then shrugged more or less in unison. None of them looked happy about it, but work was work.

'What the hell has happened to Mark?' said Richard. 'He didn't even turn up to man the bar. Has anybody seen him?'

People looked at each other, but no one had anything useful to say. And then, one by one, everyone turned to look at Alistair and Diana. Alistair smiled calmly at them and then turned to Diana.

'You were right. We are needed.'

EIGHT
Reasons and Revenges

Alistair and Diana let themselves back into the theatre lobby and found it all shadows and gloom. Alistair locked the door behind them. Diana raised an eyebrow.

'What was that for?'

'To make sure we won't be disturbed,' said Alistair.

'OK . . .' said Diana. 'That probably didn't sound quite so bad while it was still inside your head, but what came out wasn't anything a girl would want to hear in a setting where the light has to sneak in.'

'I just needed to be sure no one could get out of the theatre,' said Alistair.

'Better,' said Diana. 'But almost as worrying. Who else could be here? The police have all gone, and the cast and crew aren't budging from the hotel until we can go back and assure them their troubles are over.'

'Our saboteur and killer are still here,' said Alistair. 'Their work isn't finished yet.'

Diana scowled. 'Two dead bodies and a reign of terror wasn't enough?'

'Not to ensure this play is dead in the water,' said Alistair. 'They must know everyone is ready to try again, so you can be sure they're lurking in the shadows and planning something truly unpleasant.'

Diana smiled coldly. 'Let them try. I am really in the mood to show them how upset I am.' She stopped and looked at Alistair. 'Do you think they know we've come back?'

'Wouldn't surprise me in the least,' said Alistair.

'Good,' said Diana. 'How are we going to track them down?'

'We have to locate someone else first,' said Alistair. 'Even though they're almost certainly dead.'

Diana nodded slowly as she made the connection. 'You're talking about Mark, aren't you? The only one of us who didn't turn up at the hotel. That poor sweet old bear . . . Why would the saboteur want to kill him of all people?'

'Probably for some reason that only makes sense to the killer,' said Alistair. 'But we still need to find the body.'

Diana scowled at the shadows, and the shadows stared back, unimpressed.

'Where do we start? I mean, there's only the two of us. This is a big building, with lots of hiding places. And given how much thought went into hiding Paul's body . . .'

'They want us to find Mark,' Alistair said steadily. 'He's bait in a trap, to draw us in.'

And then he broke off as the door at the end of the lobby swung open to reveal a balding middle-aged man. He smiled and nodded, and Alistair smiled back before turning to Diana.

'It's just Griffin,' he said. 'Part of the stage crew. He volunteered to stay behind and keep an eye on things. Have you seen something, Griffin?' The man nodded.

'Given that someone wants to pin the blame on the three witches, where would be the best place to leave Mark's body to incriminate them?'

Diana smiled gleefully at Alistair. 'Their secret room, where they hid themselves away! To play around with that damned Ouija board.'

She looked to Griffin for confirmation, but he was already gone. She turned back to Alistair.

'Who was that?'

'Someone who's been with the theatre so long he knows all its ins and outs,' said Alistair. 'Just be glad he's on our side.'

Diana frowned. 'Why is the killer still so determined to point the finger at those three actresses?'

'It's all about playing games with our heads,' said Alistair. 'Keeping us off balance, so we won't see the real game plan until it's too late. This was never about the play or witchcraft. It's always been about revenge.'

Diana grinned broadly. 'You've already worked this out, haven't you?'

'Let's say I have a strong suspicion,' said Alistair.

Diana didn't push him. She knew he wouldn't say anything until he was certain.

'You're sure Mark is dead?' she said slowly. 'He couldn't just be locked up somewhere, waiting for us to rescue him?'

'Why would they keep him alive?' said Alistair as kindly as he could. 'When a third body would provide the final nail in this play's coffin?'

'Damn . . .' said Diana. 'That's cold.'

'Cold and calculating,' said Alistair. 'Right from the very beginning.'

They made their way to the auditorium and set off down the aisle. Their footsteps echoed loudly on the quiet, as though giving warning. The open stage had been cleared of everything but its painted background, a simple illusion that no longer had any power to convince. Alistair and Diana moved on into the backstage area, to find nearly all the lights had been turned off, draping everything in shadows dark enough to hide anything.

'Someone believes in mood lighting,' said Alistair.

'All the better to ambush us with,' said Diana.

'No . . .' said Alistair. 'They need to confront us, to justify themselves and rub our noses in how clever they've been.'

'And then kill us,' said Diana.

'That is probably the plan,' said Alistair. 'They must know we're the only real threat to their schemes.'

Diana sniffed. 'If they're stupid enough to show themselves, I will punch their head through a wall.'

When they finally reached the witches' secret room, Alistair put a staying hand on Diana's arm, bringing her to a halt well short of the door. She looked at him sharply.

'What's wrong?'

'The door has been left open a crack,' Alistair said quietly.

Diana glared at the door suspiciously and lowered her voice.

'You think someone could be lying in wait?'

'Someone's there,' said Alistair. 'Stick close to me. It's time we put an end to this. Whatever it takes.'

Diana looked at him. 'Hardcore, Bish.'

'I know I'm not supposed to run out of Christian charity

and forgiveness,' he said quietly, 'but there's a cold malice to everything that's happened here that disturbs me. And it stops now.'

He hit the door with his shoulder, slamming it back against the inner wall. The echoes reverberated loudly, like a statement of intent. Alistair strode in, with Diana right behind him.

Mark was waiting for them, sitting by the table with a large hand resting on the Ouija board, as though trying to send one last message. He had been stabbed repeatedly in the chest, and the whole front of his kingly costume was soaked in blood.

'Murdered, just like Duncan,' said Alistair.

'I'm not seeing any defensive wounds on his hands or his arms,' Diana said steadily. 'He never even had a chance to protect himself.'

'It must have been someone he knew and trusted,' said Alistair. 'That's the only way they could have got so close.'

'But what brought him here?' said Diana.

'He was lured to this room,' said Alistair. 'Probably with the promise of some evidence that would finally explain what's been going on. And now Mark has been reduced to just another prop in someone else's story.'

He frowned and leaned in for a closer look at Mark's clothes.

'His shirt's been left unbuttoned. Give me a hand here.'

Diana gingerly helped Alistair pull the shirtfront apart. The whole of Mark's torso was covered with bloody wounds, but that wasn't all. An inverted star had been carved into the flesh over his heart. Diana made a low angry sound.

'The bastard . . .'

'One last attempt to link the killings to witchcraft and black magic,' said Alistair. 'But I never did believe any of that stuff was real. And when I'm done, neither will anyone else.'

He raised his voice for the last few comments. Diana looked at him curiously.

'Why are you playing to the back seats, Bish?'

'Because we're not alone,' said Alistair.

Diana raised her fists and looked quickly round the room. 'I'm not seeing anyone.'

Alistair fixed his gaze on the open doorway and the shadows beyond.

'Don't be shy! Come on in and join us, and we'll have a nice little chat.'

'Who are you talking to?' said Diana.

'We were followed all the way here,' said Alistair. 'I could hear their footsteps on the quiet.'

Diana stared at him. 'And you didn't think to tell me?'

'I didn't want to frighten them off,' said Alistair.

Diana glared at the open doorway. 'Get your arse in here! Don't make me come out and get you!'

There was a pause, and then Banquo's ghost appeared at the open door. Still wearing the familiar military jacket with its fake bloodstains, and the featureless glowing mask. The grim figure advanced slowly into the room. Diana frowned suddenly.

'Aren't you a bit short to be Banquo?'

'Close enough to fool anyone who wasn't looking for it,' said Alistair. 'And a good enough actor to make all the right moves during the banquet scene.' He stared steadily at the unmoving figure. 'But that's all over now. It's time for the truth, Sarah.'

Banquo's ghost reached up and removed the mask to reveal Sarah's cold gaze. Diana stared at her, and then at Alistair.

'How long have you known?'

'Long enough,' said Alistair. 'The clues were there all along, if you looked for them. Like this.' He produced a small plastic shape from his pocket and showed it to Sarah. 'I found this on the floor, after your trick with the burning mannequin. It took me a while to realize it was one of the fake warts you wore on your face as a witch. You must have left it on without realizing, and it fell off.'

He tossed the thing at Sarah's feet, but she didn't take her eyes off him.

Diana glared at Sarah. 'You terrorized your fellow cast members. You killed three people. Why would you do that?'

'Because I have given my life to the left-hand path of the Wiccan way,' said Sarah. 'And it offended me to see this play making a mockery of witches.'

She broke off, because Alistair was already shaking his head. 'Well, maybe. But that's not why all of this has been happening.'

'How can you be so sure?' said Diana.

'Because I read up on black magic and its associated belief

patterns at the seminary,' said Alistair. 'The various forms of witchcraft I've seen since I arrived here all came from different belief systems that didn't belong together. A clear sign of an amateur at work, with only just enough knowledge to get by.

'And there were far too many stab wounds on Mark's body to be the result of a single knife, so I knew you couldn't have done this alone, Sarah. Won't you ask your partner in crimes to join us?'

She stared coldly back at him, still refusing to say anything. Alistair raised his voice again.

'I know you're out there. Please come in and join us. I'm sure you have lots to tell us, Todd.'

There was barely a pause before Todd came strolling through the open door to nod easily at everyone. All the grief was gone from his face, and his smile was perfectly steady. Diana clapped her hands, slowly and sarcastically.

'Well done, Todd. It would seem you're a better actor than I ever gave you credit for. You actually had me convinced you were heartbroken over the death of your good friend Paul. I had no idea at all that you killed him.'

Alistair showed Todd his steadiest look. 'Why did you kill Mark? I thought you liked him?'

Todd shrugged. 'He was very likeable, but what's that got to do with anything? You know, for famous investigators of mysteries, you were both far too ready to believe what you saw. But don't feel too bad about being fooled. Tom, Paul, even Mark, never had any idea how I really felt about them. Mark didn't even question me when I told him I'd discovered some interesting evidence in the witches' back room. He followed along quite trustingly and never suspected he was in any danger. Right up to the point where Sarah and I fell on him with our knives. Though I did think he looked just a bit disappointed at the end.'

Sarah smiled at the dead man in his chair. 'Who would have thought the old ham would have so much blood in him?'

'Why carve the star into his chest?' said Alistair. 'You didn't need to imply witchery in such an obvious killing.'

Todd shrugged. 'We were going to cut his heart out and do something impressively awful with it, but we ran out of time. We couldn't disappear from the hotel bar for too long; someone would have been bound to notice. So we did what we could in the time available. And yes, there is an underground tunnel that links the hotel and the theatre. I think it was originally created to allow assignations between cast members and their admirers.'

'How did you know about that?' said Diana.

Todd smiled cheerfully. 'I went online and dug up the original blueprints for the theatre and the hotel. And there was the tunnel, clearly marked, just waiting for someone to make use of it. Fortune favours the properly prepared.'

Diana tore her gaze away from Todd to stare at Sarah. 'How could you make yourself a part of this butchery? Mark was one of your oldest friends!'

'He might have thought so,' said Sarah. 'To me, he was just another man who took most of the credit for my hard work. He made this necessary by asking too many questions and trying far too hard to calm people down and reassure them. He should have kept his mouth shut.'

Diana gestured at Mark's bloody corpse. 'But how could you do this?'

'Oh, come on, darling,' said Sarah, smiling for the first time. 'Acting has always been a cut-throat business.'

A certain hardness entered Diana's gaze. 'Were you Banquo's ghost at the banquet? Did you put the poison in Tom's wine?'

'It had to be her,' said Alistair. 'Most of the cast were involved in that scene, but not the three witches. I remembered the big fuss you made, Sarah, about not being involved. You made a point of pressuring Richard in front of everybody, so he had no choice but to keep you out to preserve his authority. And it couldn't have been Angela or Jenny playing Banquo, because they were sitting together in the auditorium. You were the only one sitting on your own.'

'Did you mean to poison Tom?' said Diana. 'Or did his changing seats just put him in the wrong place at the wrong time?'

'The poison was all that mattered,' said Todd. 'Who got it was irrelevant. We just needed someone to die, to make an impression.'

Diana shook her head slowly. 'And I thought I'd seen every kind of backstabbing the theatre had to offer . . .'

Sarah looked to Todd. 'Enough talk. Kill them, and no one will ever suspect us. And two more bodies will really bury this production.'

She stopped as she realized Alistair was already shaking his head.

'Interesting that you should turn to Todd for approval. He always was the one in charge.'

Sarah glared at him. 'We were partners, right from the beginning!'

'I don't think so,' said Alistair. 'This was all his idea, and his plan. He merely used you and your limited understanding of witchery to make it happen.'

'Shut up!' said Sarah. 'You have no idea what I'm capable of!'

A long-bladed knife suddenly appeared in her hand. Todd smiled and produced his knife. The two of them moved together, blocking the way to the door. Diana moved in beside Alistair, her hands closed into fists.

'Those knives do look a bit nasty, Bish,' she said quietly. 'Please tell me you have a plan.'

'I always have a plan,' said Alistair. He fixed his gaze on Todd. 'You used Sarah as your stalking horse, so no one would suspect you. She was responsible for all the witchy business, while you stayed in plain sight. She knew all about old stage tricks, so it was no problem for her to arrange the ring of fire and the burning mannequin. She even knew how to fake footsteps on the lobby ceiling, by walking heavily on the floor above.

'She took Paul's place on stage as Banquo's ghost, risking exposure at every moment, while you were safe being Macbeth and therefore above suspicion. All someone had to do was spot Sarah was the wrong height for Paul and rip her mask off, and everyone would have blamed her for everything. And even if she did name you as her accomplice, there was no evidence against you. You'd seen to that.

'I'm guessing that you fixed the dagger in Banquo's death scene and poisoned the blade. You would have wanted that to be personal, after what Paul did to you.

'Mark's murder was the only time you actually worked with Sarah. Why was that, Todd? Didn't you trust her to handle a big man like Mark? Or did you simply want to get your hands dirty, just the once, for the thrill of it? I don't suppose it matters. Sarah might have thought she was using you, but it was always the other way round.'

'No!' said Sarah, unable to keep silent any longer. 'It was my stage experience and my knowledge of witchery and poisons that made all of this possible.'

'He let you think that,' said Alistair. 'But this was always and only about Todd.'

Sarah stared at Todd, and he frowned at her impatiently.

'Hold your nerve. Don't let him throw you.'

'You still haven't explained why Todd has been doing all of this, Bish,' said Diana, keeping a watchful eye on the two knives. 'Come on; it's time for the big speech that makes all of this make sense.'

'Let's start with why Todd was so determined to get his revenge on Richard,' said Alistair. 'It all goes back to when Todd was supposed to be part of the *Swiss Family Robinson* musical, but Paul talked Todd into demanding more money. If Todd had stayed, he would have become rich and famous. But he listened to Paul and lost out on everything. And you just couldn't let it go, could you, Todd? Richard and Paul had to be punished. Except . . . it was never their fault. You made the decision to walk away. But you could never allow yourself to believe that. It was much easier to blame Richard and Paul. That's why you decided to sabotage this production and put an end to Richard's career. Knowing the destruction of his reputation would hurt him more than anything else you could do.'

'But Richard made up for what happened by casting Todd as the lead in *Macbeth*,' said Diana. 'Why would Todd want to sabotage a play that could make him just as rich and famous?'

'Even the most successful production of *Macbeth* was never going to make the same kind of money as *The Swiss Family Robinson*. And I think that after brooding on the unfairness of it all for so long, it was more important to Todd that Richard fail than Todd should succeed.'

'You do like to talk, don't you?' said Todd.

Alistair looked at him steadily. 'I have to admit I'm still not clear as to why Paul had to die. He went with you when you left the musical, so he lost just as much as you did.'

'I had no intention of leaving until he whispered his poison in my ear,' said Todd. 'I couldn't believe it when I discovered he'd been cast in this play as well. It did make for an even better revenge – on both the people who destroyed my life.'

'But why kill Mark?' said Diana. 'Hadn't you done enough?'

'You would have thought so, wouldn't you?' said Todd. 'But even after everything Sarah and I had done, Mark kept encouraging the cast to carry on! They were actually talking about going back and trying again! So I knew Sarah and I would have to do something really dramatic to make it clear this play was doomed.'

'How did you and Sarah become partners in this?' said Diana. 'I didn't think the two of you had even met before.'

'Look at them closely,' said Alistair. 'The eyes, the bone structure . . . Sarah is Todd's mother.'

'I gave him up for adoption when he was still a baby,' said Sarah. 'There wasn't room in my life for a career and a child. Todd tracked me down earlier this year, using one of those genealogy sites, and when we were both cast in this play, it seemed like destiny. He would get his chance for revenge, and I would get to do something for the child I abandoned.'

'But . . . that means Mark was your father, Todd!' said Diana.

He shrugged. 'He was never around when I needed him.'

'And afterwards . . .' said Alistair. 'Todd could ride the publicity for surviving all the weird events surrounding this play to have an even more successful career. But who would pay any attention to a minor player like you, Sarah? What were you going to get out of this?'

'Todd said he'd look after me,' said Sarah.

'And you believed him?' said Diana.

'Someone was going to have to take the blame for the murders,' said Alistair. 'How long do you think it would have been before the police got an anonymous phone call pointing in your direction? And if you did try to take Todd down with you, well . . . who would believe a crazy old witch anyway? Todd would have called you a liar to your face, and you know how convincing he can be.

'He set all of this up from the beginning so he could get everything he wanted. And blame it all on the mother who gave him up without a second thought.'

Sarah turned slowly to stare at Todd.

'Don't listen to him,' said Todd. 'He's just trying to drive a wedge between us.'

'But he's right,' Sarah said slowly. 'What do I get out of this? You'll become a success, but I'll just lose my job. And they're not easy to come by at my age.'

'Why are you talking like this?' said Todd. 'You've never questioned me before!'

'Maybe I should have,' said Sarah.

Todd struggled to hold on to his temper.

'Look . . . just calm down and follow the plan. We're too close to getting away with everything to let it fall apart now. Just . . . do as you're told!'

He gestured with the hand that happened to have the knife in it, and Sarah lunged forward and stabbed him through the heart. She put all her strength into it, slamming the knife hilt against Todd's chest. He stared at her in disbelief.

'Mother . . .'

She twisted the blade, and blood burst from Todd's mouth. He fell dead to the floor, and Sarah glared at him.

'I never wanted a child anyway.' She turned to Alistair and Diana, and laughed softly. 'There's only room for one star in this story.'

She reached inside her jacket with her free hand and brought out a doll from the props room. It had no costume, nothing to make it appear like anyone in particular. Sarah gripped it firmly and showed it to Alistair.

'This doll is whoever I believe it to be. And I believe it's you, Bishop.'

She pressed the point of her knife against the doll's chest, but Alistair shook his head.

'I'd say it looks a lot more like you, Sarah. If you stab that doll, you'll die. Don't do it.'

Their eyes met. Alistair's gaze never wavered, but after a moment, Sarah's did. Alistair took a step forward, and Sarah thrust the knife deep into the doll's chest. Her face spasmed, and she fell dead to the floor. Alistair looked at her.

'It always comes down to who has the most faith . . .'

NINE
The Final Question

Sometime later, Alistair and Diana stood out in the street, watching as the bodies were stretchered out of the theatre. Inspector Forbes and Sergeant Hill supervised the process, while being very careful not to even glance at Alistair and Diana.

Richard and Caitlin came over to join them, and even Alistair noticed how closely they were standing together.

'I don't believe it,' said Diana. 'You two are an item, now?'

Caitlin smiled happily. 'Spend enough time with someone, and you change your mind about how you see them. He just needs looking after.'

'This is true,' said Richard. 'Someone to believe in me, when I can't always manage it for myself.'

'Josie will probably be a bit upset that she never got to add you to her collection,' said Caitlin. 'But most of that was made up anyway, to make her seem more interesting.'

'Imagine my relief,' said Richard. 'But I was always more interested in you, Cait.'

'Then why were you always shouting at me?'

'How else was I going to get your attention?'

They smiled briefly at Alistair and Diana, and then moved away, holding hands.

'People can always surprise you,' said Diana.

'Excuse me for a moment,' said Alistair.

He went over to the theatre door that was standing just ajar and looked in at Griffin, looking out.

'I'm not supposed to move this far from the wings,' said Griffin. 'But I wanted to see this through to the end.'

'Why don't you come out and join us?' said Alistair.

'Into the sunlight?' said Griffin. 'I don't think so. I don't do that anymore.'

Alistair nodded slowly. 'What will you do now?'